Praise for
Mimi Matthews

The Work of Art

"Matthews weaves suspense and mystery within an absorbing love story. Readers will be hard put to set this one down before the end."

—*Library Journal* (starred review)

"Strongly recommended."

—*Historical Novel Society*

Gentleman Jim

"Tartly elegant…A vigorous, sparkling, and entertaining love story with plenty of Austen-ite wit."

—*Kirkus* (starred review)

"Exhilarating…this page-turner shouldn't be missed."

—*Publishers Weekly* (starred review)

"Matthews ups the ante with a wildly suspenseful romance."

—*Library Journal* (starred review)

"Readers who love lots of intrigue and historicals that sound properly historical will savor this one."

—NPR

The Belle of Belgrave Square

"Shiveringly Gothic…Watching Julia blossom away from prying eyes is almost as satisfying as seeing Jasper Blunt pine for her from nearly the first page…For best effect, save this one for a windy night when trees scrape against the windowpanes."

—New York Times Book Review

"Mimi Matthews never disappoints."

—Jodi Picoult, #1 New York Times bestselling author

"Such tremendous good fun…Julian Fellowes fans will rejoice!"

—Kate Quinn, New York Times bestselling author

"This story unfolds like a rose blooming, growing more and more beautiful as each delicate layer is revealed. A tender, luminous romance."

—Caroline Linden, USA Today bestselling author

"Mimi Matthews just doesn't miss."

—Evie Dunmore, USA Today bestselling author

"A grand cross-class romance, a twisty mystery, and emotional internal struggles combine to excellent effect in Matthews's effervescent second Belles of London romance."

"An intoxicating, suspenseful romance. Highly recommended."

The Siren of Sussex

"A tender and swoonworthy interracial, cross-class romance in Victorian London...Readers will delight in this paean to women's fashion and horseback riding."

"Romance aficionados who love fashion and animals will delight in this tender romance and will be excited to see Evelyn's friends in future installments."

"Matthews brings the Victorian era to vivid life with meticulously researched details and an impossible romance made believable and memorable."

"A tender, empowering love story."

—*Shelf Awareness* (starred review)

Fair as a Star

"Historical romance fans won't want to miss this."

—*Publishers Weekly* (starred review)

"A kindhearted love story that will delight anyone who longs to be loved without limits."

—*Library Journal* (starred review)

The Matrimonial Advertisement

"For this impressive Victorian romance, Matthews crafts a tale that sparkles with chemistry and impresses with strong character development...an excellent series launch."

—*Publishers Weekly*

"Matthews has a knack for creating slow-building chemistry and an intriguing plot with a social history twist."

—*Library Journal*

A Holiday By Gaslight

"Matthews pays homage to Elizabeth Gaskell's *North and South* with her admirable portrayal of the Victorian era's historic advancements…Readers will easily fall for Sophie and Ned in their gaslit surroundings."

—*Library Journal* (starred review)

"A graceful love story...and an authentic presentation of the 1860s that reads with the simplicity and visual gusto of a period movie."

—*Readers' Favorite, Gold Medal for Holiday Fiction*

The Lost Letter

"Lost love letters, lies, and betrayals separate a soldier from the woman he loves in this gripping, emotional Victorian romance."

—*Publishers Weekly* (starred review)

"A fast and emotionally satisfying read, with two characters finding the happily-ever-after they had understandably given up on. A promising debut."

—*Library Journal*

Books by Mimi Matthews

FICTION

Somerset Stories

The Work of Art

Gentleman Jim

Return to Satterthwaite Court

Appointment in Bath

Belles of London

The Siren of Sussex

The Belle of Belgrave Square

The Lily of Ludgate Hill

Parish Orphans of Devon

The Matrimonial Advertisement

A Modest Independence

A Convenient Fiction

The Winter Companion

Victorian Romances

The Lost Letter

The Viscount and the Vicar's Daughter

Victorian Christmas Novellas

A Holiday By Gaslight

Victorian Romantics

Fair as a Star

Gothic Fiction

John Eyre

———— ❦ ————

NON-FICTION

The Pug Who Bit Napoleon:

Animal Tales of the 18th and 19th Centuries

A Victorian Lady's Guide to Fashion and Beauty

Return to Satterthwaite Court

SOMERSET STORIES
BOOK THREE

MIMI MATTHEWS

RETURN TO SATTERTHWAITE COURT
Somerset Stories, Book 3
Copyright © 2023 by Mimi Matthews
Edited by Deborah Nemeth
Cover Design by James T. Egan of Bookfly Design
Cover Photo by Abigail Miles/Arcangel
E-Book: 978-1-7360802-3-8
Paperback: 978-1-7360802-4-5

*For all the wonderful readers who
encouraged and supported me through a difficult year.
This story is for you.*

Chapter One

L ieutenant Charles Heywood came to a halt in front of the holly- and ivy-festooned window of the draper's shop. He was just about to enter—intent on purchasing Christmas presents for his mother and younger sister—when a small, filthy gray mongrel dog darted past him.

It was a busy day in Bond Street. Shoppers bundled up against the cold in heavy topcoats and cloaks hurried up one side and down the other. Their arms were laden with parcels, their puffs of breath visible in the frosty December air. Carriages and cabs rattled by them through the mud. Drivers jockeyed for position amid the heavy afternoon traffic that clogged the center of the street. Pedestrians crossed at their peril.

But the thin little dog exercised no caution.

He flew straight into the path of an oncoming conveyance, seemingly set on catching the wheels of a passing carriage and four.

A jolt of alarm spurred Charles into action. He surged into the street, narrowly avoiding being flattened by a coach himself. Vehicles veered around him. The muck from the flying hooves of the horses spattered his greatcoat

"Bloody fool!" one of the drivers shouted.

Charles didn't stop to apologize. The pup was on the move and Charles along with him.

He had many flaws, undeniably, but no one had ever accused him of failing to be a man of action. It was what he'd chiefly been known for during his time away. Eight years altogether, spent serving in Her Majesty's Navy. Always the first into the fray, no matter the risk to life and limb.

It was a quality he'd hoped to put behind him now he was finally back in England. He'd had enough of swash-buckling adventure. He was ready to settle down to a quiet, uneventful life.

His ship had only docked in London yesterday morning. It was but a brief stop in his journey. Tomorrow, he'd be traveling home to join his parents and sister at Heywood House, their family estate in Somersetshire. A long-awaited reunion. A difficult one as well.

He'd seen his family only a handful of times since leaving Somersetshire eight years ago. Just a few short visits managed while he was on leave. It had been four years since the last one. Then, Charles and his father had argued, relitigating the past with no little acrimony. His father had never wanted him to be a soldier or a sailor, risking life and limb in service to the crown. Indeed, he'd strictly forbidden Charles from joining up.

But Charles had no thought for that now. Nor for the

Christmas presents he was meant to be buying in a feeble effort to atone for the pain of his absence. There was only the dog and the immediate threat of danger.

Charles reached out to grab the muddy miscreant, but the little beast nimbly darted away, snapping first at the wheels of one carriage and then another.

The dog was in the throes of the chase, heedless of the crushing danger of the wheels or the steel-shod hooves of the horses. It was a madness in some creatures. Charles had observed it before. Raised in the country among his mother's pack of unruly dogs (a ragtag group of dubious lineage and character), he'd learned from the cradle to count animals as his friends. He'd seen them at their best—and at their worst.

But this snarling canine was nobody's friend. He didn't appear to reciprocate any fellow feeling toward humankind at all.

Reaching the opposite side of the street, the dog turned his focus on the bustling shoppers. He weaved through the crowd, snapping at a passing woman's skirts and baring his teeth in a threatening matter. Never mind that he couldn't have been more than half a stone in weight.

"Away with you!" An elderly lady in a plumed bonnet batted at him with her silk-ruffled umbrella. "Do something, Smithers," she cried to the liveried footman accompanying her, "before he ruins my hem!"

Obedient to his mistress, the footman swung his foot to kick the dog back into the street.

The wiry little mongrel was too canny. Nimbly dodging the footman's boot, the dog set his sights on another pair of shoppers up ahead—two stylish young ladies walking arm in arm. His gimlet eyes fixed on the bell-shaped mazarine velvet skirts of the smaller lady's expensive-looking carriage gown. Mayhem was plainly on his mind.

With a sigh of resignation, Charles moved to intervene.

He was thinking more of the dog than the young lady. A shortcoming of his, to be sure. It was one that arose as much from upbringing as inclination. His compassion for animals frequently overshadowed his concern for the comfort of well-to-do human beings.

"Pardon me, ma'am," he began.

The velvet-clad young lady turned to look at him in the selfsame moment the little dog latched onto her skirts. Her eyes widened in surprise.

They were blue eyes.

Impossibly blue.

Charles's words of warning died on his lips. For an instant, he forgot where he was.

It was only for an instant.

He may not be immune to the sight of a pretty face, but neither was he a green lad. He was nearly nine and twenty. A hardened sailor to the bone. He'd encountered plenty of beautiful women in his lifetime.

Though, admittedly, this female was something out of the common way.

And it wasn't only the blue of her eyes, as rich and midnight-velvety as the fabric of her gown, it was the turn of her flawless ivory-and-damask-rose countenance.

But she was no milk-and-water miss, for all that. Not if her face was to judge.

There was an air of strength in the winged arch of her mink brows and the firm line of her jaw. It was softened only slightly by the voluptuous curve of her mouth and the fetching cleft in her chin. A cupid's thumbprint, he'd some-times heard it called. The sign of a bold and sensuous nature.

It took an effort not to stare. Not to privately catalogue every contour and lilt in her vivid expression.

If she noticed the effect she had on him, she gave no sign of it. Her gaze dropped at once to the growling dog attached to her hem. A bemused smile touched her lips.

"Naughty boy." She stretched out an elegantly gloved hand to gently remove the beast. "You mustn't worry my skirts."

"Don't touch him!" Charles commanded.

The taller young lady gasped at his tone.

And no wonder.

It was the same voice he'd often used on the deck of the HMS *Intrepid*. One perfectly pitched to reduce wayward underlings into quivering masses of compliance.

The blue-eyed young lady didn't even flinch. "Nonsense." She continued to reach for the dog. "He's just a mischievous pup. He doesn't mean any—"

The dog responded to her advances with vicious speed, sinking his teeth into her gloved fingers.

"Oh!" She jerked her hand back with a startled cry. The fine leather of her kid glove was torn open. A drop of blood welled from her exposed finger, bright as crimson against her skin.

Charles's stomach tightened to see it. He shrugged off his greatcoat and, in one deft movement, threw it over the snarling dog. Using the coat as a blanket, he wrapped the little creature up and lifted him into his arms.

A good swaddle was known to work miracles on small animals who had run amok. This one was no different. The dog fought his captivity in vain for but a moment before ceasing his struggles in favor of muffled yips and grumbles.

Shoppers began to slow around them, some of them stopping to investigate the source of the commotion.

"He's bitten me," the blue-eyed young lady said in amazement.

"I told you not to touch him," Charles shot back. "If you'd listened—"

"I *beg* your pardon, sir," her tall friend interjected. "Can you not see that she's hurt?"

The first woman the dog had accosted caught up with them through the growing crowd, her footman close at her heels. She waved her umbrella about like an angry queen brandishing her scepter. "Summon the constable! That dog is a menace."

"He may have hydrophobia," her footman volunteered unhelpfully. "And now he's bitten this poor lady."

"An unprovoked attack," the older woman said. "A sure sign the beast is rabid!"

Charles muttered an oath under his breath. "He doesn't have hydrophobia," he said, holding tight to the still growling dog. "And if he does and she's contracted it, she'd have no one to blame but herself."

"*She* isn't afraid of dogs," the blue-eyed young lady retorted tartly. "Nor of trifling scratches."

"Oh, Kate!" The taller young lady's eyes welled with tears. "You're bleeding!"

"It's nothing," the blue-eyed young lady said. Kate, presumably.

Charles's heart gave a peculiar thump. Reaching into the pocket of his waistcoat, he withdrew a linen handkerchief. It was clean and pressed, thank heaven. He offered it to her, his voice gone gruff. "It *is* only a scratch, but perchance you should bind it."

She accepted his handkerchief, using it to stop the trickle of blood. "You're very obliging," she remarked dryly.

"So he should be, if it's his dog," the taller young lady said.

Kate's gaze met his in challenge. "*Is* that your dog?"

"That creature belongs to no one," the older woman declared. "It's a mongrel. A street dog. Anyone can see."

"He's filthy," the taller young lady said. "And he smells dreadfully."

Charles couldn't disagree. The stench from the dog's muddy fur was emanating all the way through the folds of his greatcoat. No doubt he'd have to burn the garment. As for the dog himself…

"He's somewhat worse for wear, I grant you," Charles said. "He's only recently arrived on a ship from Spain. The sailors should have taken better care of him."

"From Spain?" the older woman repeated scornfully. "*This* dog?"

"He is, ma'am. A rare breed. One of the only of his kind. Why do you think I was pursuing him?" Charles inwardly grimaced at so blatant a lie. But it was in a good cause. Given the chaos the dog had wrought, the interfering busybody was five seconds away from calling for the poor creature's destruction.

"He *is* yours, then?" Kate asked.

"Yes," Charles answered emphatically. "He is. Now, if you'll forgive me, I must get him home."

She continued to look at him, as though he'd said something that both bewildered and intrigued her. "You better had, sir," she said at last, "before the constable arrives."

Charles didn't have to be told twice. Offering the three ladies a rigid bow, he strode away through the growing throng, the snarling dog still cradled in his arms.

This wasn't going to go over well at Grillon's Hotel.

But no matter.

In twenty-four hours, Charles would be home. Once there, his mother and sister would take charge.

A half-starving London street dog wasn't the Christmas

present he'd envisioned for them, but knowing their feelings toward the canine race, the matted stray might yet prove to be the perfect gift.

Lady Katherine Beresford stared after the tall, raven-haired gentleman as he stalked off down Bond Street, disappearing into the crowd of Christmas shoppers.

His greatcoat had made him seem impossibly large and imposing. Without it, he somehow appeared even more so.

He was clad all in black—black wool trousers, coat, and waistcoat, with a stiffly knotted black cravat. His skin was bronzed from the sun. An oddity at this time of year. They'd had nothing but rain for weeks. This gentleman, however, must have recently returned from a more pleasant clime. He had the look of a man who spent most of his time out of doors. One who enjoyed a bit of sport—riding, fencing, and boxing. The cut of his coat set off his broad shoulders to magnificent effect.

"What a rude fellow," Christine remarked. She stood beside Kate, her narrow face the picture of ladylike outrage.

The eldest daughter of Lord and Lady Mattingly, Christine was as sensible as Kate was reckless. Her betrothal to an older baronet had been announced just last month. He was a dull sort of gentleman, but Christine was happy with him. She prided herself on being pragmatic about the future. It was a quality she'd inherited from her equally pragmatic mother, Jane.

Aunt Jane, as Kate was accustomed to calling Lady Mattingly, was Kate's mother's oldest friend. It was she who had brought them shopping today. They'd separated from her only briefly so she could purchase a new hat while they finished a fitting at the modiste. Kate and Christine had been on their way to join her at the milliner's when the little dog had appeared.

Deprived of their spectacle, the gaggle of onlookers slowly dispersed. The umbrella-wielding busybody departed along with them, uttering one final huff of complaint as she went.

"Yes, he was," Kate agreed when she and Christine were alone again. "But a handsome one."

To be sure, Kate couldn't recall when she'd seen any male so darkly attractive. Not during her season, anyway. And certainly not back home in the country, where she lived surrounded by her strapping older brothers, all of them golden-locked and ice-gray-eyed like her formidable father.

Papa was presently with Kate's mother and brothers at Beasley Park, their family estate in Somersetshire. A beautiful property. Kate had spent a great deal of her childhood there, gamboling over the forget-me-not–covered grounds. It was where her parents had met and fallen in love when they were children themselves. A special place they returned to often, bringing Kate and her brothers with them.

Their visits had become less frequent of late, with good reason. On her great-grandfather's death last year, Kate's father had lost his courtesy title. No longer Viscount St. Clare, he had become the Earl of Allendale. As a consequence, the family now resided almost exclusively at Worth House, the seat of the earldom in Hertfordshire.

They were a close-knit bunch, albeit a slightly ramshackle one as far as society was concerned. Rumors still managed to cling from the past. Whispers that Papa was illegitimate and that the title he'd inherited wasn't truly his but instead belonged to some odious distant cousin.

It was why Kate was in London alone instead of in company with her parents. Mama had thought it preferable for Aunt Jane to bring Kate out. And Aunt Jane had done so, to miserable effect. Six months later, her season at an end, Kate was still unmarried.

Still ungovernable.

Tomorrow she would be traveling down to Somersetshire to join her family for Christmas, having achieved none of the things her parents had wished for her.

Kate tied the gentleman's handkerchief tighter around her throbbing finger. Her mouth settled into a pensive frown.

She was too willful, that was the problem. And no gentleman wanted to shackle himself to a difficult wife, no matter how beautiful she might be. A man wanted a wife who was demure and biddable. A wife willing to dim her intellect and ability so that he could shine the brighter.

Kate would die, rather.

And anyway, what kind of man was intimidated by a woman merely because she could rival him in thought and deed? None worth having. Not as far as she was concerned.

"How can you call him handsome when he was so unforgivably unpleasant?" Christine wondered. "Rude, officious, and really quite—"

"Handsome," Kate said again. "Why haven't we seen him before?"

"Because he's no gentleman, clearly."

"Rubbish. He was well-spoken. And did you see how he carried himself?"

"I'm sorry, no." Christine resumed walking down Bond

Street. "I was rather distracted by his hydrophobic dog biting your hand."

Kate kept pace with her friend. "It wasn't his dog."

"He claimed it was," Christine said.

"He was lying."

"I don't know why he would. If the dog didn't belong to him, what business had he in defending it? Or in taking it away from here?"

Kate gathered her heavy skirts in her hands as she side-stepped a puddle. "He was rescuing it, of course."

Christine cast her a dubious glance. "*Him?*"

"Yes, the very man. Rude, officious, handsome, and… alarmingly tenderhearted, it seems. At least"—Kate smiled—"when it comes to dogs."

A frown puckered Christine's brow. "I wonder who he was?"

"I don't know." Kate's shoulders set with determination. "But I intend to find out."

Chapter Two

M r. Elias Catmull stood at the center of Lord and Lady Mattingly's luxuriously appointed drawing room. A slim, angular-faced gentleman with unusually close-set, shrewdly assessing eyes, he was one of Kate's most relentless admirers.

One of her most aggravating as well.

At only seven and twenty, he possessed the patronizing air—and the thinning pate—of a gentleman a full decade older.

"You must forgive the impetuousness of my visit," he said, lips twisting in a thin smile. "I couldn't allow you to leave London without paying my respects once more and bidding you a safe journey."

Kate's expression hardened. Impetuous indeed!

The two of them had met at the beginning of the season. A business associate of Christine's fiancé, Mr. Catmull had inveigled an introduction to Kate at her debut and had made a point of appearing at all of her engagements thereafter. Indeed, he'd crossed her path altogether too frequently. Not only at every ball, musicale, and theatrical, but at the shops and in the park as well.

She'd sometimes suspected he was stalking her. Impoverished rakes often employed such tactics with heiresses, attempting to catch them in a rare moment of vulnerability so they might compromise them. But though Kate was indeed an heiress, Mr. Catmull wasn't impoverished. Not that she was aware.

Whatever his motives, their acquaintance was of a long enough period for Kate to have formed a fixed opinion of the man. With his devious gaze and encroaching manner, Elias Catmull was as calculating as a poisonous adder in the grass.

And, at the moment, he was the least of Kate's concerns.

She walked restlessly to the wine-velvet–draped window, only half listening to his speech. A red-and-gold cashmere shawl was threaded loosely through her arms. She scarcely needed the warmth of it. Her cheeks were still burning from the lecture Aunt Jane had read her on the carriage ride home.

Kate had erred again, it seemed, not only by reaching out to stroke the head of that poor, wretched mongrel, but by allowing herself to be engaged in a public spectacle.

According to Aunt Jane, it was just the sort of thing the society gossips would latch on to. The kind of tale that would be added to the rapidly growing catalog of other salacious stories about Kate's wildness that were already circulating through the fashionable ballrooms, drawing rooms, and gentlemen's clubs of London.

Stories about Kate engaging in an unchaperoned dawn shooting contest with a group of gentlemen on the Heath (true), galloping her horse in Rotten Row in a ramshackle race with the disreputable mistress of a marquess (partially true), and the much-whispered-about encounter Kate had enjoyed in a candlelit library with the youngest son of the Duke of Whitney (completely and utterly false).

As if Kate would ever have deigned to kiss such a tedious, prosing blockhead!

But truth was less interesting than fiction. And society was disposed to believe the worst where a lady's reputation was concerned, especially if that lady came from a family already notorious for its wildness.

Not that Mr. Catmull cared.

The loathsome man had been awaiting Kate in the drawing room on her return from shopping, determined to force his attentions on her yet again. It didn't matter that she'd rebuffed him dozens of times. Her own feelings had no bearing on his suit. He never countenanced the opinions of females.

Kate was in no mood for his attentions. "You needn't have bothered," she said. "As I recall, you expressed similar sentiments on the last occasion we met."

"At Lady Billingham's soiree, yes," Mr. Catmull said. "I attribute the discouraging words you spoke to me then to the oppressive crush. You were agitated by the heat and not thinking clearly. A common complaint among ladies who become overstimulated."

"I was perfectly sensible," Kate replied. "Really, sir, how can I make myself plainer—"

"You're returning for Lady Chesham's ball in February, I understand?"

Kate broke off. How on earth had he learned *that*? She'd only accepted the invitation last week, at the urging of Aunt Jane and Christine.

The Dowager Duchess of Chesham was planning an extravagant celebration ball for her sixtieth birthday. There were whispers that members of the royal family would attend, including, very possibly, the Queen herself. It was an event not to be missed. Certainly not by a young lady whose family was looking for her to make a favorable match.

"I am," she admitted.

"After which you'll remain to take part in the season?"

She gritted her teeth. "Presumably."

Odious man, to make reference to the fact that she must embark on a second season.

"Then I shall preserve hope." He sketched her a bow. "I'm not a man who gives up easily, my lady. Ask anyone who has done business with me and they will attest. I always prevail, one way or another. You'd be wise to get used to the idea."

Kate bit her tongue as Mr. Catmull took his leave.

Get used to the idea? The devil she would!

Elias Catmull was everything she despised most in the male sex—overbearing, officious, and disposed to treat her like a porcelain trinket to be acquired for his mantelshelf.

Kate had the suspicion he'd do anything to obtain her hand, even if he must resort to despicable tricks and traps. Indeed, Mr. Catmull didn't strike her as being a stranger to scheming.

She *hated* being alone with the man.

He'd no sooner departed than Christine entered the room. She offered Kate an apologetic smile. "I didn't like to interrupt."

"I wish you would have done," Kate said feelingly.

"What did he want?"

"Me." Kate turned back to the window. "Heaven knows why. I've conveyed my dislike for the man by every possible method."

"He *is* an odd fish," Christine allowed, "but one of

considerable fortune. I've heard he claims a viscount for an uncle."

"I've heard the same," Kate said. "From *him*."

"He wants to impress you."

"With petty boasts?" Kate made a dismissive noise. "I'd rather a man prove his worth with deeds, not words."

"Many of your suitors have tried," Christine said.

"Yes, but they're so painfully *obvious* about it." She wrapped her shawl tighter around her shoulders. "If I could find but one worthy gentleman—a man of noble character and firm convictions—who would *be* a hero rather than acting the part for personal advantage... that's the man I'd wed."

Christine's lips pursed with ready disapproval. "I pray you're not referencing that rude fellow in Bond Street again."

Kate frowned. In truth, she hadn't even been thinking about the man. But now Christine mentioned it... The gentleman's actions *had* been heroic. And he certainly hadn't been performing for Kate's approval—or anyone's, for that matter.

It didn't hurt that he was dashingly handsome. Or that his deep, commanding voice had sent a delicious tremor down her spine.

If only she'd had the presence of mind to ask his name.

"No," Kate said. "I'm merely referencing my ideal. A man that hasn't yet appeared at any society event, I might add. If he had, I'd be happily engaged like you instead of a perpetual disappointment to everyone who knows me."

"You're not a disappointment." Christine joined Kate at the window. "You mustn't take my mother's scolding to heart."

"How should I take it? She's right, anyhow. I'm always doing something to make myself infamous."

"It wasn't entirely your fault," Christine said. "It was that other lady who created the worst of the scene; waving her umbrella about and shouting until half the street was staring. When she left us, I thought we were done with the business. I'd no idea my mother would hear of it."

"Neither did I," Kate said glumly.

They'd gone no more than a few steps farther up Bond Street before Aunt Jane had emerged from the milliner's shop. At once ascertaining the situation, she'd quickly shepherded them into the carriage and ordered the coachman to drive them home.

"She blames herself," Christine said. "In the brief time we were out of her sight, you were attacked by a feral dog, you exchanged words with a strange man in the street, and you attracted the unfavorable notice of a crowd."

"Scandal upon scandal," Kate muttered under her breath. "It seems I can't help but be embroiled in them." She leaned her hip against the window embrasure. "I suppose I must be grateful the story hasn't yet reached my parents."

"As to that..." Christine touched Kate's sleeve in consolation. "I'm afraid my mother is even now writing to yours, conveying all the unfortunate details. Her letter will doubtless precede you to Somersetshire."

"Oh." Kate's already-flagging spirits fell even further.

Her parents wouldn't censure her overmuch for her behavior. They rarely did. But Kate knew when she had erred. And she knew when they despaired of her.

"I don't expect it matters in the end." She lifted her throbbing finger. The gentleman's handkerchief was still tied snugly around it. "It isn't as if I could keep the story secret from them. Not with this to explain."

Christine's face contorted in a sympathetic grimace.

"I'm amazed Mr. Catmull didn't insist on summoning a surgeon."

Kate snorted. "It would never occur to him. He only ever looks at my face and figure. The remainder of my person doesn't merit noticing."

"Foolish man. We should go down to the kitchens and ask Cook to look after you. She'll fit you up with a proper bandage."

Kate didn't intend to give up the handsome stranger's tribute so easily. "Bosh. This handkerchief is the height of propriety." She slowly unwound it, wincing as the dried blood on the fabric tugged free of her wound. "The linen is exceedingly fine." She examined it more closely. "And look—there appears to be a monogram."

Christine drew closer. "C.H.," she read. "What exceptional embroidery."

"Some lady's done it," Kate said. "His wife, I daresay."

"Does it matter?"

Kate fell silent.

A dawning look of suspicion clouded Christine's brow. "Good Lord, I knew it! That insolent gentleman has stolen your heart away!"

Kate was surprised into a laugh. "Hardly. You should know by now that my heart isn't so easily won."

Christine gave her a long look. "No, I suppose not. Nor how could it be? You've set the bar so high no man can hope to meet it. Not when measured against the standard set by your brothers."

Kate smiled at the mention of her overbearing, overprotective, and frequently irritating older brothers James, Ivo, and Jack. Despite their constant interference in her life, she was excessively fond of the three of them. "What have they to do with anything?"

"They're all of them dashing and well favored. Like

three golden princes out of a fairy tale. My mother says James is the image of your father at that age."

"They're *all* the image of my father," Kate said distractedly. She traced the pad of her thumb over the letters of the monogram. "Though Jack does have Mama's temper."

"As do you, my dear," Christine pointed out gently.

Kate's mouth quirked. "A lady needs a bit of temper. She'd lose herself otherwise." She turned from the window, the bloodstained handkerchief still twined in her fingers. "And you're wrong to say that no man can measure up to my brothers. Not that I'm blind to their finer points, but... I'm not looking for some masculine ideal. I've never sought it."

"Then what?"

"I told you, I want a hero."

Christine smiled dryly at the impossibility of it. "Is that all?"

"Very well then," Kate said, goaded. "If that's too much to ask, I at least require a gentleman who will provide a bit of a challenge. I can't abide being bored."

It was the unfortunate truth of it; one Kate had finally come to accept after her lackluster season in London. She knew now that she could never spend her days stitching silently in a drawing room, content to be admired by some respectful adoring spouse. She was made for the storm. For braving the mad currents of life, not sheltering in the shallows.

"Life can't always be exciting," Christine said. "Sometimes we must put our heads down and get on with the business of a lady's day-to-day. There's happiness to be found in the quiet moments. In being industrious and obliging mothers and wives."

"In needlework and crochet patterns, you mean." Kate

twisted her shawl more securely through her arms. "I can do both well enough, thank you very much. I don't need to make a life's work out of it."

"You'll do neither with that wound festering on your finger," Christine said. "Pray God that miserable cur didn't infect you with some dread disease."

"That dog was no cur." Kate's words held an impish twinkle. "He was a rare Spanish import."

"So I heard," Christine replied without humor. "Do you truly think that gentleman rescued him?"

"I know he did," Kate said. "It was quite the most heroic display I've witnessed since arriving in London."

"What's this about a heroic display?" The door swung open and Christine's cousin Gilbert Trumble sauntered into the drawing room.

Gilbert was a thin, fair-haired gentleman with a loping gait and an easy manner. He expended most of his time hunting, shooting, and riding to hounds. What leisure hours he had left were spent at his club in St. James's Street—a veritable hotbed of society gossip. It kept Gilbert remarkably well informed. He could always be relied upon for the latest tittle-tattle.

"Gilbert!" Christine crossed the room to greet him. "What are you doing here? I thought you were leaving for Surrey this morning?"

"That dashed bay hunter of mine has sprained his hock." Gilbert took Christine's outstretched hands. "I've been in the stable physicking him since dawn." He kissed her cheek. "And missed the fun, it seems." He glanced at Kate. "What's this about heroic deeds?"

"Heroic might be overstating the matter." Christine released her cousin's hands. "Kate claims a gentleman stranger rescued a dog in Bond Street."

Gilbert came to greet Kate, first with a bow and

then—a little sheepishly—with the same cousinly kiss on the cheek with which he'd greeted Christine.

Kate may as well be his cousin. She'd known Gilbert Trumble all of her life. He was an amiable fellow and sufficiently capable on horseback. Granted, he was at times a trifle awkward with her—particularly in recent years as she'd grown into a young lady—but he'd never once stepped a toe out of line. Kate trusted him almost as much as she trusted her brothers.

"He did rescue it," she said. "And then he disappeared into the crowd."

"We have no notion who he was," Christine said.

"Save for his initials," Kate added. "C.H."

"C.H.?" Gilbert cocked his head with interest. "What did he look like?"

Christine answered: "Tall. Black hair. Quite impolite, really."

"C.H.," Gilbert repeated. "I say...I wonder if it was Charles Heywood? He's recently back in England."

"Charles Heywood?" Kate's curiosity was instantly piqued. "Who is he?"

"Grandson of the Earl of Gordon," Gilbert said. "I was at Eton with him."

"You and he were friends?" Christine asked.

"Only nodding acquaintances," Gilbert said. "He was a more serious sort than I ever was. We ran in vastly different circles. But I knew *of* him well enough. Heywood had a fondness for dogs. For most animals, come to think of it. Once, as I recall, he even managed to nurse an injured crow back to full health. God knows how—or why."

Kate looked at Gilbert expectantly. No longer merely curious, she was downright intrigued. "Is that all you remember about him?"

"Not much else *to* remember. Excepting that he was the finest marksman I've ever encountered. Could shoot a half penny off of a fence post, with either hand, at fifty paces. Ambidexterity, they call it. It's a rare skill. A lethal one, too. Remarkable to behold. I gather that's why he joined up in the end, to put his talents to good use."

Kate stilled. "He's a soldier?"

But she already knew the answer.

It had been evident in the way he carried himself and in the gruff bark of command that had edged his voice when he'd ordered her not to touch the dog.

"A sailor," Gilbert said. "He had a place at Cambridge, same as me, but he gave it up at the last minute to attend the Royal Naval College at Portsmouth. After that, he went to sea. He's back in London, I've heard. Likely stopping off on his way to Somersetshire. His father has an estate down there."

"Somersetshire!" Kate marveled at the coincidence. "I wonder that I've never met him before."

"Can't say you're missing much," Gilbert said. "When I knew him, he was a man of few words. No sense of humor, Heywood. Quite rude on occasion, if I'm honest."

"So," Christine murmured, "it *was* him."

Kate exchanged a speaking glance with her friend. She couldn't dispute Mr. Heywood's rudeness, but she suspected that he *did* have a sense of humor. Why else would he have told them the stray dog was a rare Spanish breed? However serious he was on the surface, underneath, the man must have a keen appreciation of the ridiculous.

There was only one way to find out.

Somehow, during her holiday in Somersetshire, she'd have to arrange to cross paths with Mr. Heywood again. It wouldn't be easy. On the contrary, it would be a distinct challenge.

The prospect boosted Kate's spirits. Not because Mr. Heywood had stolen her heart (the very thought!), but because he'd captured her imagination.

And because she was bored.

She'd be returning to the country tomorrow. The long winter months stretched ahead of her, secluded inside the house against the sleet and the snow, celebrating Christmas with her family. She'd need a bit of diversion.

Who knew but that Mr. Heywood might prove just the person to provide it?

Chapter Three

C harles rested a gloved hand on the curve of the little dog's narrow back as the hired carriage rolled down the remote West Country road that led toward the village of Heycombe. Now sporting a leather collar and lead, the mongrel was curled up beside him on the padded seat, dozing contentedly.

Outside, the sky was clear and bright, with no trace of warmth in it. A chill wind whistled over the bleak winter landscape. It was the kind of weather that foreshadowed a heavy frost or possibly even snow.

Perhaps this would be a white Christmas?

Charles gave the prospect scant consideration. His attention was too occupied with thoughts of home.

He wasn't anxious. After eight years at sea, he rarely experienced anything like nerves. Nevertheless, a part of him had been dreading this reunion.

It wasn't because he didn't wish to see his family. He loved them, just as he knew they still loved him. But his decision to go to sea had caused a rift between them. The announcement that he'd resigned his commission, leaving the Navy under less-than-ideal circumstances, wasn't likely to go over any better. Not after all he'd put his family through.

There would inevitably be questions. Questions Charles still wasn't entirely certain he had the answers to.

Church bells rang out in the distance, sounding the five-o'clock hour. A familiar sound, followed by an equally familiar sight: the high steeple of the village church rising over the hills ahead. It wouldn't be long now. Heywood House lay just beyond the rise.

Charles glanced down at the still sleeping dog. He'd given the creature a thorough bath yesterday. By the end of it there had been more soapy water on the hotel carpet than there had been in the metal tub that the two liveried footmen had hauled up to his room at Grillon's.

The dog was clean, at least. Clean, fragrant, and rather well-behaved now he was away from the lure of the busy street. On entering the hotel room, he'd quieted down at once. His large brown eyes had taken in his surroundings with cautious optimism. He'd seemed to recognize that he'd been rescued. After a brief meal—which he ate with gusto—he'd even gone so far as to bestow a grateful lick on Charles's cheek.

He was just a puppy under all that mud and filth. No more than eight months old, if Charles was to guess. Starving and wretched, but no longer repulsive. The muddy gray had been rinsed away, revealing wiry hair that was an attractive shade of brindle.

"I'm not going to name you," Charles informed the dog as the carriage rolled on. "That's Hannah's province."

It was his sister's greatest pleasure to bestow names on the animals in the Heywood family's ever-increasing menagerie. She'd been fifteen on his last visit home. A burgeoning beauty, with the same mass of dark auburn hair and the same mismatched eyes—one blue and one golden brown—as their mother, but one whose shyness often got the better of her.

Charles had always been protective of Hannah. It was a consequence of there being so many years between them. Children hadn't come easily to his parents. Only two in the end, both of them unreservedly adored. It had made Charles's decision to join the Navy even harder to forgive.

Heywood House appeared as they crested the final hill in their path. It was a classical Palladian structure, built of weathered stone, with proportions that spoke less of grandeur than of quiet elegance and gentility. A grand old place, full of warmth and familial happiness, set back amid a lush expanse of untamed parkland.

Home.

It was the dearest sight in the whole word. Charles's heart swelled with emotion to see it.

The coachman slowed his team as the carriage rolled up the expansive drive.

Charles's arrival was no surprise. He'd written ahead, informing his family of every stage of his journey. They awaited him at the top of the granite steps, the doors to the house open behind them.

His parents, Arthur and Phyllida Heywood, stood side by side beneath the arched entryway. Hannah was next to them, a grizzled pug dog and a three-legged black spaniel milling around the full skirts of her twilled silk gown.

Charles swallowed hard.

He had always been the mirror of his father. Not so much anymore.

Arthur had celebrated his sixtieth birthday last year. Though still tall and well made, with granite-hewn features and penetrating gray eyes, his hair was now liberally streaked with silver. He balanced some of his weight on his cane. His right leg often ached in the winter months—a consequence of an injury he'd suffered as a cavalry captain in the Peninsular Wars.

Philly's arm was twined lovingly through her husband's. The intervening years had been gentle with her. A full nine years younger than Arthur, her dark auburn hair was free of all but the faintest hint of gray. She wore it confined in a haphazard roll at her nape, stray curls framing a sweetly beautiful face that was bright with anticipation as she looked down the drive.

A smiled tugged at the corner of Charles's mouth. His parents were holding hands. They often did, though outward displays of affection had long been considered unfashionable.

But Arthur and Philly had never cared much for fashion—or for the opinions of fashionable people. They were a love match. The kind local people still talked about with something like reverence. During her first London season, Charles's mother had famously refused an offer from a wealthy duke in order to elope with Charles's father, a wounded soldier of modest fortune, somber disposition, and legendary skill with a pistol.

Their early life as a married couple had been fraught with scandal. With danger, too. More of it than Charles's parents had ever been willing to share with their children. But ultimately there had been happiness. A surfeit of it.

Nearly thirty years later, Arthur Heywood was still deeply in love with his wife, and she with him. It was the sort of love that, as a young man, Charles had aspired to one day have with his own bride.

That hope had diminished over the years.

Indeed, as he'd grown older, Charles had begun to feel that, when measured against the standards set by his parents, he'd fallen woefully short in every way that mattered. It was one of the reasons he'd left home.

He'd been restless here. Impatient to strike out on his own and discover what he was made of. It had seemed important at the time. More important than his parents' feelings on the matter. More, even, than his sister's tears when she'd begged him not to go.

"*I know you'll be killed,*" she'd said. "*Then what will I do? What will Mama and Papa do?*"

Charles had thought of her words often these past years, with more regret than Hannah would ever know.

As the carriage came to a halt, she ran down to meet him. The pug and spaniel ran along with her, barking at her heels. They were joined by three other dogs from the house, all of them familiar; an aged lemon-and-white setter named Flurry, a scruffy old Scottish terrier known as Twig, and an ancient mastiff fondly called Ignatius.

"Charles!" Hannah cried. At nineteen, she was taller now and even lovelier than she'd been as a girl.

He opened the door of the carriage and climbed out, pausing only long enough to extract the little dog.

The other dogs raced around Charles's feet in a chaos of excitement. The pug and spaniel sniffed cautiously at his trousers, while Flurry, Twig, and Ignatius jumped against his legs, pawing at him and nudging him with their heads, demanding his attention

Excited by the pack of strangers converging on him, the new little dog yipped and barked, wriggling to be free.

"Oh!" Hannah said. "You've brought a puppy home!" She went straight for it, all thoughts of greeting her brother forgotten. "May I hold him?"

"Of course, you may," Charles handed the dog to his sister. "He's yours."

"Mine?" Hannah gathered the small dog up in her

arms. Her voice softened to a soothing murmur. "Poor dear. You're so painfully thin. You must be starving." She glanced at Charles. "Where did you find him?"

Charles briefly crouched to pet the dogs clamoring for his attention. He acknowledged them in turn, scratching ears and rubbing backs and shoulders, murmuring their names. "How have you been, Ignatius? And you, Twig? Easy, Flurry. Don't lick me to death." He cast a look at his sister. "He was chasing carriages in Bond Street. He's also exhibited a fondness for attacking ladies' skirts."

An image of the blue-eyed young lady who had fallen victim to the dog's temporary foolishness sprang, unbidden, into Charles's brain.

Kate.

His blood warmed at the thought of her.

She'd been so bold. So singular. Any normal lady would have succumbed to hysterics at being bitten by a street dog. Kate, however, had taken the insult in stride.

A rarity.

But there was no point in dwelling on her finer qualities. He and Kate—whoever she was—weren't likely to meet again.

"That one's Tippo," Hannah said, introducing Charles to the pug. "And this is Evangeline." She urged the spaniel to hop forward for her brother to pet. "She's shy."

"Pleased to meet you, Tippo," Charles said. "And you, Evangeline." He stroked the two new dogs gently on their heads, careful not to be too familiar just yet. Many of the dogs at Heywood House had started their lives in less-than-ideal circumstances. It often took time for them to trust new people.

"What do you call him?" Hannah asked, admiring her new puppy.

Charles stood, brushing the dog hair from his trousers

as his parents descended the steps to join them. "I haven't named him yet. I'll leave that to you." He leaned down to drop a kiss on his sister's head. "I've missed you, little one."

Hannah hadn't only grown in height since he'd seen her last. She'd matured in countless other ways. Her letters had attested as much. She'd written frequently, telling him about her studies, her support for a newly formed organization devoted to the prevention of cruelty to animals, and how her love of animals had prompted her to adopt a vegetarian diet.

"You shouldn't have gone back to sea after your last visit," she said. "Not with a war brewing. Though Papa says I must try to understand. Something about your having to prove yourself."

Charles smiled. He'd long ceased being surprised by his father's perception. "Something like that."

"You've brought us another dog?" Arthur said. "Good God." His gruff tone was belied by the warmth in his eyes as he beheld his son. He pulled him into a hard embrace— brief but heartfelt—just as he'd often done when Charles was small. "Is this how you make amends?"

A lump formed in Charles's throat. "It's a start."

"A poor one, given what's past."

"I'm aware."

Arthur's gaze held a hint of steel. "You and I are due for a long talk, lad."

"I'm aware of that as well," Charles said.

His mother came to him next. She hugged him fiercely. "My darling, how I've longed to see your face!"

Charles enfolded her in his arms, holding her tight. There was a different kind of strength in his mother's embrace. One born of grace and tenderness.

She was the gentlest lady he'd ever known. Wherever

he'd gone in life, however far he'd roamed, her kindness and compassion had been his lodestar.

"Do we have you a month this time?" she asked. "Or dare I hope you've been given longer?"

"A bit longer." Charles wasn't yet ready to tell them the truth. Not here on the front steps, only seconds after his arrival.

"Thank heaven," she said. "And you won't cut it short like last time?"

He inwardly winced at his mother's delicate reprimand. After arguing with his father during his last visit, Charles had departed Somersetshire with two weeks of his leave still remaining. His mother and sister had wept when he'd left.

"I'm sorry about what happened then," he said, his words for her ears alone. "I never meant to cause you pain."

"Hush, love. You're here now. That's all that matters. There's time enough for the rest of it." She drew back to look at him. Her mismatched eyes glistened with tears of pure happiness. "Oh, what joy we shall have this Christmas now you're home!"

"Grandfather isn't joining us this year," Hannah said. "Nor Mrs. Ogilvy."

Mrs. Ogilvy was the longtime mistress of Charles's grandfather, the Earl of Gordon. Grandfather refused to travel without her companionship. When Charles was a boy, they'd visited Heywood House together often. To the outward world, Mrs. Ogilvy's inclusion in the family was a minor scandal, but Charles had been raised to look on the lady almost as a grandmother.

"Why not?" he asked.

"They're staying with Uncle George in Northumberland. We might have gone, but Aunt Prudence doesn't like me to bring all the dogs."

George Heywood, Viscount Carlisle was the earl's heir. A former rake, known for his disastrous affairs with women, he'd long since settled down into respectable marriage and fatherhood.

"A pity," Charles said. "I would have liked to see them."

"You will soon, darling, I promise," Philly said. "When next you have leave, we'll arrange it so all of the family can be together."

All.

Their extended family wasn't very many in number. Though Charles's father had relations still living, his mother had none. Philly had been raised by her beloved grandfather, Sir Charles, at Satterthwaite Court in Devonshire. Both he and the estate had been lost well before Charles was born. But his great-grandfather hadn't been forgotten. Charles was his namesake.

"In the meanwhile"—Arthur slapped his son on the back—"come inside. You'll be wanting your tea."

"Sara has laid out a feast for you," Philly said.

"Iced gingerbread, almond cakes, and all of your special favorites," Hannah informed him. "She means to spoil you rotten."

Their housekeeper, Sara, and her husband, the Heywoods' butler, William, had been seeing to the smooth running of the household since Charles was in leading strings. They were practically family.

"What tragedy has befallen Evangeline's leg?" Charles asked as the three-legged spaniel hopped past him up the steps.

"She lost it in a shooting accident at the abbey,"

Hannah explained. "Their gamekeeper was going to have her destroyed."

The neighboring estate belonged to an unpleasant couple, known for hosting raucous house parties that attracted the worst of London society.

"Fortunately," Philly said, "your sister and I persuaded him to abandon the idea and give her to us instead."

"*Papa* persuaded him." Hannah cast a meaningful glance at her brother.

Charles suppressed a grin. He well knew his father's powers of persuasion. There was little Arthur Heywood wouldn't do to ensure the happiness of his daughter—and nothing he wouldn't do for his wife.

"It was all to the good." Philly linked her arm through Arthur's as they ascended the steps. "Evangeline has been exceedingly happy with us."

"This dashing fellow will be happy as well." Hannah settled the little stray more firmly in her arms. "I shall call him Odysseus." She flashed her brother another look. "He was a wanderer too. A sailor, like you, Charles, who eventually found his way home."

"WHAT THE DEVIL ARE YOU DOING IN HERE?"

Kate's fingers stilled on her crochet hook as her brother, Jack Beresford, third son of the Earl of Allendale, strode into the morning room at Beasley Park.

He was dressed for a ride—a sturdy broadcloth coat molded to his shoulders and cord breeches hugging his long legs. Sunlight filtered through the tall windows, gleaming in the golden threads of his hair. At one and twenty, he was the spitting image of their father.

"By God, are you *knitting?*" He looked at his sister in horrified amazement.

Kate repressed an uncharacteristic surge of embarrassment "It's not knitting," she said. "It's crochet-work."

A copy of the December issue of *The Lady's Museum and Domestic Magazine* lay open beside her. There was an illustrated pattern on the left-hand side. She quickly turned the page before her brother could see it.

"But…why?" he asked.

Kate's mouth compressed with irritation. Jack's astonishment at finding her thus engaged wasn't very flattering. "I'm making a Christmas gift for someone," she said, resuming her chain of stitches. "Is that so surprising?"

"Yes," he replied frankly. "This gift isn't for me, I hope?"

"No, not for you."

"Good. Because I don't want some ugly knitted scarf that I'll be obliged to wear all winter so as not to hurt your feelings."

"I told you, it's crochet, not knitting," Kate said. "And since when were my feelings so fragile?"

"How am I to know? You've been away in London. James says you'll be changed now you've come home."

"I haven't changed," Kate said.

"And that's the problem," James said.

Kate looked up from crocheting as her eldest brother entered the room to join them.

James Aldrick Nicholas Beresford was the newly minted Viscount St. Clare. He'd assumed the lesser title on Papa's elevation to the earldom. Like Jack, James was tall, lean, and powerfully made. A copy of their father to an uncanny degree. But if Jack resembled Papa as a reckless young blade, then James resembled him as a man in his prime—cold, formidable, and capable of anything.

Were Kate anyone else, she might have been intimidated by him. She wasn't, thank heaven. Quite the reverse. "Can none of you leave me alone for five seconds? I came in here because I wanted some peace."

"A pox on your knitting," Jack said. "Put on your habit and come riding with me."

"Ivo can go with you," Kate said. "I must finish this before Christmas."

Ivo was her second eldest brother. At three and twenty, he wasn't quite as wild as Jack, but he was far more fun than James. He'd recently returned from a lengthy grand tour of Europe and was keen to reacquaint himself with the local flora and fauna.

"Ivo is down the lane calling on the blacksmith's daughter," Jack said. "Someone should tell him she's already had half the young squires in the West Country."

James hit the back of Jack's head with the flat of his hand as he walked by him. "Don't be crass. Not in front of our sister."

"Kate would say the same," Jack grumbled under his breath. "Indeed, she'd say worse."

"Don't embroil me in your quarrels," Kate shot back tartly. "Can't you see I'm sewing?"

James studied her face. At five and twenty, he considered himself to be responsible for all of his younger siblings, never mind that he was only a scant few years older. "What are you up to, Kate?"

"Nothing. What are *you* up to?" She examined her brother with a critical eye. He was clothed in a dark suit with a freshly pressed shirt and an immaculately tied cravat "You're dressed exceptionally fine for a morning indoors."

James was silent for a long moment. And then: "I'm taking the carriage to fetch Ivo home."

Jack scrunched his face in confusion. "I thought Ivo was wooing the blacksmith's daughter?"

"I never said so." James's expression became grim. "I believe he's at Letchford Hall, calling on Miss Burton-Smythe."

Kate's mouth fell open. "He would never!"

"You can't be serious!" Jack exclaimed at the same time. "He knows how Mother and Father feel about that family."

Sir Frederick Burton-Smythe owned Letchford Hall, the estate that bordered Beasley Park. He and Kate's father were enemies of old. Kate didn't know the specifics, only that, at one time, Sir Frederick had been in love with her mother, Margaret.

Not in love. *Obsessed.*

He still was, Kate suspected. Why else would he have named his daughter after her mother?

Margaret Burton-Smythe, known as Meg hereabouts, was a willowy, freckle-faced redhead of eighteen. Kate had no particular quarrel with her, but all the same…

What was Ivo thinking to even consider courting such a person?

"Mother and Father can never know." James stood by the window, his voice as implacable as his posture. "Do you hear me, Jack?"

"I'm not going to tell them," Jack said defensively. "But they're bound to discover it for themselves if Ivo continues in this manner."

"I'm taking care of it." James moved to leave. "In the meanwhile"—he gave Kate and Jack the sternest of looks before departing the room— "try not to cause any other scandals."

Kate arched a brow at Jack. "Where *are* Mama and

Papa today?" she asked after James had taken his leave. "I've not seen either of them."

"Still in their room," Jack said.

Unlike most fashionable married couples, Kate's mother and father didn't hold with separate bedrooms. They shared a room; a place they retreated to often. Indeed, they were always slipping away together somewhere, whether to their bedchamber or off riding, driving, or strolling the grounds.

In warmer weather, when in residence at Beasley, they could often be found stretched out on the forget-me-not covered banks of the stream that ran through the park. Once, Kate had unexpectedly found them there embracing.

An awkward encounter.

She'd quietly slipped away before they could remark her presence.

"I heard them laughing as I came through the hall," Jack said. "We won't see them for another hour or two at least. Plenty of time to go riding." He gave an impatient kick to the leg of the sofa, rattling Kate in her seat. "Enough of your ridiculous needlework! Whatever scheme you're brewing can wait. Let's have a gallop across the park. I'll wager you ten pounds I can beat you to the gnarled oak."

Kate was up from the sofa before she could think, her every instinct primed for the challenge. The spirit of competition was in her blood. She couldn't have refused even if she'd wanted to. "I accept your wager. But not for a meager ten pounds."

"How much, then?"

She hesitated a split second before fixing on a way to turn the challenge to her advantage. "I want a forfeit. After Christmas, I want you to take me somewhere."

He gave her a suspicious look. "Where?"

"To call on a friend of mine. It's not far. Only twenty miles each way, by my calculation."

"*Twenty miles each way?* Good Lord, Kate. Where *is* this friend of yours? In Devonshire?"

"Does it matter?"

"No, but—"

"Unless, of course, you're afraid I'll win? We both know I'm likely to do so."

Jack immediately took the bait. "Very well. On the remote chance you prevail—and you must concede it's *very* remote—I shall accompany you to see this friend of yours. But you won't beat me, Kate. Not this time."

She smiled. "We shall see about that."

Chapter Four

C harles rose early the next morning, well before the sun had risen and the household had come to life. Lighting a lantern, he donned his clothes, collected a warm coat, and made his way downstairs for a quick cup of tea before heading out to the stables.

Flurry, Twig, and Ignatius stirred from the hearthrug to accompany him. Their nails clicked softly as they crossed the brick-and-mortar stable yard in Charles's wake.

The wind bit at his face. He paid it no heed. He was accustomed to rising before dawn, regardless of the weather. It was a time of rare peace and quiet. One he'd always relished, whether far out at sea or camped on the fringes of some remote battlefield.

As a boy he'd often awakened before sunrise to gallop his stallion, Nero, through the rolling mist that blanketed the grounds of the estate. It was Nero that Charles had now come to see.

He found the old dark bay stallion much as he'd left him, safe and snug in the warmth of the stable. He stood in a loose box not far from the ones that held the riding horses belonging to Charles's parents and sister.

Nero was the son of Charles's father's late and much-mourned stallion, Hyperion. Large, hot-tempered, and mercurial, Nero had once been something of a handful.

At the ripe old age of two and twenty, he was all but retired now. A well-deserved retirement. He'd been a faithful mount in his time and an equally faithful friend. Catching sight of Charles, he swung his head over the door of the loose box, giving a low whicker of greeting.

Charles crossed the hay-strewn floor of the stable. "Nero. You old devil." He stroked the stallion's muscular neck. "You haven't forgotten me, have you?"

Nero raised his head to Charles's face in answer. He lipped at Charles's cheek, his breath warm and his whiskery black muzzle soft as pressed velvet.

There were still a few remnants of hay in the stallion's manger, but in the loose box behind him, his water pail lay on its side. He must have kicked it over in the night.

Charles immediately entered the box to retrieve it. A horse couldn't be without water in weather like this, not for any length of time. It was the sort of thing that could lead to colic.

He carried the empty pail out to the pump in the yard. The dogs trotted with him, interested in his every move-ment. So interested that, as Charles worked the pump handle, Flurry jumped up against the half-filled pail, tipping it with his paws. Icy cold water spilled straight down the front of Charles's shirt and trousers.

He sucked in a sharp breath. "*Bloody hell.*" His shirt and coat were soaked through. "Blast it, Flurry." He shot a reproving look at the setter. "Have you lost all sense of decorum in my absence?"

An amused chuckle sounded behind him.

Charles turned sharply to find his father standing in the hazy glow of the lantern.

Arthur was bundled against the cold, his weight leaning heavily on his cane. A wry smile curved his mouth as he took in the state of his son's sopping clothing. "Miss the sea that much already, do you?"

Charles's scowl transformed into a swift grin. Righting the pail, he resumed pumping water into it. "Did my letters give you the impression that I was enamored of the sea?"

"There weren't many letters to speak of this time around."

Charles's grin faltered at the subtle rebuke. "I hadn't much time to write on the *Skylark*. Even less on the *Intrepid*. When I did, there wasn't a great deal to write about."

"Nothing you could share, presumably."

"Precious little," Charles said. His last visit home had coincided with the outbreak of war in Syria. It was that which had taken him back to sea, despite his family's strenuous objections. They'd wanted him to resign his commission. Instead, he'd returned to his ship early, determined to be part of the fight, even at the risk of his own life.

He finished filling the pail. Water sloshed over the rim of it as he carried it back to the stable.

His father walked alongside him, holding the lantern aloft. He waited in silence while Charles deposited the pail inside Nero's loose box.

Bestowing a final pat on the stallion's neck, Charles withdrew, latching the door securely shut behind him. A shiver coursed through him. Winter in the West Country was no place to be in wet clothing. Not on a frosty morning such as this.

"Come," Arthur said. "We'd best go inside before you catch your death. We can light a fire in the kitchen. Get some more tea into you."

Charles shot him an alert glance. "How did you—"

"Because your character hasn't altered as much as you may think." Arthur's cane clacked on the bricks as they navigated their way back to the house. "You're still the same restless boy who was up before dawn, sneaking cups of tea in the kitchen before slipping away to gallop your horse over the moors. The same boy who used to worry his mother sick."

Charles's conscience twinged. "I never meant to worry her. Not then. Not now."

"It doesn't change the fact that you *have* worried her." There was no overt censure in his father's words, but they were nevertheless a reprimand. "We neither of us wanted our only son to go off and get himself killed. A not unreasonable desire, you'll agree."

Charles opened the back door to the house. Taking charge of the lantern, he waited for his father and the dogs to precede him into the kitchen. "I'm here now. I've not returned any worse than when I left."

"Better than when you left, I'd say." Arthur glanced back at him. "Your prize money is substantial."

Charles had accumulated his fair share. Forty thousand pounds at last count. All sailors received a portion of the spoils from enemy ships they captured, and Charles had assisted in capturing more than most. Indeed, his tenure, first on the HMS *Skylark* and then as first lieutenant of the HMS *Intrepid*, had been extraordinarily lucrative.

He placed the lantern on the mantel. Crouching down, he lit a fire in the hearth. "It's sitting in the bank at present. I've not touched it yet."

Two chairs were arranged in front of the kitchen fireplace. His father took a seat in one while Charles brewed a fresh pot of tea. The three dogs stretched out on the hearth rug, eagerly soaking up the warmth from the freshly laid fire.

When the tea was ready, Charles brought them each a mug. "Is Mother still abed?" he asked as he sat down.

"She was when I left her." Arthur raised his mug to his lips, unwilling to have the conversation diverted. "Forty thousand pounds is a great deal of money."

Charles's muscles tensed imperceptibly.

The two of them had yet to talk candidly since his return. Charles had been reluctant to do so, and his father had so far refrained from pressing him. But no longer, it seemed. His father's patience was apparently at an end.

"Yes," Charles replied. "I know."

There was a lengthy silence between them.

It was taut with all the things left unsaid since Charles's last visit home. The lingering disappointment at the choices he'd made and the anger and frustration at his stubborn determination to diverge from the path that had been set out for him since birth.

"Do you have any plans for it?" his father asked.

"I mean to purchase a property of my own," Charles said.

He would have to. Heywood House wasn't coming to him in his father's will. It wouldn't go to his mother, either. His father merely had a life estate in the property—a fact which had remained firmly at the back of Charles's mind since he came of age.

"A wise idea," Arthur said. "Though, perhaps, a trifle premature given your current occupation." He continued to look at Charles with the same inscrutable expression. "Do you have a location in mind?"

"Somewhere close."

"I confess, that surprises me."

"I don't see why it should."

"Eight years ago, you couldn't leave Somersetshire quickly enough. And four years ago, you couldn't even stomach spending the entirety of your leave here." His father's gaze became stony. "Your mother and sister were deeply grieved."

"For which I'm heartily sorry," Charles said. "But there was no point in remaining only to rehash the same old arguments. What good would it have done? A sailor must return to sea. It's part of the job. One doesn't give up their post simply because the danger becomes too great."

"No, indeed. I daresay that, for you, the danger was the bulk of the attraction."

Charles stiffened. But he couldn't argue the point. He'd always yearned for more excitement in his life. It hadn't been enough to be the best at fighting or shooting when there were no consequences to be had. Actions had to mean something. There had to be risk—*serious* risk—to justify the reward.

"You've been chasing adventures since you were a boy," his father went on. "But war isn't a contest of skill or a feat of strength. It's brutal and pitiless. It changes a man."

"As I'm well aware," Charles said tightly.

"Yes, I believe you are. I can see it in you." The rigidity in his father's countenance was edged with a glint of sadness. "I'd have spared you that look."

Charles felt an answering twinge of sorrow. It was accompanied by no little guilt. "You couldn't shield me from everything in life. I never wanted you to."

"I had no idea of doing so. But you're my son. My *only* son. More importantly, you're your mother's only son. If she were to lose you—"

"She hasn't lost me. I'm alive and well and in possession of a sizeable fortune. My years at sea *have* changed

44

me, I won't dispute the fact, but I was damned successful as a sailor."

His father's attention sharpened, narrowing in on the single word with hawklike intensity.

Too late, Charles realized his mistake.

"*Was?*" Arthur repeated. "What do you mean *was?*"

Charles steeled himself for the argument to come. The one he'd been dreading since he'd parted ways with the Navy. "I've resigned my commission," he admitted.

His father went unnaturally still. At length, he set his mug down on the small table beside him, his every movement precise. "I see."

Charles's stomach knotted. "I was going to tell you when I arrived, but I didn't want to ruin the holiday with bitterness and recriminations."

"Because you've put us through eight years of anguish for nothing?"

"It wasn't for nothing."

"Quite so. You have your forty thousand pounds."

Charles's brows lowered. "I didn't mean the money. I meant—"

"When you decided to go to Portsmouth instead of Cambridge, without regard for my wishes or those of your mother, you told us you intended to make the Navy your life."

"It was the truth."

"I recall you making an impassioned argument about your duty to King and country. About the honor you'd bring to the family name and how you'd be putting your skills to good use rather than moldering in the country—"

"I *know* what I said then."

"And now?"

Charles hated to admit that all of his arguments had come to nothing. That rather than honor, he'd ultimately brought disgrace on the Heywood name. "It's past time I settled down," he said instead. "In future, my energies can be better expended managing an estate."

His father gave him a dubious look. "Am I to believe you've given up the Navy in order to marry and start a family?"

Charles downed a swallow of tea. The brew left a bitter taste in his mouth.

The conclusion his father had drawn wasn't entirely inaccurate. Though it hadn't been Charles's reason for leaving the Navy, marriage was certainly a consideration now he was home. It was all part and parcel of the quiet, peaceful life he envisioned for himself. A life he'd imagined with increasing frequency during his final years at sea.

That fact made it no less tedious to contemplate.

He'd had no childhood sweetheart awaiting him in England. No one who had been writing to him all these years, anxiously anticipating his return. When he embarked on the business of courtship and matrimony, he'd have to start from scratch.

"I've no plans to marry in the immediate future," he said. "Not until I've found a suitable property."

His father made no reply.

Charles couldn't tell whether his silence was disbelief or disapproval. "Do you object to the idea?"

"Not in theory," Arthur said. "The life of a gentleman farmer is an admirable one."

"But?"

"It's hardly sufficient to entice an officer away from a successful career at sea. You could have easily had another ten years in the Navy. A command of your own. It's what you claimed you wanted. Not an estate. Not a dull life in the country." Arthur studied his son's face. "Why would you give it up? And please, do me the courtesy of sparing me anymore half-truths and evasions."

Outside, the sun was beginning to rise. The servants would soon rise along with it. What privacy Charles and his father had wouldn't last much longer.

There was no more point in dissembling.

"Because I was tired of politics," Charles said. "I was a sailor. I had no interest in statecraft."

"A good sailor does what he's told."

"And when he can no longer obey in conscience?"

Charles had reached that point in the summer of 1840. His ship had been patrolling the Lebanese Coast, protecting British interests against the occupying forces of Egyptian ruler Muhammad Ali Pasha. When the citizens revolted against Muhammad Ali's occupation, his soldiers had brutally retaliated, burning towns and villages up and down the coast.

Britain had moved to intervene. Charles's ship was first on the scene. His commodore was tasked with leading the land force—an assemblage of British, Ottoman, and rebel troops. Charles was among them. He'd helped to protect the coastal cities from the marauding Egyptian soldiers.

And then the allied fleet had joined the battle.

Rather than defending the civilians, the allies had bombarded them. Many innocent people had been killed in the action.

Charles and the rest of the commodore's army had entrenched themselves in the city, ultimately compelling its surrender. Later, he'd learned that the allies claimed their flag of truce had been fired upon. It was that which had prompted their merciless assault.

By then it was already too late. Charles had lost faith. He'd begun to doubt what it was they were doing there. What it was *he* was doing there.

The following years at sea had done nothing to restore his confidence. He'd seen bad men decorated and good ones ordered to relinquish their commands. It had little to do with heroism or the lack of it. It was all politics and influence and the ever-increasing focus on expansion of the British Empire, regardless of the innocents harmed in the pursuit of it.

Charles explained it to his father as best he could.

Arthur listened in silence, his expression of concern deepening as Charles relayed the circumstances under which his dissatisfaction with the Navy had come to an unfortunate head.

"I couldn't stomach it any longer," Charles said. "I was frustrated and angry—challenging my superiors at every turn and questioning their commands. Captain Bright summoned me to his quarters to meet with Admiral Dixon. They told me I had a promising career ahead of me if I could get myself in order. They even held out the lure of a ship of my own. I was almost tempted until they began talking about our God-given mission to extend British rule across the globe. That was what scuttled it. I all but laughed in their faces."

Arthur winced. "I trust you didn't take it that far."

"I may have." Charles couldn't remember everything he'd said or done during that fateful interview, only that one moment he'd been an officer and the next he hadn't. "Admiral Dixon offered some choice words about my lack of patriotism and my general want of discipline. The captain responded with a few words in my defense. I interrupted them both to tell them I was done with it. Done with the scourge of Imperialism. Done with cowards issuing orders from behind their desks."

"Good God, Charles."

"I know." Charles stared bleakly into his tea, recalling

the way the two officers' faces had gone from red to white with fury. "The Admiral told me to tender my resignation. So I did, with extreme pleasure. And then I walked out of there. Captain Bright had one of the men escort me from the ship while another tossed my trunk and the rest of my belongings onto the dock."

The fire crackled in the hearth, sparks flaring up into the chimney. Charles no longer felt the heat of it. The memory of his ignominious departure from the Navy left him quite cold to the heart.

"I booked passage on a merchant ship home," he said. "The news of my behavior is sure to follow when the *Intrepid* returns to England. Grandfather will be furious. So will Uncle George."

"You'll write to them both and explain," his father said. It wasn't a request.

"I scarcely know what I'll say."

"Tell them the truth. Tell them you were too idealistic."

Charles huffed a bitter laugh. "That's your conclusion?"

"It's your nature. I saw it in you when you came to me and informed me you wouldn't be attending Cambridge. You wanted to prove yourself in a noble fight. But the reality of war is rarely noble. It's more often tragic."

"Then you comprehend why it was time for me to depart."

"Comprehend it? I could have foreseen it. That doesn't excuse the toll your quest for adventure has taken on the family."

Charles set down his mug with a troubled frown. "I intend to make amends."

"I look forward to it." Rising from his chair, Arthur set a hand on Charles's shoulder, giving it a hard squeeze. "Come. Your mother and sister will be up soon and eager to see you at the breakfast table. They'll be pleased beyond measure to hear you're out of harm's way at last." He paused, adding, "I'm pleased as well."

The knot in Charles's chest began to ease. His father's disappointment was evident, but it paled in comparison to his love for his son. Charles knew then, just as he'd known as a boy, that whatever he'd done, he would always have his father's unconditional support.

It wasn't enough.

Charles wanted his respect, too.

"Is that all you mean to say on the subject?" he asked. "You were right, after all. I shouldn't have gone. It's done nothing but distress the family and leave me right back in Somersetshire, worse off than when I started."

"Hardly worse off," his father said. "You're older and wiser, now. Richer, too."

Charles stood. "Poor compensation, all things considered."

"Is it? You took a stand against what you perceived as injustice. I might argue with the manner of it, but I can't be ashamed of your principles."

"Grandfather and Uncle George won't be so forgiving."

"They'll come around. In the meanwhile, it's you who must reconcile yourself to what's happened, not any of us."

The dogs remained by the fire, refusing to relinquish its warmth, as Charles and his father departed the kitchen.

"I should have resigned my commission after the *Intrepid* departed Syria," Charles said. "I could have left with dignity, then. Instead, I let my anger and unhappiness fester until I could contain it no longer." His shoulders slumped. "I feel as though I've failed."

His father gave him a fond smile. "You'll soon rouse

yourself from your disappointment. A new adventure will beckon and you'll set out after it, just as you always have."

Charles shook his head. "I've had enough of adventure. From now on, it's peace and tranquility I want."

He meant it.

It didn't matter that leaving the Navy had left him unmoored. That he was restless and out of his element back on land. A few more weeks in the bosom of his family and surely his spirit would calm and the proper course for his future would become clear.

It had to.

Chapter Five

"This one is from me as well." Charles passed a tissue-wrapped box to his sister. She sat next to him on the overstuffed sofa, the skirts of her dressing gown pooling around her in a spill of soft pink wool. "It's just a trifle. Something I picked up at a bazaar in Cairo."

Hannah had only just awakened. Her dark auburn hair, so difficult to tame, had been temporarily subdued into a thick plait, secured with a velvet ribbon. Odysseus wore a matching ribbon around his scrawny neck. He dozed peacefully at Hannah's slippered feet, well-fed and contented, amid the growing pile of torn paper and tinsel.

"What is it?" she asked.

"You must open it and see," their father said.

"Yes, do," their mother encouraged.

Arthur and Philly Heywood sat across from their children on the drawing room settee, their hands held in an intimate clasp. Behind them, stretching all the way to the drawing room ceiling, stood the Christmas tree in all its splendor. It was a new addition to their holiday celebrations. A fashion only recently brought to England, courtesy of Queen Victoria's German husband, Prince Albert.

Philly and Hannah had taken to the idea at once. Since Charles's arrival a fortnight ago, he'd been kept busy finding a suitable tree for them, cutting it down, and hauling it back to the house to decorate. Together, the Heywoods and their longtime retainers—Sara, William, and the rest of the servants—had trimmed the tree with candles, gilded fruit, red ribbons, and tinsel.

The entire room smelled of new pine, fresh oranges and cloves, and of the spice cake Cook was baking for their Christmas tea.

Philly had been determined to spare no effort in celebrating the holiday, now that Charles's was home and finally free from danger. She'd received the news of his resignation from the Navy with tears of happiness and relief. Hannah had been equally overjoyed. There were no arguments or recriminations. The past was forgiven in exchange for the promise of a safe and hopeful future.

Charles wished he could feel as optimistic about that future as his mother and sister so obviously did.

A fortnight in residence and he was still as unmoored as he'd been when he arrived. It was an unsettling sensation. A familiar one, too. This same sense of restlessness— of incompleteness—had prompted him to leave Somersetshire eight years ago. It had followed him across the sea to Lebanon, Egypt, and beyond, a constant companion as he'd journeyed to the ends of the earth and back again. Adventuring hadn't quelled the feeling. Perhaps nothing ever would.

Hannah opened the box he'd given her to reveal a dainty, hand-painted porcelain perfume bottle. "Oh, look, Mama! Isn't it beautiful?" She flung her arms around Charles's neck in an impulsive embrace. "Thank you. I love it." She kissed his cheek before releasing him. "I shall put it on my dressing table."

"Are ladies wearing much perfume abroad these days, my love?" his mother asked.

"I didn't meet many ladies during my travels," Charles said. "Certainly no one of fashion."

"Hadn't the sailors any dances or parties?" Hannah asked. "There were balls when you were a soldier, weren't there, Papa?"

"A few," Arthur said. "But I was in the Army, not the Navy, sweetheart."

"We sailors spend a great many months at sea," Charles said. "A grim business. We have no one but each other for company."

Hannah returned her gift to its box. "You must have been very lonely."

Charles didn't answer.

The truth was, he *had* been lonely. Time had hung heavy when the fighting had stopped. He'd begun to crave a return to action. But when that action came, it was never of the sort he'd wanted. In the end, there had been no true heroes there. No genuine villains. Only men fighting other men for reasons none of them wholly understood.

"Soldiers and sailors aren't the best source of information on what transpires at social events," Arthur said, turning the subject. "You'd be better served consulting a lady."

"The only one I know who has had a season is Mama," Hannah said.

"And then only a single ball," their mother replied. "Hardly worth remembering."

Arthur brought his wife's hand to his lips. "No," he said gravely, "it isn't."

It had been a dark time in Charles's mother's life. On

her grandfather's death, Satterthwaite Court had passed out of her hands, going instead to a distant male relation— a ruthless London financier by the name of Edgar Townsend. He'd removed Philly from Satterthwaite Court and brought her to town, ostensibly to give her a season. In reality, he'd been conniving to marry her off to a notorious duke.

Charles didn't know the whole of it. His parents hadn't wished to burden him or his sister with distressing tales from the past. But Charles knew that his mother had been made unhappy and that only his father's intervention had prevented her coming to harm.

"In that case," Hannah said. "I shall have to rely on Charles's betrothed to be my guide."

Charles gave a surprised laugh. "Have I missed something? The last I checked, I wasn't betrothed to anyone."

"You will be soon," Hannah replied with unshakable confidence. "It's all but guaranteed. Is it not, Mama?"

Philly smiled. "I don't know about a guarantee, but it does seem likely that your brother might soon find himself engaged."

Hannah flashed Charles a grin at having her suspicions endorsed by their mother.

"Pray don't encourage her, Mother," Charles begged. "I've already told you all that I don't plan to marry until I've found a suitable estate."

"When it comes to romance," his father said, "a man's plans have a way of going straight out the window. Especially if that man is young and has just returned from nearly a decade at sea."

Charles scoffed.

"It's true, love," Philly said. "You have a good name and a good-sized fortune. The minute the snow melts, matchmaking mamas from Truro to Berwick-on-Tweed will be throwing their daughters at your head. Your father and I expect it. We only ask that, when you make your choice, you choose a lady worthy of your affections. Don't make the mistake of tying yourself to the first pretty girl who crosses your path."

Charles's treacherous emotions once again conjured a vision of Kate. The way she'd looked at him so archly. As though she'd found him as intriguing as he'd found her.

A rare prickle of heat crept beneath his shirt collar. "You and father have nothing to worry about on that score."

Arthur's gaze sharpened. "Good God, lad, have you met someone already?"

"Absolutely not," Charles replied quickly.

A little too quickly, perhaps.

He cleared his throat. "Was that the last package?"

His mother took pity on him. "No, indeed." She rose and went to the tree. "There's another here somewhere." She rummaged beneath the branches. "Sara brought it in yesterday along with the post."

Hannah's attention was temporarily diverted. "For me?" she inquired eagerly.

"No, dearest. It's for Charles. Ah!" Philly's face lit with a triumphant smile. "Here it is." She withdrew a small parcel from beneath the tree. There was a cream-colored envelope tucked beneath its ribbons, with Charles's name and direction written across the front in a spidery hand.

"Who is it from?" he asked as his mother passed it to him. The parcel was soft beneath the printed wrapping paper. It felt rather like an article of clothing.

Odd, that. Charles didn't know anyone outside his family who would feel compelled to send him any gift, let alone something as intimate as clothing.

"I've no idea," Philly said. "It didn't have a return

address. Whoever sent it desires to remain anonymous. Unless they've included their name inside the card?"

Charles tore open the envelope. It contained a letter on plain-woven stationery, written in the same spidery hand-writing.

To Lieutenant Charles Heywood:

I write to you as an act of conscience at great risk to my own safety and beg you to tell no one of this letter. A grievous wrong has been done to your mother. You may yet make it right. Look for Mr. Arbogast on the eighth of January at ten o'clock in Gold Street, Tiverton. Employ the utmost discretion. You will know best how to proceed.

Signed,
One Who Wishes You Well

A peculiar feeling of uneasiness settled in Charles's veins as he finished reading. What in blazes could be the meaning of it?

"Who is it from?" his mother asked. "Did they include a name?"

Refolding the letter, Charles tucked it into the inner pocket of his coat. He had no desire to alarm his family. "A well-wisher," he replied. "Nobody important."

"Open the gift," Hannah urged.

With a burgeoning sense of foreboding, Charles unwrapped the parcel. Given the contents of the letter, it could be anything. But on folding back the tissue paper, he discovered that the mysterious gift was only a folded piece of crochet-work fashioned in a soft red yarn.

A scarf? A muffler? It was impossible to tell.

He lifted it out to inspect it.

Philly inhaled a surprised breath. "My goodness. It's a crocheted dog muzzle!"

The four Heywoods leaned forward in unison to examine the offending article.

"What a strange thing to give someone," Hannah said. "It's not meant for one of *our* dogs, is it?"

"I doubt that. It doesn't look very sturdy," Arthur observed. "More for show than for substance, I'd guess."

"Someone's idea of a jest, perhaps?" Philly suggested.

Hannah craned her head to peer into the box. "Look, Charles! There's another note inside."

Charles's brows knit. There was indeed another note. This one was in an even smaller envelope. He opened it. The writing within was as bold as the script on the previous letter had been spidery.

For your rare Spanish dog, until he learns to recognize the difference between a carriage wheel, a skirt, and my fingers.

And suddenly, Charles understood exactly where the gift had come from.

It was from Kate, his blue-eyed Bond Street lady. Some sort of odd jest, as his mother had suggested, undertaken for Kate's own amusement. A crocheted dog muzzle of all things!

In other circumstances, Charles might have laughed. She was teasing him. Making sport of the fact she'd been bitten.

But there was nothing funny about the first letter she'd sent.

Quite the reverse.

There was an implied threat about it. Something vaguely malicious.

"Is it from a lady?" Hannah asked, looking over his shoulder. "It looks like a lady's handwriting."

Charles quickly folded the note away, tucking into his

pocket along with the other letter. "Yes," he said. "I suspect so."

His parents exchanged a weighted look.

"Who is she, my love?" Philly asked.

A devil, Charles was tempted to reply. She must be to have written the first letter.

But he had no intention of involving his parents in the affair.

"I don't know her," he answered truthfully. "Nor do I wish to."

Chapter Six

Somerset, England
January 1844

"How did you say you know these people again?" Jack asked his sister as their carriage rolled up the drive of the sprawling granite house.

"I don't know them," Kate admitted.

Jack's head jerked to look at her. *"What?"*

She sat across from him, dressed in a carriage gown of dusky blue glacé silk and a black velvet cloak. Her hair had been artfully arranged, parted at the center and smoothed back into an elegant chignon at her nape. She looked rather well, or so she'd thought when she checked her reflection in the glass before departing Beasley Park two hours ago.

It had been a long journey, made as comfortably and expeditiously as possible. The Earl of Allendale's black-lacquered carriage, with the family crest gilded on the door, was extraordinarily well sprung.

"Don't work yourself up into a state," she said to her brother. "I'm not a complete stranger to the Heywoods. We simply haven't been properly introduced, that's all."

"But you *are* acquainted with them?"

She gave a dismissive shrug. "A passing acquaintance." It was mainly true. She *had* passed Lieutenant Heywood on the street. "Anyway, we're in the country now, not London. We needn't stand on ceremony."

"Kate…" Jack groaned. "If we've come all this way only to make arses of ourselves…"

The carriage came to a halt in front of the stone steps that flanked the entrance.

"We might have done," she conceded as the footman opened the carriage door. "But it's too late to turn back now."

Jack jumped out first, offering his hand to assist Kate down. His brows were set in a furious line.

He was still angry about losing that race to her. And now, even angrier to discover that the Heywoods were, effectively, unknown to them.

Kate didn't regard his foul temper. She was here, wasn't she? That was all that mattered. Her hand on Jack's arm, she ascended the stone steps to the arched entrance of the house.

Jack rapped twice on the door, imbuing all his ire into the summons. The loud thump-thump echoed in the stillness of the cold January morning. "We can't stay above half an hour," he muttered. "There'll already be hell to pay when we return."

She smoothed her skirts. Mama, Papa, and James believed she and Jack were joining acquaintances of theirs for an outing to Dunster Castle. A flimsy lie that could easily be disproven. Kate was disappointed she hadn't thought of a better one. But there were few other ways to explain a half day's absence from home at this time of year.

"It will be worth it," she said, as much to herself as to her brother.

Jack's brows dipped into a scowl. He raised his fist to knock again. The door was opened before he could do so.

A frowning manservant stood on the threshold. He glanced first at them, then at the crest on the carriage, and back again. "May I help you, sir?"

Jack removed his hat. "Mr. Beresford and Lady Katherine Beresford to see——"

"Lieutenant Heywood," Kate said.

Jack's gaze shot to her face. He had been aggravated before. Now, he was positively appalled. "*Lieutenant* Heywood?"

She affected an innocent expression. "Is he at home?" she asked the butler.

"Yes, my lady." The man bowed to them before stepping back to admit them into the house. "This way, if you please."

Kate followed him up the curving marble staircase.

The inside of Heywood House was fashioned in the same classical style as its stately Palladian exterior. There were molded ceilings with ornamented plasterwork and white-paneled walls spaced with Ionic pilasters. Enormous landscape paintings covered every available surface; scenes of dogs, horses, and the pristine English countryside. Along with the thick Aubusson carpets and sumptuous furnishings of walnut and mahogany, they brought a richness to the house that spoke less of cold elegance than of warmth and familial affection.

Kate took it all in with avid curiosity as the butler led her to the drawing room.

Jack lagged behind them, his irritation with her radiating off of him in waves. It was one thing to maneuver him into making an unsolicited call on strangers, but to trick him into accompanying her to call on a gentleman—well. That was something else entirely.

Kate couldn't be sorry for the deception. She'd been eagerly anticipating her next meeting with the handsome Lieutenant Heywood ever since she'd first encountered him in Bond Street. With luck, he'd be expecting her. She had, after all, sent him the crocheted dog muzzle.

It had been a stroke of inspiration.

The pattern had appeared, rather auspiciously, in last month's edition of the *Lady's Museum and Domestic Magazine*. Kate had found it quite by chance; a darling little design, displayed on an illustration of a lady's lapdog. The instant she'd beheld it, she'd known it would be just the thing to get the lieutenant's attention.

What gentleman could fail to be intrigued by such a humorous gift? Unless he was a simpleton, he'd easily deduce who it was from. It was sure to keep her in his thoughts until she could manage a visit.

That had been the plan anyway.

Conversation floated out from the drawing room; the sounds of deep male voices and the answering softness of feminine laughter.

Kate recognized one of those voices—a dark, rich, baritone. It had the same immediate effect on her that it had had when she'd first heard it in Bond Street. Her heartbeat quickened with anticipation.

"Mr. Beresford and Lady Katherine Beresford," the butler announced.

Kate entered the drawing room along with her brother.

It was a graceful room, comfortably worn, with silk-papered walls, blue brocade draperies, and sofas and armchairs upholstered in faded velvets and soft-striped damasks. At the heart of it, a small family was seated, completely at their ease, around the crackling flames in an enormous marble fireplace. A tinsel-covered Christmas tree towered behind them and a motley assortment of dogs lay at their feet, stretched out on the carpet in various states of repose.

The dogs stirred to life as the drawing room's occupants stood to receive their guests.

There were four people altogether. Two were beautiful auburn-haired ladies: one older and one younger. Mother and daughter, Kate guessed. They both shared the most extraordinary feature: eyes that didn't match, one blue and one brown. Kate had never seen the like of it.

The other two were men. The more senior—a stern, raven-haired gentlemen with silver at his temples—rose from his seat with the aid of a cane. Not far from him, his back to the fireplace, stood Lieutenant Heywood.

A flush of warmth spread through her.

He was as handsome as she recalled, though no more welcoming.

His posture was rigid, his face impassive. Only his gray eyes betrayed any feeling, and then merely the barest flicker. A flash of surprise, followed swiftly by a flare of… Good Lord, it was annoyance!

Kate's spirits sank.

Thank goodness for Jack. He had the natural Beresford ability to rise to any occasion.

"Forgive the presumption," he said. "We were in the neighborhood and thought we may as well pay our respects. My sister and Lieutenant Heywood met briefly in London, I believe."

The older, auburn-haired lady looked at her son with gentle curiosity. "Are you acquainted with this young lady, Charles?"

There was a long silence.

A pit of anxiety formed in Kate's stomach. It was in Lieutenant Heywood's power to humiliate her. To disavow the connection, thus making her appear ridiculous. She hadn't considered the possibility. She'd thought—

But heaven knew what she'd thought anymore.

All her girlish ideas of flirtation had vanished the moment they'd entered the drawing room and she'd seen the look on his face.

He may have been annoyed with her in Bond Street, but he'd also been fascinated. She'd recognized the signs. She had seen them often enough during her London season. But there was nothing of fascination about the way the lieutenant was looking at her now.

"Yes," he said at last. "Though we've yet to be properly introduced."

Kate exhaled a breath. Whatever his feelings for her, it seemed he was disposed to play the gentleman.

"Lady Katherine, is it?" he asked.

"It is." She pasted on a brilliant smile. "We have a mutual friend in Mr. Gilbert Trumble. A schoolmate of yours at Eton, I understand."

Lieutenant Heywood's brow arched in sardonic acknowledgement of Kate's over embellishment. He forbore to point out that Gilbert was many years below him at school or that the two of them had barely qualified as acquaintances, let alone friends.

Another gentlemanly courtesy.

Kate could have done without it, frankly.

Christine had called Lieutenant Heywood rude, and she hadn't been wrong. Perhaps Kate had misremembered his brief look of masculine interest in Bond Street? The way he'd turned gruff and solicitous as he'd handed her his handkerchief to bind her hand?

It wouldn't be the first time she'd over-romanticized an event. One had to on occasion. Life was so dull and dreary otherwise. Still…

She was beginning to regret having come here.

"Mr. Trumble and his family are friends of longstanding," Jack explained, oblivious to the undercurrent passing between Kate and the lieutenant. "I'd no idea you were on terms with them."

"Yes," Lieutenant Heywood said dryly. "It is surprising, isn't it?"

Kate's smile dimmed. She clenched her teeth against a sharp retort. "May I have the pleasure of meeting your family, sir?"

"Of course." Lieutenant Heywood's manner was no warmer as he dispensed with the introductions. "I have the honor of presenting my parents, Captain and Mrs. Heywood, and my sister, Miss Hannah Heywood."

"Sir. Ma'am. Miss Heywood." Kate curtsied. "I'm pleased to make your acquaintance."

"Perhaps you know my parents?" Jack inquired after sketching a bow. "My father is John Beresford, Earl of Allendale. Our family seat is at Worth House in Hertfordshire. However, my mother was formerly Margaret Honeywell of Beasley Park. We're in residence there for the holiday."

"Beasley Park is a distance away," Captain Heywood said. "But the name of Honeywell isn't wholly unfamiliar." He gestured to the sofa. "Will you not sit down?"

"Yes, do," Mrs. Heywood said. "I'll order the tea tray." She went to the tasseled bell pull by the fireplace and gave it a firm tug.

The dogs approached to sniff the flounce of Kate's silk skirts as she took a seat. One dog in particular caught her eye—a brindle mongrel pup with a velvet ribbon around his neck.

"Good gracious!" Her gaze lifted to the lieutenant's face in astonishment. "Can this be your imported Spanish dog?"

Lieutenant Heywood remained standing. "It is," he said stiffly. "His name is Odysseus."

Mrs. Heywood returned to her place on the overstuffed sofa. "Spanish, did you say?"

"A poor joke," Lieutenant Heywood replied to his mother.

Kate extended a hand to pet the little dog, only to pause. She cast another glance at the lieutenant. "Dare I risk it?"

"He's quite gentle," Miss Heywood volunteered, resuming her seat. It was the first she'd spoken since Kate had entered the room. She seemed a shy sort of girl, not much used to company.

Kate offered her a smile of genuine warmth. "Then his character has reformed since our last meeting." She stroked Odysseus gently on the head. He received the tribute with every sign of enjoyment, displaying no evidence of the wild-eyed aggressiveness he'd exhibited in Bond Street. "He bit me then."

"Did he?" Captain Heywood gave his son a measured look as he sat down beside his wife. "I begin to understand."

There was an awkward pause.

It was interrupted by the arrival of a young maidservant at the door of the drawing room. She wore a starched apron over a plain black stuff gown. "You rang, ma'am?"

"Would you bring in the tea tray, please, Mary?" Mrs. Heywood asked.

"Yes, ma'am. At once." With a curtsy, the maid withdrew.

Lieutenant Heywood cleared his throat. He addressed Kate: "You've, ah, recovered, I trust?"

"Oh yes," Kate said. "It was only a scratch. I scarcely regard it. Isn't that so, Jack?"

"My sister is made of stern stuff," Jack said. "She's always getting into scrapes with her dogs and horses. Not to mention those two cats of hers. Selfish, ill-tempered beasts. If I wasn't so attached to them myself, I'd bar them from the house."

"You're fond of pets, my lady?" Miss Heywood asked.

"I couldn't live without them," Kate said. "No doubt it's why I prefer the country. I had an abominable time during my come-out. Meeting your brother was the only interesting thing to happen all season."

Lieutenant Heywood appeared unmoved by her assertion. He remained by the fire, looking as grave and implacable as a sailor standing at the prow of a 56-gun frigate.

"Hannah will be making her debut this year," Mrs. Heywood said.

"You're going to London?" Kate asked with interest. Perhaps Miss Heywood's brother would be accompanying her?

Not that Kate half cared any longer.

Insufferable man!

Had his declaration that the mongrel was a rare Spanish breed been nothing more than a one-time bout of insanity? Had he, in truth, no sense of humor at all?

Kate was beginning to suspect so.

"London or Bath," Miss Heywood said. "We haven't decided."

"You *can't* go to Bath," Kate replied at once. "The prospects are poor enough in London. I shudder to think what they might be in Bath. You'd have no one to choose from but aged gentlemen gone to take the waters."

"I say, Kate," Jack murmured. "Steady on."

"Mind you, I've nothing against aged gentleman," Kate continued. "I'm sure there are very nice ones about in Bath or Ramsgate or wherever it is they go to cure their many infirmities. But an aged fellow would never do as a husband for someone of our age. You're so sweet and lovely, Miss Heywood. Truly, you mustn't settle."

Lieutenant Heywood regarded Kate steadily, an unreadable expression on his face. She couldn't tell whether he was amused by her or as appalled as Jack was. Perhaps neither. Perhaps the lieutenant wasn't thinking of her at all. He may well be contemplating politics, or his correspondence, or deciding what it was he'd have for supper.

Kate nevertheless made an effort to still her tongue.

It lasted all of a second.

"A pity London isn't merrier for young ladies," she said. "But it can never measure up to our revels in the country. We haven't a ball in the offing, regrettably, but there's plenty of music and dancing. You must come to Beasley and waltz with my brothers. I have three altogether."

A red flush swept up Jack's neck. "*Kate,*" he said in a pleading undertone. "I'm sure Miss Heywood doesn't wish to—"

"Wouldn't that be terribly entertaining?" Kate asked. "While you're there, I could show you my horses and dogs. I have the most valiant hunter, Ember, and the sweetest pair of spaniels. I'll even introduce you to my cats, unless you have an aversion?"

"I-I don't mind cats," Miss Heywood said, stammering a little. "I should like to meet them."

"Then you shall," Kate declared. "I'll fix a date and send you an invitation. If your parents don't object?"

Captain Heywood and his wife exchanged a brief look. It seemed to contain an entire unspoken conversation—a question, an answer, a silent agreement. Indeed, except for her own parents, Kate had rarely beheld a couple so much in harmony.

"We have no objection," Captain Heywood said. "Providing the weather permits."

"The weather was well enough today," Jack said. "We even have some sun. It puts us quite at our leisure in terms of travel time."

"You might like to stay for luncheon," Mrs. Heywood offered graciously.

"Oh no," Kate protested. "We wouldn't wish to put you to the trouble. But it's such a beautiful clear day and I'm longing to stretch my legs. Perhaps, after, tea, Miss Heywood might be persuaded to give us a tour of the gardens?"

"If you like," Miss Heywood haltingly agreed, but not before flashing an anxious glance at her brother. "Will you accompany us, Charles?"

Lieutenant Heywood inclined his head. He didn't seem eager, but nor was he entirely unwilling. On the contrary, his jaw was hard, his shoulders set, as though he'd resolved himself to deal with an irksome piece of unpleasantness.

With a sinking feeling, Kate realized that unpleasantness was her.

Chapter Seven

Charles accompanied his sister and their guests along the curving tree-lined path that edged Heywood House's apple orchard. At this time of year, the branches were barren and the fruit but a distant memory. A layer of frost covered the hard ground, undiminished by the winter sun shining in the sky above.

Mr. Beresford walked beside him, while Hannah strolled ahead, arm-in-arm with Kate.

But not Kate any longer.

The young woman in the shapely blue dress, silk skirts swaying provocatively with every step, was Lady Katherine Beresford, daughter of the Earl of Allendale.

Naturally she was.

Only a lady of wealth and breeding would evince such confidence. Such decisiveness. Not only had she discovered who he was, she'd contrived to call on him as well. Granted, it was on the flimsiest pretext (a fact which had been plainly evident to Charles's parents), but still she'd come, arriving at Heywood House as bold as you please.

Aggravated as he was, Charles couldn't help being

impressed by such blazing self-assurance. Almost as impressed as he was with her kindness. It was a rare quality—as wholesome as it was unexpected. Fashionable people were often polite, in his experience, but they were seldom possessed of genuine warmth.

Not so, Kate.

The goodness of her character was evident in the way she greeted the dogs, the manner in which she addressed his parents, and the honest sympathy with which she'd conversed with his sister. When coupled with her beauty and bearing, Charles couldn't help feeling himself captivated all over again.

She walked with his sister awhile before the turn of the path separated them. Mr. Beresford fell in with Hannah then, and Kate hung back until she was, quite naturally, strolling at Charles's side. She didn't mince words.

"Did you receive my gift?" she asked.

Charles ignored the sensation of her full skirts brushing the leg of his trousers. "I did."

"And did you not think it amusing?"

"I might have done," he said, "if it hadn't been accompanied by that note."

She shot him a bewildered glance from beneath the brim of her blue velvet bonnet. "What was wrong with my note? I said nothing that wasn't true. Your dog did chase carriage wheels and ladies' skirts. And he did bite my finger."

"Not that note," he said. "The other one."

"What other one?"

"The note where you dared make implications about my mother."

Kate stopped abruptly. "I *beg* your pardon?"

Charles came to a grudging halt. His sister and Mr. Beresford had rounded the bend in the path ahead.

Charles and Kate were effectively alone. What words they exchanged would be entirely private, providing neither of them raised their voices.

"Do you deny sending it?" he asked quietly.

"I most certainly do," she answered in a forceful undertone. "Why would I make insinuations about your mother? I've never met the lady before. And she seems a nice enough person."

"She is," he said. "One I won't have meddled with for the amusement of fashionable people."

Kate's expression tightened. "You must think very little of me, sir."

"I don't know you, ma'am."

"Then how——"

"The letter came with your gift," he said. "It was attached to the package."

"The only letter I wrote was contained inside the box," she retorted. "I wrote no other. Why should I?"

Charles studied her face. There was no deception in it. No slyness or sparkle of mischief in her eyes. If she was telling the truth, he'd just accused her—*insulted* her—for nothing.

His jaw tightened at the prospect.

"I don't know why," he said. "Why do fashionable people do anything?"

"I do wish you'd stop referring to me as *fashionable people*," she returned. "I'm not a *people*. I'm a *person*. The fact that I claim to a bit of fashion doesn't mean I'm some malicious London nitwit engaging in mean-spirited pranks." Her eyes kindled. "Would you ever accuse a man of such? I think not. And yet it's gentlemen who are to blame for the lion's share of these larks. Look at any of the betting books at their clubs and tell me I'm wrong."

"You're not wrong," Charles acknowledged when she

at last paused for breath. "My accusation didn't arise from your gender."

"No," she huffed. "Merely my character."

"If I've been mistaken, I apologize."

"*If?*" Her gaze narrowed. "What did this other letter say exactly?"

"Insinuations, as I told you."

"I'd like to see it."

"I think not."

"Yet you blame me for writing it? Come." She held out her gloved hand. "I demand to see that of which I'm being accused. It's the least you owe me for making such assertions."

Charles hesitated a fraction of a second. He'd collected the letter before they departed on their walk, tucking the envelope into the pocket of his overcoat. He'd meant to confront her with its contents. To wring an explanation out of her. But it increasingly appeared there was no explanation to be had. Not from Kate, in any event.

He reluctantly withdrew the letter and gave it to her.

"This isn't my handwriting," she said at once.

"How was I to know that?"

She shook the letter at him. "Did you not notice the difference between the style of writing in this note and the one I sent? Anyone could see they're not the same."

"I did notice," he said. "However, at the time, I was more concerned with what the note contained than the style in which it was written."

Kate turned her attention back to the letter, swiftly reading its contents. Her eyes widened. "Extraordinary," she murmured. "What is it they're implying?"

"I haven't the slightest notion. Something sinister, I suspect."

"Evidently. But what?" She looked up at him, her

curiosity piqued. "Will you go to Tiverton on Monday to find out?"

Removing the letter from her fingers, Charles returned it to its envelope and tucked it back into the interior pocket of his coat. Naturally he was going to Tiverton. He wasn't the sort of man to let a threat to his family go unchallenged. If Kate hadn't written the letter, he'd have to find out who had.

But that was no business of hers.

"I doubt it," he said vaguely.

"But you must!"

"Whether I do or don't is surely no concern—"

"Have you no curiosity?"

His brows lowered. "About my mother? No. I don't, frankly."

Kate stepped closer to him, her skirts bowing against the front of his legs. She dropped her voice. "But it could be anything! A missing will. A lost heir. A secret—"

"You read novels, I take it."

"I read everything, sir. I'm not ashamed of it." She searched his face. "We've already established that you have no curiosity. Do you lack imagination as well?"

Heat prickled under Charles's collar. She was too bold. Too close. Altogether too much. The fragrance of her perfume and the faint scent of starch from her petticoats was muddling his senses. "My imagination, or lack of it, has no bearing on the situation. Whatever this person intends—"

"Aha!" She pointed a gloved finger at him, her face brightening with triumph. "You admit, then, that I didn't write it?"

Charles stared down at her. A frown worked its way between his brows. "I admit that it doesn't seem as likely now as I thought it must be. For that, I can only beg your pardon."

"Freely given. I don't believe in holding grudges. However…" Turning away from him in a swirl of skirts, she resumed walking down the path. "I do love a mystery. And I'm part of this one now. I should like to see it through."

Charles caught up with her in one stride. "On no account," he said. "I told you, I'm not going to Tiverton."

"Indeed, you did," Kate replied cheerfully. "But that doesn't mean I can't go myself."

Chapter Eight

"How did you meet her, Charles?" Hannah asked as the black lacquered carriage rolled away down the drive.

Charles ushered his sister back into the warmth of the house. "Unexpectedly," he said.

Indeed, the entirety of his brief acquaintance—or whatever it could be called—with Lady Katherine Beresford had been unexpected. Her brashness. Her kindness. The abject impropriety of her behavior. At every turn, she'd subverted his expectations.

Such that he *had* expectations.

The lady was still nine tenths a stranger to him.

"Yes, but how?" Hannah looked back at him impatiently. "Was it at a—"

"Go back to the drawing room, little one." Charles urged his sister toward the staircase. "I need to speak with Sara."

The housekeeper was just emerging from the servant's door to the kitchens. Originally his mother's lady's maid, Sara's once hard features had been softened by the years, and her formerly slight figure replaced with a comfortable plumpness. She paused, hearing her name.

Hannah mounted the steps "Very well, but you must join us as soon as you're done. Mama and Papa will be as curious as I am."

Charles suppressed a grimace. He had no doubt he'd been spending the next half hour explaining who Kate was and—more importantly—who she was to him. He didn't relish the prospect.

"You have need of me, Master Charles?" Sara asked.

"Just a question," Charles said. "That Christmas package that arrived for me in the post had a card attached to the top of it. Did you, by any chance, put it there?"

"Weren't they from the same person?" Sara asked. "Only I thought they must be, which is why I stuck them together. Did I do wrong, sir?"

An inexplicable surge of relief went through him.

So, Kate had been telling the truth. She hadn't sent the letter.

"No," he assured Sara. "You haven't done wrong."

If anyone had erred, it was him. He'd levied an accusation at Kate, one she hadn't deserved.

He'd already offered a qualified apology. *"If I've been mistaken…"* It wasn't anywhere near good enough. When he saw her again—when she made good her threat to invite them to Beasley Park—he'd apologize properly.

Unless, of course, he saw her before then.

Did she mean what she'd said about traveling to Tiverton on her own?

The interfering little baggage.

He wished to God he hadn't shown her that letter. The last thing he wanted was someone meddling in his family's affairs. It was bad enough that his mother's name should be mentioned in connection with some mysterious injustice. Charles wouldn't have gossip about her being spread all over the West Country.

As for the letter itself—

"I couldn't tell who sent it," Sara said. "There was no return direction on the envelope."

"No," Charles acknowledged. "Its origins are a bit of a mystery."

Sara's eyes went round. "Never say so, sir."

Charles couldn't fathom why she'd appear so alarmed. "I'm sure it's nothing."

"It may be so, but don't let your parents hear of it. They wouldn't like to know we're receiving anonymous letters again."

He gave her a sharp look. "*Again?* Do you mean to say they've received letters like this before?"

"One," Sara said. "A great many years ago, before you were born. It were a threat, like. Your father and mother haven't forgotten."

"What kind of a threat?"

"Against your mother's life," she said. "Didn't they never tell you?"

He shook his head, stunned, even as a grim possibility occurred to him. "Perhaps this letter came from the same person?"

"Oh no, sir. The gentleman what wrote the last letter is long dead. Your father—" She stopped herself. "But I'll not be telling tales about the past. Captain and Mrs. Heywood have been good to me. Like family they are. I wouldn't have them worried over another anonymous letter."

"Nor would I," Charles said.

Certainly not now he knew it would cause them distress.

Indeed, when he returned to the drawing room, he

found his parents and sister sitting together in such joyful harmony, he was reluctant to give voice to anything that might disturb their peace.

"Come and join us," his mother said. "Hannah has been singing your Lady Katherine's praises."

Charles crossed the room to sit down beside his mother. "She's not *my* Lady Katherine."

His protestation fell on deaf ears.

"Do you suppose she'll be returning to London in the spring?" Hannah inquired. "I know so few people there. It would be nice to have a friend when I make my come-out."

"I thought you were resolved on having your season in Bath," Arthur said. "Don't say that one young lady's opinion has been sufficient to change your mind?"

"She made many good points, you must agree, Papa." Hannah turned back to her mother. "She was so beautiful, I wonder that she wasn't betrothed in her first season."

"When did *you* meet her, Charles?" his mother asked.

"She must be a new acquaintance," his father said, "given that your ship only docked a fortnight ago."

"A very new acquaintance," Charles replied.

He would offer no more on the subject. To do so would only cast Kate's behavior in a poor light. Aggravating as she was, he had no wish for his parents to think ill of her.

His father didn't press him. His eyes nevertheless held a glimmer of sympathetic amusement. He alone seemed to understand the tenor of his son's predicament. For the first time in his life, Charles was being pursued by a lady. And such a lady!

It was unhinged. Unheard-of. Men were the ones who did the pursuing, not the reverse.

Courtship must have changed a great deal during Charles's time away from England.

"She's a comely young lady," his father remarked a

short while later after Philly and Hannah had departed the drawing room with the dogs. "Though her temperament may prove to be at odds with your plans for peace and tranquility."

"Lady Katherine Beresford doesn't figure into my plans at all," Charles replied. "I have more pressing concerns." He paused. "I wanted to ask you about something." He held his father's gaze. "Did mother really receive an anonymous letter once that threatened her life?"

His father's expression sobered. "Who told you that?"

"Is it true?"

Arthur lapsed into silence. "Yes," he said at length. "But it was I who received it, not her." A deep line etched his brow. "Forgive me, it's not the happiest of memories."

"Why on earth would someone threaten mother?" Charles asked in bewilderment. "She's never harmed anyone."

"Not directly, no. Certainly not purposefully. But when your mother and I met, she was intended for someone else."

"The Duke of Moreland. Yes, I know. I've heard the story."

"Not the whole of," Arthur said.

"Then tell me."

"What can I say? He was a powerful man, with many enemies to his name. It was one of them who targeted your mother. I dealt with it, of course, but the memory is an unpleasant one. I'd not have you mention it in her hearing."

"I won't," Charles assured him. "But this man who sent the letter—"

"Long in his grave," Arthur said. "He's no threat to her anymore."

"Then...mother has no enemies remaining?"

Arthur seemed to consider. "I suppose we both do," he said. "Our marriage affected a great many people. Not only Moreland, but those who had arranged the match between him and your mother. Her guardian, Edgar Townsend, chief among them. When your mother and I eloped, Moreland was humiliated. He took out his ire on Townsend, effectively ruining him. Townsend and his daughters lost almost everything."

Charles frowned. The names were all familiar to him, but the details were entirely new. "I'd no idea."

"It isn't something we enjoy reminiscing about. There's little point. Townsend and Moreland are dead. The past is behind us. So long as your mother and I keep out of London, she won't be hurt by any of the old gossip that might still linger about."

"I can't believe anyone would still be talking about it. Not with Moreland, Townsend, and this letter-writer all in their graves."

"Gossip lives forever," Arthur said. "It's why, all things considered, your mother and I would prefer your sister make her debut in Bath. If you can exert any influence in that sphere—"

"I will," Charles said. "I'll even accompany her if she wishes. It will save you and mother the trouble of escorting her everywhere."

"A splendid notion." Arthur's mouth lifted in a faint, weary smile. "Tell me, what's this sudden fascination with the past?"

Charles could have told his father about the letter then. Confided in him and sought his counsel just as he'd intended to do.

But no.

He wasn't a lad any longer. He was a man grown. A former lieutenant of Her Majesty's Navy, for God's sake.

"Just something I heard from one of the servants," he answered instead. "I'm sorry if my curiosity has raked up bad memories."

"I suppose it can't be helped," his father said. "Though, for your mother's sake, I'd rather we didn't dwell on all that unhappiness."

"Indeed," Charles replied. "I won't mention it to her."

There was no need to involve his parents. No need to give his family a moment's pain.

On Monday morning, Charles would make the journey to Tiverton to meet this Arbogast person in Gold Street. And if it turned out there was something sinister going on…

Charles would deal with it himself.

Chapter Nine

Kate's brother had predicted there would be hell to pay when the two of them returned to Beasley. He wasn't wrong. The moment Kate stepped into the hall, she was met by her mother.

Margaret Beresford, Countess of Allendale, was a vibrant lady whose strength of will was rivaled only by her great beauty. Now two and fifty, she was no less striking than she'd been when she'd sat for the gilt-framed oil portrait that hung over the drawing room fireplace—a magnificent depiction of a stunning, sapphire-eyed hellion in her prime.

Kate had always been a little in awe of her mother. Perhaps it was because they were so much alike. Not only in looks, but in temperament. Indeed, Margaret had stamped her glossy mink hair, vivid blue eyes, and stubbornly set cleft chin on her only daughter as surely as she'd stamped her willful personality.

She stood in the entry hall, barring the way to the stairs. She was clothed in a smartly cut black riding habit, her dark hair caught up in a woven net. A riding crop was tucked under her arm.

Jack faltered on the threshold, looking for the barest instant as though he would lose his nerve. He recovered himself quickly. "Are you going riding, Mother?" he asked with an overbright smile. "A capital idea. The weather is——"

Margaret silenced her youngest son with a point of her riding crop. "Not a word." She glared at Kate. "Go straight up and change into your habit. You and I are going to have a talk."

"Mama," Kate protested. "If you'll——"

"At once," her mother interrupted in a tone of iron. "Or you'll have both your father and me to deal with."

Jack gave Kate a grimacing look of sympathy. He was all too familiar with parental lectures and knew that the ones delivered by both of their parents were always the worst of the lot.

Catching up her skirts, Kate raced up the stairs to change.

Not fifteen minutes later, mounted on her bay warm-blood gelding, Ember, Kate rode alongside her mother away from the Beasley Park stables.

"Miss Colfax called this morning, inquiring whether you'd like to join her for luncheon at the vicarage," Mama said, deftly maneuvering her elegant black mare through the stable yard gate. "Imagine my surprise to learn you weren't already with her, halfway to Dunster Castle."

Kate's gloved fingers fidgeted on her reins. She might have known she'd be caught out on so feeble a story. Though really, how was she to guess the vicar's daughter would come calling? "I'm sorry I lied."

"It's not only the lie. Though that's vexing enough. It's the fact that no one knew where you'd gone. Hours I've waited, imagining every grim accident that might have befallen you. Hours of having to restrain your father from going to look for you—"

"I was with Jack."

"Worse and worse! As if being chaperoned by your brother is any excuse for what you've done. Upon my word, Katherine. He gets in more scrapes than you do!"

Kate's stomach sank like a stone. Mama never used her full name unless Kate was thoroughly in her black books. "We didn't get into a scrape. We only paid a call on some-one. They live a distance away, near the village of Heycombe. That's why we've been gone so long."

"A call on whom?"

"The Heywood family," Kate said. "Captain Heywood is the son of the Earl of Gordon."

Mama shot Kate a look of alarm. "The Earl of Gordon is ancient. His son must surely be older than your father. What business had you with him?"

"Not with him. With his…" Kate was tempted to lie and say she'd gone to visit Miss Heywood. But Mama was no fool. "Captain Heywood has a son," she admitted. "A naval lieutenant, recently returned from abroad. I met him briefly in London."

Her mother's brows rose higher. "I see." She slowed her horse. "I understood from your Aunt Jane that you'd met no gentlemen you liked during the season. Quite the opposite."

"I didn't say I *liked* him. And we didn't meet. Not formally. It was more of an accidental encounter." Kate gave her mother an abridged version of the events in Bond Street. "Was that not heroic?" she asked when she'd finished. "To rescue a poor wretched street dog in that manner? No other gentleman of my acquaintance would have done so."

"It's a sort of heroism, certainly," Mama allowed. "But my dear, when it comes to marriage, you must set the bar higher than that."

"I'm not interested in marrying the lieutenant."

"What, then?"

Kate shrugged. "I find him interesting, that's all."

"Stern silent types often are," Mama said. "Do you know why?"

"I suppose it's because their silence is more tolerable than empty compliments and sad attempts at flirtation."

"No, dearest. It's because a young lady's imagination fills in that silence with all manner of romantic daydreams. Those daydreams result in her crediting that gentleman with a depth of feeling he doesn't possess."

"I haven't—"

"You encountered this Lieutenant Heywood on your last day in London when you were feeling particularly discouraged about your matrimonial prospects."

"I wasn't—"

"And then he appeared: handsome, silent, and inscrutable."

"Heroic," Kate reminded her.

"Vaguely heroic," Mama conceded. "The ideal masculine canvas on which to paint your idea of a perfect gentlemen. It's no wonder you felt compelled to call on him today. I daresay the idea of the man you've conjured has captured your fancy. But trust me, my love, these sorts of men aren't worth the effort."

"How do you know? You've only ever loved Papa."

Her mother's countenance softened just as it always did at the mention of her love for Kate's father. "I have. Which is exactly how I know that genuine affection isn't one-sided. A gentleman who cares, who's truly worth your effort, will make an effort of his own. He'll seek you out. He'll endeavor to win you."

"Who says a lady must allow herself to be won?" Kate asked, nettled. "You didn't raise me to be anyone's prize."

Her mother's gaze turned thoughtful. "Indeed, I did not."

"Then why must I sit still and wait for the gentleman I fancy to come to me? Why must I settle for prosing old windbags, lecherous lords, or devious snakes like Mr. Catmull? Why can't I go after someone I like? I'm no less capable of choosing my future partner than a man. *More* capable, for I know what sort of person I might happily tolerate for the next forty or more years."

"You *do* like this Lieutenant Heywood, then?"

Kate turned her attention to the bleak winter landscape ahead. The setting sun kissed the curves of the barren hills, streaking the empty brown fields in cold shadow. "It isn't at all what you think. I'm not enamored of him. I'm only intrigued. It amuses me to tease him a little. Why shouldn't I?"

"Take care," Mama warned. "Country gentlemen aren't as sophisticated about flirtation as London gentlemen are. They're far more likely to be offended by such things."

"I don't seek to give offense."

"Your intentions matter little among those who don't know you."

Kate frowned. She didn't like to imagine Lieutenant Heywood thinking ill of her.

But he already had, hadn't he?

He'd accused her of writing that strange note. Of daring to mention his mother—a grievous sin by any measure. One didn't involve a man's mother or sisters in a jest. It simply wasn't done. Kate would never—

But he hadn't known that.

Her mother was right. The lieutenant knew nothing about Kate's motives *or* her character. Nothing except that she'd had the temerity to send him a humorous gift and to seek him out at his parents' home uninvited.

"No, he doesn't know me," Kate said. "Which is why the two of us must become better acquainted."

Her mother considered the matter. "If you're resolved on it, I suppose your father and I could invite the Heywoods to dine."

"I already have," Kate replied promptly.

Mama took the pronouncement in stride. "Naturally you have. When might we expect them?"

"I've asked them to join us next week." Kate urged Ember into a trot. "Once the lieutenant has dined and danced with me, I'm confident he'll recognize my finer points."

Her mother easily kept pace on her ebony mare. "After which you'll grow bored of him just as you have the others."

Kate gave an exaggerated wince. "Really, Mama. You're too cruel."

"It's not I who can be cruel. You're too careless with gentlemen's hearts, my dear."

Kate gave a short laugh. "I'm not. I've never had anyone's heart. In truth…" She hesitated a fraction of a second, hating to give voice to the niggling suspicion. "I sometimes think gentlemen don't like me at all."

"Nonsense. You're enormously likable."

"You wouldn't know that by what happened in London. I met no one who could tolerate me as I am."

"That's not what your Aunt Jane said in her letters. She claims a multitude of gentlemen called on you in Duke Street."

"Oh yes, they paid court handsomely enough. They thought me pretty. They also thought me strident, over-bold, and excessively opinionated." As they approached the top of the hill, Kate brought Ember back down to a walk. "I know for a fact my personality grated on them."

Mama slowed her mare. Her expression was troubled. "How can you know?"

"One hears things. And one has eyes enough to see them." Kate circled Ember back to her mother. The wind whipped at her net veil. "I'm tired of playing by society's rules. They weren't designed for a lady's happiness."

"No," Mama said. "But we must all play by the rules at some time or other. To flout them occasionally may be forgiven, but to disregard them entirely—"

"You would have done."

"It was a different time. And I wasn't the daughter of an earl, merely the wayward only child of a bombastic country squire."

"Nevertheless…" Kate cast a contemplative eye toward the horizon. The icy air filled her lungs on a deeply indrawn breath.

It wasn't even about Lieutenant Heywood. Not really. It was about the exercise of her own free will. She wanted the unbridled independence to choose her future husband for herself.

"Take care," Mama said again. "You have your reputation to consider. It's already received a beating during your time in London, deservedly or not. I won't review what transpired then. You've been scolded enough on that score. But I beg you, for once, spare a thought for your good name. If not for your own sake, then for your father's. Your conduct reflects on the earldom. It does him no credit when you behave as though you don't know any better."

Kate's gaze returned to her mother's. She'd heard this

particular lecture before. If pressed, she could probably recite it by heart. "I've done nothing wrong. I've only called on Lieutenant Heywood in company with my brother. A perfectly respectable call, I might add. There was nothing of romance about it. And even if there were…" Ember stamped his hooves beneath her, sensing her restlessness. "What harm could it do if I were to pursue him a little?"

"A great deal of harm if he doesn't reciprocate your intentions. Society tolerates boldness far more readily than it does foolishness. If you make yourself ridiculous—"

"I've no plan to do so." Kate turned Ember back toward the house. "You needn't worry, Mama."

"I won't worry." Mama rode up alongside her. "Not so long as you promise to behave."

"I promise," Kate said, "to do nothing more scandalous than what you might have done yourself when you were my age."

Her mother's mouth curved in a dry smile. "That, my darling girl, is precisely what I'm afraid of."

Chapter Ten

On the morning of January eighth, Kate rose early and, after donning her riding habit and fetching her horse, embarked on the eleven-mile journey to Tiverton in company with her groom, Jonas. It was a ride she'd made several times over the years, but never with such a sense of excitement.

Look for Mr. Arbogast on the eighth of January at ten o'clock in Gold Street…

A proper mystery! Whatever could it mean?

Kate could think of a dozen different answers, all of them more unlikely than the last. How could Lieutenant Heywood not be intrigued? He must, indeed, have no imagination at all. If it were a letter about her own mother, she'd have been champing at the bit to get to Tiverton.

As it was, she arrived in good time, crossing the boundary into Devonshire at exactly half past nine. She'd just entered Gold Street when she felt it—an alarming hitch in Ember's stride.

She was off of him at once.

Jonas rode up alongside her. He dismounted. "Something wrong, my lady?"

"I fear so." Kate ran a gloved hand down Ember's right front leg, prompting him to pick up his foot for her inspection. The problem was immediately evident. A small, sharp-edged pebble had lodged itself in the groove of Ember's frog. "Blasted thing," she muttered, prying it loose. "How long has that been stuck there?"

"You didn't feel anything afore now?" Jonas asked.

"Not until we came onto the street." Kate led Ember a few steps. He bobbed his head as he walked. It was a sure sign of lameness. "Double drat," she said under her breath. "I fear he's bruised his hoof."

Jonas didn't argue with Kate's assessment. He trusted her judgment when it came to horses. "That's the case," he said, "you won't be riding him back."

"No, indeed." Kate turned, frowning. There was a coaching inn at the top of the street—The White Horse. She'd have to leave Ember there in Jonas's care and hire a carriage to take her back to Beasley. It was either that or ride Jonas's gelding back alone. Even she wouldn't be so foolish.

"What a dreadful nuisance," she said.

Her words were drowned out by the clatter of a curricle thundering around the bend. A young gentleman was driving with abandon. He slashed his whip in the air with a startling crack.

Ember reared, tearing the reins from Kate's fingers. She reached for them again, but it was too late. With a toss of his head, Ember lunged forward. He might have galloped away if a gentleman hadn't appeared out of nowhere to catch hold of his bridle.

Not just any gentleman.

Kate blinked up at the commanding figure of Lieutenant Heywood.

"You!" she exclaimed.

"You were expecting someone else?" The lieutenant addressed her briefly before turning his attention to settling her horse. "Easy lad," he murmured to Ember. "You're all right." He stroked the gelding's neck with one large, black-gloved hand. His touch was surprisingly gentle for a man so formidably built.

The young sprig in the curricle slowed a fraction as he approached them. "I say," he called out amiably. "Is anything amiss?"

Lieutenant Heywood leveled a glare at the reckless idiot. "You careless fool." Though he didn't raise his voice, the deep, implacable tone of it nevertheless caused the fellow to recoil. "Did no one ever teach you how to comport yourself in a public street?"

The young gentleman reddened at the reprimand. "Beg pardon. Didn't mean to startle—"

"Drive on, sir," Kate said impatiently. "We have no need of your apologies."

Shame-faced, the fellow continued past them at a quick clip. His curricle swiftly disappeared around the corner, leaving Kate alone in the street with her horse, her groom, and the soberly clad (and irritatingly handsome) lieutenant.

She took charge of Ember's reins. "You said you weren't going to come."

Lieutenant Heywood didn't reply. Not directly. "Your horse is lame."

"I'm well aware." Kate soothed Ember with a pat on his shoulder.

Horses had no sense when it came to their physical limitations. When spooked, a lame horse would bolt as surely as a sound one, often causing himself irreparable damage in the process. It was why a horse with an injury must be confined to a loose box.

"Jonas?" She turned to address her groom. "Take him to the White Horse and soak his hoof. I'll not have him lamed on my account."

"Yes, my lady." Jonas took hold of Ember. The fiery-tempered bay promptly attempted to bite Jonas's gelding. "None of that," Jonas chided. And then to Kate: "Will you be needing me to put your sidesaddle on Smokey?"

"No," she said. "I shall walk."

"All the way back to Somersetshire?" Lieutenant Heywood inquired blandly.

Kate shot him a dark look. He appeared serious enough—solemn, even. She nevertheless had the distinct feeling that he was laughing at her. "When I'm ready to return home, sir, I shall hire a carriage. It's no concern of yours."

"You've made it my concern," he said.

The nerve of the man!

Kate waited to respond until Jonas led the horses away. The moment he was gone, she turned on the lieutenant. "Why are you here?"

He didn't reply. He only stared down at her, frowning.

Kate was aware she didn't look her best. Though her black wool riding habit had been clean and pressed when she'd departed Beasley, her heavy skirts had fast become rumpled and her tightly fitted bodice, with its long row of small black cloth-covered buttons, was now streaked with dirt. Her face was dirty as well. A strand of perspiration-damp hair had come loose from her chignon to cling to her cheek.

A surge of self-consciousness threatened.

She ignored the sensation. "When last we spoke, you—"

"I changed my mind," he said.

She cast a cursory glance around. There was no sign of a horse or carriage nearby. No conveyance from which he could have alighted in time to catch Ember's bridle. He must have been walking along the street when he saw her.

Dratted man!

She *hated* that she hadn't noticed him first. That he'd somehow managed to surprise her.

"How did you get here?" she asked. "You didn't ride, surely. Not the entire way from Heycombe."

"I hired a post chaise."

"You have a carriage, then?"

His black brows lowered. "If you're about to suggest—"

She cut him off with a dismissive wave of her hand. "I suggest nothing. I'm merely remarking on the fact that you have a post chaise at your disposal, while I have no means—"

Before she could finish her thought, the bell on the parish church tower rung out, signaling the hour. It was ten o'clock. The precise time mentioned in the anonymous letter.

Kate eagerly scanned the street. Aside from a smattering of ladies exiting the linen-draper's shop, arms full of packages, there was no one else about.

Her shoulders drooped with disappointment. "I don't see anyone who might be this Mr. Arbogast person."

"The man's not likely to appear out of nowhere."

"Why not? You seemed to do so."

"I was walking from the White Horse. You'd have noticed me if you weren't so absorbed with concern for your horse."

"Of course I was concerned. I've had Ember since he

was a foal. I'd never forgive myself if my decision to ride here today resulted in his being lamed."

"It was a stone, nothing more. Horses pick them up regularly." Lieutenant Heywood gestured for her to precede him to the left side of the street, safely out of the path of an oncoming carriage. "It could have happened anywhere."

"I suppose so." Draping the skirts of her habit over her arm, Kate crossed the road ahead of him.

Lieutenant Heywood followed, shadowing her like some great, broad-shouldered stoic knight of old guarding the lady to whom he'd pledged an unwilling fealty.

She was conscious of his every step.

He didn't like her overmuch, that was plain. He didn't want to be in her company. When they reached the side of the street, he nevertheless walked along her right, shielding her from the dirt and traffic of the road. For all his rudeness, the lieutenant knew how to act the gentleman. Like her or not, he was resolved to do his duty.

The fact made Kate cross as a cat. She didn't want to be any man's duty. Not his, certainly. "Have you learned anything more about this Mr. Arbogast?" she asked.

"No."

"And the letter said nothing about the man's premises or—"

"You know it didn't."

"So…? What do you propose to do next?"

The lieutenant's frowning gray gaze drifted over the placards that hung above the doors of the shops that lined the way. "I propose to walk up one side of the street and down the other until I find the man. If there's an establishment that bears his name, I'll see it soon enough."

Kate snorted.

Lieutenant Heywood's gaze cut to hers. "You have a better idea?"

"An infinitely better one. Why don't we just *ask* somebody?" Kate didn't wait for the lieutenant to agree with her. Sidestepping a puddle of winter slush, she entered the linen-draper's shop.

What was it about gentlemen that prevented them asking for help? One would think there was something inherently bad in inquiring after directions. Kate's brothers were just the same. It made the simplest tasks far more difficult than they need be.

The bell on the door rang shrilly as they passed through it, announcing their arrival to the grizzled shopkeeper at the wooden counter. Bolts of fabric lined the walls around him, along with a small selection of ribbons, fringes, and buttons.

"May I help you, madam? Sir?" he asked.

"I hope you can." Kate approached the counter.

Lieutenant Heywood stood stern and silent at her back. He might have been her brother for all the shopkeeper knew.

Or her husband.

The thought provoked a trill of butterfly wings in Kate's stomach. She refused to credit the feeling. Not when the man was being so surly and disobliging.

Granted, he may not have said anything outright, but he didn't need to. Disapproval was evident in every inch of his towering frame. Disapproval of *her* and her involvement in what was—admittedly—his own private problem.

Kate felt a twinge of remorse for meddling in his affairs. She didn't credit that either. It was the lieutenant's own fault she was here. If he hadn't accused her of writing that letter, she'd never have known about any of this.

"We're looking for the premises of a Mr. Arbogast," she said. "We'd be obliged if you could direct us to them."

"Arbogast," the shopkeeper repeated thoughtfully. "Might be that's the new man Mr. Crale has taken on."

"Crale?"

"The solicitor down the road." The shopkeeper emerged from behind his counter to accompany them back out the door. He pointed to a small brick building with a slate roof located at the end of the street. The door of the establishment was painted a bright bottle green. "Can't miss it."

Kate thanked the man. "A solicitor?" she whispered to the lieutenant as they continued down Gold Street. "Perhaps it *is* about a lost will."

The lieutenant was still frowning. He always seemed to be doing so. Kate began to wonder if he ever smiled. If he ever laughed.

"Don't be absurd," he said.

"What else can it mean? A great wrong, the letter said. It must be about an inheritance. In novels, someone is always being done out of their money or property or some such thing."

He narrowed his eyes at her. "Does your family know where you are?"

"I don't see why that matters."

"It matters a great deal. You're miles from home. You've lamed your horse. Your groom has left you and you have no chaperone to lend you countenance."

"I don't require a chaperone."

"Every young lady requires a—"

"How very straitlaced you are. I wouldn't have thought it after the circumstances of our first meeting. You seemed rather out of the common way, then."

"As did you, my lady," he replied.

Her eyes flew to his. For a full three seconds, she could think of no way to respond.

"Ah," he said. "Here it is. Oldsmuir and Crale, solicitors."

Kate's momentary lapse into girlish self-consciousness was instantly forgotten. She gave the lieutenant a look of unvarnished excitement. "Shall we go in together?"

"I don't think that's—"

But it was too late. Kate was already pushing open the door.

Chapter Eleven

C harles stifled a muttered oath as he followed Kate into the interior of the solicitor's office. He was half-tempted to toss her over his shoulder, carry her back to the coaching inn, and put her bodily into a carriage that would take her straight home to Beasley Park.

An alarming impulse.

He'd never in his life laid hands on a lady. A gentleman wouldn't even think of doing so.

But the feelings Charles was having for Lady Kate Beresford weren't at all gentlemanly.

From the moment he'd set eyes on her standing in the middle of Gold Street, diligently examining her horse's hoof, with seemingly not a care in the world for her reputation, he'd experienced an odd tightness in his chest. It was merely worry for her safety, he'd assured himself. That, and aggravation that she'd made good on her threat to come to Tiverton.

But that wasn't all it was.

Charles wasn't too proud to admit it to himself. Like it or not, he was captivated by the girl.

An uncomfortable state of affairs.

Lovely as she was, she was also as brash and unpredictable as wildfire. Being around her had lit something equally unpredictable within him—some rogue spark of emotion he didn't quite know what to do with.

He had no intention of revealing it to her.

If this was how she behaved when she believed him indifferent, Lord only knew what she'd do if she learned how thoroughly she'd already captured his attention.

And not only his.

The pasty-faced law clerk who greeted them appeared similarly smitten. On seeing Kate, he turned a dull red, cleared his throat, and rose hastily from his chair, nearly knocking over the cup of tea on his desk in the process. "May I help you, madam?"

The plain black wool of Kate's form-fitting riding habit and the fine net half-veil of her little black hat did nothing to disguise her beauty. "We have come to see Mr. Arbogast," she said with all the imperiousness of a duchess. "Please inform him we're here."

"May I have your name?"

Kate opened her mouth to answer.

"Charles Heywood," Charles informed the man before she could do so. He wouldn't have her bandying her name about the town unnecessarily. Not when she was in company with a gentleman unchaperoned. The less attention she called to herself the better.

"Heywood?" The clerk checked the leather-bound diary on his desk. "I don't seem to have you down—"

"We don't have an appointment," Charles said. "But we'd appreciate five minutes of Mr. Arbogast's time. It's a matter of some importance."

"Yes, of course, sir. One moment, if you please, while I see if he's at liberty." The harried clerk scurried off through the door to the interior offices.

"*A matter of some importance?*" Kate echoed under her breath. "Pray he won't ask us to explain what that matter is. I'd have to tell him——"

"You'll tell him nothing," Charles replied quietly. "I'll do the talking."

"But——"

"No buts. Count yourself lucky I've permitted you to accompany me this far."

She glowered at him. "It's *you* who have accompanied *me*. I'm the one who——"

"Mr. Heywood?" The clerk came back through the door. "Mr. Arbogast will see you now. If you'll follow me?"

Kate's mouth clamped shut. Chin held high, she preceded Charles through the door.

He came after her, ignoring the tantalizing hint of her perfume that drifted to his nose as she passed.

The little termagant.

Didn't she realize the mess she could be getting herself into? Tiverton wasn't so far from Beasley Park that gossip about her behavior wouldn't reach her parents.

"Mr. Heywood?" A stocky gentleman in a neatly pressed suit stood from behind the curve of a large mahogany desk to extend his hand to Charles. A row of bookcases stretched to the ceiling behind him. The shelves were lined with leather-bound law books. "I don't believe I've had the pleasure."

Charles shook the man's hand. "No indeed. Thank you for seeing us."

"Not at all. You find me quite at my leisure." Relinquishing Charles's hand, Mr. Arbogast acknowledged Kate with a bow. "Mrs. Heywood. How do you do."

Kate inclined her head. "Mr. Arbogast," she replied without missing a beat. "My husband and I are pleased to make your acquaintance."

Charles's stomach clenched.

Her husband?

Good Lord.

"Please, sit down." Mr. Arbogast directed them to the pair of leather-upholstered chairs across from his desk.

Charles briefly met Kate's gaze as they took their seats. She looked back at him, a flash of devilry in her eyes. He could have happily throttled the woman. No matter that her words had unexpectedly fired his blood.

Mr. Arbogast resumed his seat. "I was led to believe I might expect interest before I announced the listing." He riffled through a disorganized stack of loose papers on his desk. "But I never imagined I'd be visited quite so soon. You do realize the property won't be vacant until the spring?"

Kate's eyes widened. She exchanged another look with Charles. She'd been right. The mysterious letter *had* been referencing a property.

Or so it appeared.

She opened her mouth to speak.

Charles gave her an infinitesimal shake of his head. The only way to find out anything was to let the man keep talking.

Blessedly, Kate understood him. She closed her mouth again without uttering a word.

"The current tenant has possession through April," Mr. Arbogast went on. "Which gives us ample time to complete the repairs. Only small ones, mind, but—" He continued to shuffle through his papers with growing frustration. "My apologies. The documents only came into my possession a fortnight ago. I've not even finished the inventory of the estate." He glanced up. "You wouldn't care to come back—?"

"We're anxious to settle on a place," Charles said.

"And this property suits, does it?" Mr. Arbogast's mouth curled in a satisfied smile. "I won't argue with your assessment. It's a pretty village, is Fox Cross, and Satterthwaite Court is but a—"

Charles gave the man an arrested look. "Did you say...*Satterthwaite Court?*"

Mr. Arbogast's hands stilled on his paper. "That *is* the property you're inquiring after? Oh dear. I'd assumed—"

"It *is*," Charles replied sharply. Seeing Mr. Arbogast flinch, he moderated his tone. "Forgive me, but I understood it to be entailed?"

It was how his mother had lost it. On her grandfather's death in the winter of 1813, the estate had gone to Edgar Townsend.

"It was indeed entailed." Mr. Arbogast paged through one of the folders on his desk. His frown deepened. "I don't have copies of the official documents in my possession, but according to my notes, a legal mechanism was employed to break the entail several years before it came into my client's possession."

"An entail can be broken?" Kate asked, astonished.

"In certain circumstances," Mr. Arbogast said. "If the current owner of the estate and the next male heir both agree. The property then returns to freehold status and may be sold or left to whomever the owner chooses, as was the case here. My client came into legal possession of the estate in 1834. Title now resides with him, unencumbered."

"Just who is your client?" Charles asked.

"I'm acting on behalf of Mr. Elias Catmull, lately of Russell Square, London."

Kate's lips parted in an expression of surprise. "*Elias Catmull?*"

The name meant nothing to Charles.

"Yes, ma'am," Mr. Arbogast said. "He owns the property outright, though he's never resided there. Satterthwaite Court has been tenanted since the death of the last Satterthwaite some three decades ago. But its maintenance hasn't been neglected. If you mean to have the property, you can rest assured all will be in good order."

"Oh, I mean to have it," Charles said. "And no mistake."

KATE DISCREETLY STUDIED LIEUTENANT HEYWOOD'S FACE through her net riding veil. He'd been preoccupied when they'd entered the solicitor's office, more attentive to her and to her taking the reins of their informal investigation than to the mystery itself.

But not anymore.

His expression had changed the instant Mr. Arbogast mentioned the name of the estate. No longer distracted, the lieutenant was unequivocally determined.

He must be acquainted with the place. Though he didn't appear to know its owner. That much, at least, was unsurprising. Kate couldn't imagine Charles Heywood and Elias Catmull as friends. She'd never met two gentlemen more dissimilar.

"I can't recall, my love," she said, making the most of her limited time as Mrs. Heywood. "Have you visited Satterthwaite Court before?"

Lieutenant Heywood's gaze jerked to hers. His black brows notched in a repressive frown. "I have not."

"It's fortunate you should arrive today, then," Mr. Arbogast said. "I have an appointment at the steward's lodge in an hour to discuss the accounts. If you can spare the time to ride over, I'd be happy to show you the exterior of the house." He glanced at Kate's rumpled habit. "You might even have a canter over the grounds if you like. I'm sure the tenants would have no objection."

"Thank you," Kate replied. "We'd love to—"

"Riding out to Satterthwaite Court won't be possible today," Lieutenant Heywood said before she could finish. His voice took on an unmistakable note of meaning. "You forget, dearest, that your horse has been lamed."

Dearest.

In other circumstances, the husbandly endearment might have quickened Kate's pulse. But not now. Lieutenant Heywood's tone held no affection in it, only an unspoken warning about compromising situations, potential scandals, and the growing risk to her reputation.

Those risks were real, admittedly, but Kate refused to be dissuaded by them.

"Yes, it is rather a nuisance." She gave Mr. Arbogast a dazzling smile. "I suppose we shall just have to accompany you in your carriage."

Chapter Twelve

Twenty minutes later, the three of them were settled snugly inside Mr. Arbogast's clarence carriage, rattling their way past the quaint little village of Fox Cross and through the filigree iron gates of Satterthwaite Court.

Kate gazed out the carriage window. "Oh, look at it!" she exclaimed as the house came into view. "What a glorious rambling, hodgepodge of a place it is!"

The expansive structure appeared to have been built in several competing styles. Elegant Palladian lines contrasted with Gothic arches and intricate Baroque stonework. It should have resulted in chaos. Instead, the countless architectural additions to the house created an oddly appealing symmetry.

Lieutenant Heywood sat beside her in the carriage, as unmoving as a figure chiseled from granite. He'd been largely silent since they'd left Tiverton, no doubt biding his time until he could administer a stern lecture on her reckless behavior. But though he often gave a fair impression of being so, the man wasn't made of stone.

"Here." She drew back in her seat so he could lean across her. "Isn't it grand?"

As grudgingly obedient as the husband he was pretending to be, Lieutenant Heywood stretched over her to look out at the looming façade of the house. His expression turned thoughtful. "Yes," he said quietly. "It is."

"Aye," Mr. Arbogast agreed. "I'm sorry I can't allow you the benefit of seeing inside today, but I'm under strict instructions not to trouble the tenants. Mr. Catmull would be none too pleased if he should hear of them being disturbed."

"We shall have to come back in the spring when the property is vacant," Kate said.

"Oh no, madam, there's no need to wait that long," Mr. Arbogast replied. "The tenants will be leaving for a brief visit to Bristol next month. They're expected to remain as long as a fortnight. It's only a small window of opportunity, I realize, but if you're at liberty, I could show it to you then."

Lieutenant Heywood sank back in his seat. "I'd like that. Thank you."

Kate folded her hands in her lap. There was no mention of her accompanying him. Nor should there be. She wasn't really his wife, after all. Even so, she lamented being excluded. This was her adventure now, too. Not just his, but theirs together. She wanted to share it with him.

The carriage slowed as it navigated the curving, tree-lined drive. Rather than continue toward the house, it veered left down a dirt track that led to a stone lodge with a neatly thatched roof. A diminutive gentleman with a heavy brown beard stood in front of the door. The estate's steward, Kate presumed. Another vehicle was parked nearby: a small gig hitched to a large, raw-boned bay with a fuzzy winter coat.

"There's Mr. Peartree." Mr. Arbogast's brow creased as he caught sight of the gig. "And it appears he has company." He gathered his briefcase and walking stick as the carriage rolled to a halt. "I must part ways with you here. My visits with Mr. Peartree are often two hours or more." He opened the door of the carriage. "Merion?" he called to his coachman. "Take Mr. Heywood and his wife round the old oak road." He glanced back at Kate and the lieutenant. "It circles the better part of the estate and will give you a good overview of the grounds. Once you've looked your fill, Merion will drive you back to town."

"We're obliged to you," Lieutenant Heywood said.

Kate added her thanks to the lieutenant's, ignoring the knot of apprehension forming in her stomach as the solicitor disembarked from the carriage and sent them on their way.

But there was no ignoring the cause of it.

She was alone in a closed carriage with Lieutenant Heywood. It was worse than scandalous. It was ruinous. No respectable young lady ever rode in a closed carriage with a gentleman, not unless he was her husband or other close family member. To do so was to cast one's reputation to the four winds.

Anything could happen in a closed carriage. A kiss. An embrace. A full-out assignation.

But Lieutenant Heywood appeared in no mind to seduce her. The moment the carriage rolled off, he rose from his place beside Kate and moved to the seat opposite. His jaw was clenched, his mouth pressed into a forbidding line.

Kate knew that look. It was the look of a man about to administer a thorough—and very possibly well-deserved—scolding.

She had no interest in receiving one.

"You're familiar with this place?" she asked before he could begin. "Satterthwaite Court? You seemed to recognize the name of it."

The lieutenant lapsed into scowling silence. He was no doubt deciding whether to soldier on with his planned lecture or to allow her to divert him down another, more desirable, path.

Fortunately for Kate, he chose the latter.

"I did," he replied grimly. "It was my mother's childhood home. Satterthwaite is her maiden name."

"Fascinating," Kate murmured. "And the house itself? I presume it was entailed away from the female line."

"It was. My great-grandfather, Sir Charles, would have left it to my mother otherwise. Instead, it went to a distant relation. A man by the name of Edgar Townsend."

"You must have been close with your great-grandfather."

"I never knew him. He died before I was born."

"But you're named after him, aren't you?"

Lieutenant Heywood gazed out the window, surveying the passing landscape. He was in an odd mood, both self-possessed and distracted. "My mother christened me in his honor. Sir Charles was the only family she ever knew. A good man, I'm told. He was knighted for services to the crown at the end of the last century. My mother loved him dearly."

"Is that why you want to buy the house?" Kate asked.

The lieutenant hadn't yet presented an offer, but neither had he flinched when Mr. Arbogast had disclosed the amount Mr. Catmull was asking for the property—some fifteen thousand pounds. It was no small sum.

Lieutenant Heywood must have a sizeable fortune to his name.

Kate had never before given the matter any thought.

She'd been more interested in the lieutenant's heroism than in the size of his bank account. But it didn't hurt that he was a man of means. If she decided to continue pursuing him...

If.

Mama had warned her against making a fool of herself. Kate feared she'd already done so. It wasn't an attractive quality, to be seen desperately chasing after a gentleman who was indifferent to oneself.

Kate slid him another assessing look as the carriage continued its slow circuit around the estate. *Was* he indifferent? She couldn't entirely tell.

He bore no resemblance to the fawning admirers she'd had in London. Gentlemen who had sent her flowers after dancing with her at a ball. Who had complimented her and flirted with her in the established manner, though they'd never seemed to like her very much as a person.

Unlike the lieutenant.

He hadn't flirted with her *or* complimented her. From the first, he'd been curt, gruff, and downright rude. Insulting, even. Any other young lady would have washed her hands of him the instant he accused her of writing that letter.

But Kate was accustomed to rudeness. She'd been raised amid the rough and tumble of her three older brothers. She flattered herself that her skin was as thick as a horse's hide.

And anyway, she hadn't yet acted out of desperation. Her recent decisions had been made with the same assertiveness a gentleman might employ when conducting his pursuit of a lady.

A successful pursuit by all accounts.

She was here now, after all, alone in a closed carriage

with the same heroic soldier who had captured her fancy in London.

And there was a mystery in the offing.

She wouldn't ruin the experience by second-guessing herself.

"I do want the house," Lieutenant Heywood said. "I intend to make an offer for it, once I ascertain that this Catmull person has the legal right to be selling the place." He cast an unreadable glance at Kate. "You recognized his name."

Her lips compressed. She hated to think of Mr. Catmull at any time, least of all when she was in company with Lieutenant Heywood. "Mr. Catmull is an associate of my friend Miss Mattingly's fiancé, Sir Lawrence Glade. They're investors in a canal scheme together."

"You don't know him personally?"

"Well enough. He was introduced to me during the season and has been chasing after me rather relentlessly ever since. I understand he's seeking a rich wife."

Lieutenant Heywood evinced no reaction to this information. Indeed, his face was suddenly absent expression.

"Have I shocked you?" Kate asked.

"Why should you have?"

"Because I had the indelicacy to mention that he was interested in my money."

"Ah. That."

"Yes, that. It's no secret that most gentlemen who come to London for the season are looking to better their financial situations. And even if they aren't—even if they already have a fortune of their own—no man wishes to marry an impoverished lady."

"You believe Catmull wants you for your fortune?"

"Among other things," she said. "Though it isn't for

lack of his own. As far as I understand it, he's handsomely situated."

"Is he, indeed."

"Well connected, too. His uncle is a viscount, apparently."

"Yet you dislike him?"

"I didn't say that."

"No," Lieutenant Heywood replied. "You've only said he's been chasing you. And hasn't caught you, presumably."

"Nor will he," Kate muttered. "Despite his best efforts."

He studied her face. "What is it you object to about him?"

"To his being a snake," she said frankly.

A flare of repressed laughter danced in the lieutenant's eyes. It wasn't enough to soften his mouth into a smile. Indeed, the rest of his face was composed in the same mask of soldierly sternness as it always was. But he was laughing all the same.

Laughing at *her*.

Kate stiffened. She despised being laughed at.

"You don't mince words, do you?" he said.

She resumed gazing out the window, on her dignity. "I speak as I find."

The carriage rolled on over the isolated road that curved around the park. Lieutenant Heywood joined her in admiring the passing landscape. There were acres of rolling brown fields and fenced pastures. A lush woodland was visible in the distance, a long, ragged scattering of oak trees marking the boundary to it as distinctly as a row of soldiers standing guard.

One of the trees was far larger than the rest. Older, too. It stood taller and wider than the others, its massive gnarled branches curved downward in a vast, sheltering arch.

Lieutenant Heywood pounded once on the ceiling of the carriage. "Stop the coach!"

The coachman immediately brought the carriage to a halt.

"What is it?" Kate asked in alarm. "Did you see someone you recognize?"

"Not someone," Lieutenant Heywood said. "Some*thing*." He opened the carriage door. "I know that tree."

THE MOMENT THE CARRIAGE WAS STATIONERY, CHARLES leapt out. He turned to assist Kate down, gripping her gloved hand tightly. "Mind your step. It's muddy."

Kate jumped out of the carriage without hesitation, her boots sinking into the wet earth. A lopsided smile tilted her mouth. "I'm a country girl. Mud doesn't scare me."

Charles stared down at her a moment, briefly diverted. Her riding habit was rumpled, her bodice and skirt streaked with dirt. She didn't seem to regard it. On the contrary, she looked eager and unpretentious. The kind of girl who could find pleasure in every situation. One who would fit in anywhere.

It was a rare quality in any living creature, especially if that creature was a fashionable young lady.

She'd warned him not to think of her in those terms, but it was difficult to stop. Everything about her outward appearance—from her clothing, to her accent, to the elegance of her carriage—proclaimed her a lady. It would take more than a few wrinkles and a bit of mud to change that.

"What do you mean you know that tree?" She draped the skirts of her habit over her arm. "Know it how?"

He crossed the field with Kate at his side, heading toward the woodland. It was a gradual downward slope from the road where they'd left the carriage. "My mother described it to me."

She'd frequently spoken of Satterthwaite Court when he was a boy, telling him of her happy childhood on the estate, where she'd lived in isolation with her beloved pets, her doting grandfather, and their ramshackle staff of aged servants. It had been an idyllic time for her by all accounts. One that had ended abruptly when her grandfather had died and she'd been forced to remove to London.

Charles had treasured her stories, not least because they'd had a fairy-tale quality to them. In hearing them, he'd often envisioned his mother as an enchanted princess and Satterthwaite Court as the magical castle where she'd lived out her youth.

The oak tree had featured in many of her tales. It loomed ahead now, its enormous size and imposing branches unmistakable.

Kate accompanied him over ground made uneven by the roots of the tree. "Was it important to her somehow?"

"It was. She told me about it when I was a boy. About how she'd come here on her own." He paused. "Well. Not entirely on her own. She kept a great many mongrel dogs. They'd gather round her as she sat beneath the branches. She used to read aloud to them."

"To her dogs?" Kate's eyes twinkled.

"Yes, I know. Some might call it eccentric."

"I wouldn't." She walked closer to the trunk. "I think it's charming."

Charles set a hand on one of the bare branches. He imagined the privacy the tree would offer in the spring and summer when the leaves were in full. "My mother said she was happiest when she was here, sheltered under the branches with her dogs and a book. She was shy, like my sister. It was her sanctuary."

"A very pretty one. It's the kind of hiding place I'd like myself."

"You enjoy reading, I believe," he said. She'd mentioned novels to him more than once. He'd marked it, just as he had everything she'd told him.

"I love reading." She wandered around the trunk, trailing her fingers over the bark. "And riding, and shopping, and dancing."

Charles belatedly realized he was staring at her. Clearing his throat, he focused his attention back on the tree. "She carved a pair of initials. They should be here somewhere."

"Is this them?" Kate drew his gaze to a small, waist-high carving. The chiseled grooves in the trunk were so faint Charles might have missed them otherwise.

He came to join her. "Good Lord. It must be."

"F. S.," she read aloud. "Is that her?"

Affectionate amusement softened Charles's mouth as he examined the carving. "Not her, no."

"Was it her sweetheart?"

"It wasn't a person at all," he said. "The F. S. stands for Fox Satterthwaite. He was a terrier she rescued in the village."

Kate smiled. "A dog?"

"One of the many who were dear to her. He passed away when I was five, but I well remember him. He was a little rogue, still full of mischief into his old age. He's buried on the grounds of Heywood House."

"I believe you must love dogs as much as your mother."

"I daresay," Charles replied. "When I was a lad—"

A rifle shot rang out, cutting off the rest of his words.

It wasn't abnormal to hear such a noise in the country-side. But this shot was unusually close. Too close. It whizzed past them in a rush of icy air, striking a branch only inches from where he and Kate stood.

Charles reacted instinctively.

Seizing Kate around the waist, he hauled her straight down to the ground.

Chapter Thirteen

Kate found herself pinned beneath Lieutenant Heywood's not inconsiderable weight. Her riding hat had been knocked askew in the descent. It tipped over one of her eyes at a rakish angle. "Did someone just *shoot* at us?" she gasped.

"Not *at* us," he replied. "But too near for my comfort."

"And for mine. Look." She stared at the branch where the lieutenant had been standing only seconds before. It hung, broken, overhead. The bullet had splintered it nearly in half. "Good heavens. It's a miracle you weren't hit!"

"Bloody stupid poachers," he muttered.

"Is that who it was?"

"Or the gamekeeper," he said. "The shot came from near the woods."

There was a dense line of trees in the distance, marking the boundary of an overgrown woodland. Kate waited for someone to emerge from it, but though the branches rustled, no errant hunter or gamekeeper appeared. Whoever had fired in their direction, the culprit didn't seem keen to reveal himself.

She looked up at the lieutenant, still winded from her fall to the ground. "Whoever it was," she said, breathing hard, "I believe you may have just saved my life."

He cast the broken branch a narrow glance. "My own, more like it. One inch to the right and I'd be——"

"Don't say it." She clutched at the fold of his coat. "Please. It's too horrid to think of."

Lieutenant Heywood's brows notched. Now the immediate danger had passed, he seemed to register the impropriety of their position—the two of them together on the ground, practically in a lover's embrace. "You shouldn't be here, Kate," he said.

Her pulse quickened at the unexpected intimacy of his address. "Kate, is it? You're very familiar, Lieutenant Heywood."

He levered himself over her. A thick lock of black hair flopped over his forehead. It softened his stern features, making him appear almost boyish. "It's not Lieutenant Heywood any longer. I've left the Navy."

"Have you?" It was news to her. *Happy* news. She wasn't keen to marry a sailor who promptly returned to sea. "Mr. Heywood, then."

"Charles," he said. "If you please."

Her blood fizzed with warmth. "Very well. Charles."

He nodded once, as though the entirety of their relationship was now established on mutually acceptable ground.

Kate impulsively reached up to smooth his hair from his brow. He stilled at her touch, but he didn't object to it. "A wife's privilege," she said.

The cheeky statement was somewhat ruined by the breathlessness in her voice. She'd never before been this close with a gentleman.

He gazed down at her steadily, a look in his eyes that was hard to read. "You're playing with fire, you know."

"By teasing you?"

"Is that what you're doing?"

It took an effort not to blush. "Perhaps at first," she confessed, "before you became so unpleasant."

Moving off of her, he regained his feet. "What can I say? I'm an unpleasant fellow."

Kate struggled to a sitting position. She recalled how he'd looked standing in Bond Street, holding the filthy street pup wrapped in the folds of his greatcoat. "Yes," she said. "An absolute ogre."

He extended his hand to her.

She took it, allowing him to help her up. "If teasing you is playing with the fire, then——"

"I didn't mean me." He looked in the direction of the woods once more, scanning the tree line, before urging her back toward the waiting carriage. "I was talking about your coming to Devonshire, first to Tiverton and then here, to Satterthwaite Court, where anyone might recognize you."

Kate trudged alongside him. "No one knows me at Satterthwaite Court," she informed him as she brushed the dirt from her habit. "I never heard of the place until this morning. As for Tiverton, I don't visit with enough frequency to be remarked."

"You'd be remarked wherever you go," Charles said.

She hid a smile. "Would I? Even when wearing a veil?"

"If you're fishing for a compliment——"

"I would never. Besides," she added, "I'm fully aware I'm not at my best at the moment."

He flashed her a glance. "Rubbish," he said. "You're beautiful."

Kate's heart thumped hard. Not you *look* beautiful, but you *are* beautiful. The distinction wasn't lost on her.

She was tempted to compliment him in kind. To tell him how heroic he was. How excessively brave. The way he'd reacted to that rifle shot! He'd pulled her to safety so swiftly it had made her head spin. His reflexes were truly something marvelous to behold.

But Charles Heywood didn't seem like the kind of gentlemen who would appreciate excessive praise. He was too self-effacing. Too noble.

And Kate had no desire to make a ninny of herself.

"You're very generous in your praise," she said instead.

"No one's ever accused me of that before," he replied as they returned to the carriage.

"Everything all right, sir?" the coachman called down to them. "I heard a shot."

Kate avoided the man's eyes. The giant oak was visible from the road, albeit at a distance. It was entirely possible the coachman had seen Charles haul her to the ground and cover her body with his. As compromising positions went, it couldn't get much worse.

"Some careless fool was shooting in the woods." Charles opened the door of the carriage. He helped Kate into the cab. "If you would be so kind as to return us to The White Horse in Gold Street."

"What about seeing the rest of the estate?" Kate asked.

Charles climbed in after her. "Another time. We've lingered too long already."

Settling back in her seat across from him, Kate owned to a bit of disappointment. She wasn't yet ready for their adventure—or for their newfound closeness—to come to an end.

But whatever intimacy their near brush with death had conjured dissipated rapidly during their return journey to

Tiverton. Kate's attempts at rekindling it proved futile at best.

"Why did you leave the Navy?" she asked once the carriage had left Satterthwaite Court behind them and was well on its way back to town.

"It's complicated," Charles said. He didn't appear keen to discuss the matter.

Kate was undeterred. "You were a sailor for a long while, weren't you?"

"Nearly nine years."

"Nine years!" she repeated. "And all of them at sea?"

"I spent the first two at the Royal Naval College at Portsmouth."

"Oh yes," Kate recalled. "Mr. Trumble mentioned something about that."

Charles gave her a dangerous look. "Did he."

"He said you gave up your place at Cambridge."

An endless pause. "I did."

"Why? Did you have a sudden yen to take to the sea?"

He gazed out the window with an impassive frown. "I had a thirst for adventure. More fool I."

"There's nothing wrong with enjoying an adventure."

"No. Not so long as nobody gets hurt."

"Is that what happened? Did someone get hurt?"

"A great many people," he said. "And not only those who signed up to fight."

Kate couldn't pretend to imagine the things he must have experienced during his years in the Royal Navy. "It doesn't make your service any less heroic. You fought on the side of good. The British side."

"You assume they're one and the same."

She frowned. "Weren't they?"

"Not always," he said. "Regrettably."

The rest of Kate's attempts at conversation were met

with monosyllabic replies. Charles was no longer disposed to encourage her. Indeed, he didn't seem interested in her at all except as a problem he must solve.

Approaching Gold Street, he was once again somber, dignified, and—rather aggravatingly—overtly focused on minimizing the damage to her reputation.

"You can't ride back to Beasley Park," he said when they disembarked outside of the White Horse. "You can't return alone in a hired chaise either. We'll have to find a maidservant to accompany you."

She nearly came to a halt. "*We* don't have to do anything. I shall sort things out on my own."

Mr. Arbogast's carriage rolled away behind them, kicking up a cloud of grit in the street as it clattered off, returning to Satterthwaite Court to collect its owner.

"*I'll* sort them out," Charles said. "The less attention you bring to yourself the better."

"I don't mind bringing attention to myself. If anyone recognizes me, they'll merely chalk it up to the Beresford recklessness. I'm always—"

He cocked a brow. "Out in company, unchaperoned, with a gentleman?"

"No," she admitted, temporarily chastened. "You're not to think I make a habit of doing this."

"I'm pleased to hear it." He opened the door of the inn for her. Loud voices drifted out, punctuated by harsh laughter and the clatter of tableware from the dining room. "Though, as you've said, it's no concern of mine."

"No indeed. All the same…" She passed by him to enter the smoke-filled front passage. Her voice was very small. "I shouldn't like you to think ill of me."

"I don't," he said.

The deep timbre of his words brushed her ear, sending a thrill down her spine.

She would have liked to respond, but there was no opportunity to do so. The moment they entered the busy coaching inn, Charles summoned the innkeeper and set about making arrangements for her departure. He promptly hired a carriage and engaged a serving maid to act as Kate's companion, his manner as brusque and efficient as an aged guardian dispensing with his obligation to a troublesome ward.

A lowering comparison, but an apt one, Kate feared.

It wasn't until they were back on the street and he was handing her into the carriage that Kate managed to convey another private word. "You will keep me apprised of developments, won't you?"

"If you wish," he said.

"When?" she asked, still standing on the carriage step.

The young maidservant he'd hired gawped at them from inside the cab.

Charles didn't seem to notice the girl's indecorous curiosity. His attention was wholly fixed on Kate. "When next I see you," he answered.

She squeezed his hand. "Yes, but...*when?*"

His fingers curved gently around hers. A glimmer of humor softened his stern expression. "You tell me, ma'am."

Kate's heart beat hard, understanding his meaning.

He wasn't going to discourage her interest in him. Not any longer.

Quite the reverse.

Her mouth tipped into a smile. "I shall," she vowed. "You may depend upon it."

Chapter Fourteen

The clock at the end of the hall echoed faintly, chiming ten o'clock. It was still early for an evening in the country. In the normal course of events, Charles would have remained downstairs with his family for another hour or more. Instead, he'd retired early.

His bedroom was cloaked in a flickering pattern of shadows cast by the candles that blazed on the fireplace mantel, the bedside table, and on the small walnut writing desk where Charles sat, composing a letter to Mr. Inch, the family's solicitor in Taunton.

It would be up to Inch to verify the legality of Mr. Catmull's ownership of Satterthwaite Court. Once he'd done so, Charles had instructed the solicitor to make an offer on the property. A generous one. Charles had no intention of losing his chance to reclaim his family's ancestral estate.

As for the identity of the mysterious letter writer...

Whoever they were, it appeared they'd written with good intentions rather than bad ones. They had, after all, alerted him to the sale of Satterthwaite Court. For that, Charles supposed he must be grateful.

But he couldn't be easy on the subject.

For one thing, there was the 'grievous wrong' done to his mother. The loss of her childhood home, he presumed. But if that was indeed the wrong that the anonymous letter had referenced, it wasn't a legal one. On Sir Charles's death, Satterthwaite Court had passed to Edgar Townsend according to law.

Hadn't it?

And what about the rifle shot that had nearly taken Charles's head off today?

He'd told Kate it was poachers or possibly even the gamekeeper. A careless shot, merely. That hadn't stopped Charles's blood from surging with the same keen sense of battle-tested awareness he'd felt when enemy fire had come too close during a hostile encounter at sea.

Good God. Had someone purposefully shot at him?

It was outrageous to even contemplate such a thing. And yet...

Charles couldn't shake the feeling. It was why he'd cut short their tour of the estate. Why he'd shepherded Kate back into the carriage and ordered the driver to return them to Tiverton. It was one thing for Charles to find himself in danger, but to contemplate Kate being hurt was another matter entirely.

Not that Kate wanted—or needed—his protection.

She was wild and willful, with a spirit as formidable as any man. Indeed, on the three occasions they'd met, they had quarreled as much as they'd conversed. The only time she'd shown him anything other than the sharp side of her tongue had been when she'd smoothed the hair from his brow as he'd loomed over her beneath the old oak tree at Satterthwaite Court.

Her touch had been as soft as butterfly wings dancing over his skin. It had soothed the anger that had rushed through his veins after he'd hauled her to the ground. The fury he'd felt at the thought of anything—or any*one*—causing her injury.

But she hadn't been injured. She'd been unhurt.

Unchastened.

"A wife's privilege," she'd said as she'd smoothed his hair.

The cheek of her!

More than seven hours later, he was still thinking about it. About *her*. The feel of her fingertips. The teasing tilt of her mouth. The lush curve of her body beneath his.

But it was Satterthwaite Court that deserved his attention at present, not the antics of a vexatious girl.

Frowning, he dipped his quill pen into the inkpot and, tapping it once to remove the excess, signed his name to the bottom of the letter. There was little else to be done at present aside from writing to Inch. Until Charles heard back from the solicitor, his options regarding the estate were limited.

"Am I interrupting you?" His mother's voice sounded from the doorway of his room.

Charles hastily blotted his signature before folding the letter and tucking it into an envelope. He'd post it to Inch first thing in the morning. "Not at all," he said. "Come in."

Philly entered, with Flurry, Twig, and Ignatius following close behind her. "You've been busy today," she said. "Did your absence have anything to do with Lady Katherine?"

He turned in his chair. His parents hadn't yet quizzed him about Kate's interest in him, but he had no illusion that they were in ignorance of it. They'd likely already discussed the matter between them. There was little the two of them didn't share.

Theirs was a relationship built on love and trust—feelings they had transmuted to their children. As a boy, Charles had often shared his secrets with his mother and father, not because they demanded his confidence, but because they inspired it.

The impulse still lived within him.

On returning from Tiverton this afternoon, he'd been tempted to go straight to his parents to tell them what he'd learned about Satterthwaite Court.

But they neither of them needed the burden of the knowledge. Not with so much mystery—and perhaps even danger—still attached to the business.

"Not particularly," he said as he stroked Ignatius and Flurry on their heads in greeting. "I have other matters to attend to now I'm home."

"Yes, I'm aware." Philly took a seat in the wingchair beside his desk. Candlelight played across her face. "You're searching for a suitable house."

Charles stilled.

But his mother didn't appear to possess any knowledge of his visit to Satterthwaite Court today. If she did, she wouldn't speak about it in riddles.

"Have you confined your search to Somersetshire?" she asked.

Twig pawed at Charles pant leg, and Charles bent to pick him up. "I'm looking in Devonshire as well."

"Devonshire!"

"You were happy there, weren't you?"

A smile touched her lips. "To be sure, until I met your father, the happiest moments of my life were spent in Devonshire. Do you think you might find a suitable property thereabouts?"

"Possibly."

Flurry and Ignatius sat down at Philly's feet. She reached to pet them.

Charles held Twig in his lap, ruffling the little terrier's wiry hair. "It must have been hard to leave Satterthwaite Court."

"Oh yes." His mother straightened, her blue and brown eyes soft with memory. "It was a great shock. I was even shyer than Hannah, then, and London was vastly different than anything I'd ever known. The people I was obliged to stay with didn't help in that regard. They were far outside my experience."

"The Townsends."

Her smile dimmed. "My Uncle Edgar and his daughters, Elizabeth and Abigail."

Charles had no recollection of Edgar Townsend or of his eldest daughter, Elizabeth, but he vaguely remembered meeting Abigail and her husband when he was a boy.

"Abigail Townsend came here once, did she not?" he asked, scratching Twig's ears. "I seem to recall her giving me a set of carved wooden soldiers."

"She visited in company with her husband, Lord Darly. The two of them were newly married and making their way back to London after their wedding trip. I'm amazed you can recall it. You weren't much above three at the time."

"They never came again?"

"No. I'm afraid the past was rather hard to forgive, on both our parts. Once Uncle Edgar's fortunes fell and Elizabeth was obliged to marry in order to save him, it was easier to cast me as the villain of the piece."

"You have nothing to reproach yourself with," Charles said. "It's they who were in the wrong."

"They were." His mother smiled once more. "But I

can't regret any of it. If I hadn't gone to London so long ago, I'd never have met your father." She held out her hand to him across the surface of his desk. "I'd never have been blessed with you and your sister."

Charles clasped her hand warmly. "I've not made life easy for you."

"Nothing worth having is easy," she said. "Indeed, the strongest bonds in life are forged by fire."

"I'd prefer a little less fire at the moment," he replied wryly.

"Yes, I know. Your father claims you're desirous of a quiet, peaceful life."

"I am," he said. "It's why I've come home. I thought you understood."

She pressed his hand. "My darling boy, I still don't entirely understand why you left."

Charles sighed. How he could explain to her what he scarcely comprehended himself? "I was restless," he said. "Dissatisfied, I suppose. Being here, in the shadow of so much contentment..." He paused before admitting, "Happy as I was...there were times I found it hard to live up to your example. To be as good as you, as heroic as father."

His mother's expression softened. "You've had your share of heroics."

"In the Navy perhaps."

"I'm not talking about soldiering. Do you recall rescuing that tomcat out of the tree when you were five? You went straight up to the topmost branches before your father could stop you. And then you came down again with the thankless cat balanced over your shoulder, hissing and spitting, very nearly scratching your eyes out."

Charles uttered a short laugh. "I remember."

"And what about that holiday we took in Cornwall?

You saw that boy struggling in the waves and you swam out to help him. You nearly drowned yourself."

"I was twelve."

"Exactly my point. You'd no need to leave England to prove yourself. You've been showing us exactly who you are since you were a boy."

"Spoken like a mother," Charles said.

"Perhaps." Philly rose, giving his hand a final squeeze before releasing it. "But no less true."

Chapter Fifteen

The invitation to Beasley Park arrived a week later. It was contained in a letter from Kate to Hannah, written in the most eloquent terms, expressing Kate's wish that the Heywood family join the Beresford family for three days of riding, dancing, and post-Christmas merriment.

It couldn't have come at a worse moment.

"It's only a trifling head cold," Charles's mother said. "I shall be better in a day or two."

Charles stood in the doorway of her room, regarding her with concern. His father was already within, seated on the edge of the bed where Charles's mother lay propped against a fluffy pile of pillows. Her nose was red, her hair tucked under a lace-trimmed muslin cap.

She was right. There was no need to worry. She'd only been coughing and sneezing a bit—a natural result of being caught in the rain while riding yesterday morning.

Her symptoms had nevertheless set the entire household on its head.

"You must rest the week." Arthur held Philly's hand.

He hadn't left her side since the onset of her cold. "I'll not have you risking your health."

"No indeed," Philly said. "But the children shouldn't have to miss their outing on my account. If you were to accompany them in my absence, dearest—"

"There's no question of that, my love," Arthur said. "And no need for it. It's Charles who's wanted, not the pair of us. He's perfectly capable of chaperoning Hannah for three days' time."

An irritating flicker of heat crept beneath Charles's cravat. "I'm sure I'm not the only one who's wanted," he said gruffly. "The letter was for Hannah, if you recall."

"Yes, and very nicely done," his father said. "You won't mind accompanying your sister?"

"No," Charles said. "Of course not."

He could hardly refuse. Not just because of what he owed his sister, but because of what he'd promised Kate.

He blamed the rifle shot. It had knocked him off-balance where she was concerned. Made him overattached and overprotective.

And not only the rifle shot.

When they'd returned to Tiverton, when he'd handed her up into the coach that would take her safely home, she'd clasped his hand so tightly, her blue eyes for the first time uncertain.

That rare flash of vulnerability had prompted Charles to do something rash. Something stupid. *Good God.* He'd effectively told her that he was at her service! That all she had to do was snap her elegantly gloved fingers and he would come running.

And that's exactly what he was doing.

"Should I have worn my brown carriage dress instead of my green one?" Hannah asked him when they departed Heywood House four days later. "Or would it have been best to wear my new bronze cloak?" She sat across from him in the carriage, both anxious and excited by turns. "Mama said they were equally suitable, but still…I fear I'll make a poor impression."

"Impossible," Charles said.

His sister didn't seem to hear him. "And what about the dogs? Evangeline won't know what to do with me gone from my room for two whole nights. She trusts me so. And Tippo is bound to miss me dreadfully."

"It isn't too late to send our regrets," he told her as their carriage rolled down the drive. Outside, the ground was blanketed in a pristine layer of new-fallen snow. "If you'd prefer to stay home—"

"It isn't that." She folded her hands tight in her lap. "Though I do hope Mama will be feeling better soon. Indeed, she seems to be better. Only this morning, Papa remarked that—"

Charles let his sister run on until she'd exhausted herself, no more enlightened at the end of her speech than he'd been at the beginning. "What is it, then, that's making you so fretful?" he asked when she'd finished. "Is it the prospective company?"

"Yes. What if the same thing should happen at Beasley Park that happened at the vicar's musical evening?"

"What happened?"

"I've already told you. It was in my last letter." She frowned. "Didn't you receive it?"

"The one with your latest suggestions for my giving up meat? Yes, very amusing."

"It was no jest, Charles. And neither is this. I was meant to sing an Irish air at the vicarage and I went completely blank. I couldn't remember my own name, let alone the words to the song. And that was only among the villagers. What if the same thing should happen at Beasley

Park? Lady Kate is so vivacious and Mr. Beresford so witty and worldly. How can I hope to keep up my part in the conversation?"

"You kept it up well enough when they came to call on us."

"Lady Kate did most of the talking then," Hannah confessed. "And when I walked with Mr. Beresford, he spent the whole of the time telling a story about a race he'd run in his new curricle. I wasn't obliged to say more than three words put together. What if..." Her words trailed away as she turned to look out the window. Snowflakes clung to the glass, obscuring her view.

"You'll have me to talk to," Charles said. "And Lady Kate has promised to introduce you to her pets."

"What about her older brothers?" Hannah turned back to him. "She has three altogether."

"They'll behave themselves."

"How can you know? They might tease me or—"

"They'll behave themselves," Charles repeated firmly. His tone brooked no argument.

Kate may be flirtatious and overbold, but if one of her brothers acted so with Hannah, Charles would soon set him straight. He had no hesitancy when it came to protecting his sister.

Two and a half hours later, the Heywood carriage rolled up the drive to the honey-colored limestone manor house at Beasley Park. It was a graceful structure, with a classical grandeur to its portico and Ionic columns that seemed well-suited to the lush, sloping parkland that surrounded it.

On applying at the front door, they were greeted by an aged butler who welcomed them into the house's expansive marble-tiled hall.

"Lord and Lady Allendale are in the drawing room," he said. "If you will accompany me?"

Charles and Hannah followed the man up a grand, curving staircase to the drawing room. Twice the size of the drawing room at Heywood House, it was elegantly furnished, boasting richly carpeted floors and silk-papered walls covered in oil paintings of horses and hounds.

The Beresford family were within, gathered in lively harmony, all of them talking, laughing, and making merry. Two glossy-coated and excessively well-fed black spaniels snored on the carpet near the fire. A pair of plump tabby cats dozed on a nearby chair, as much a part of the familial group as the dogs were.

On entering, Charles at once found Kate. She was seated at a small inlaid table by the window, engaged in a spirited game of cards with her brother Jack. A second golden-haired gentleman, distinguished by a pair of silver-framed spectacles, stood behind Jack, peering over his shoulder and offering advice.

"Stubble it, Ivo!" Jack said, scowling back at the man. "I don't need your help!"

"He needs all the help he can get," Kate replied as she turned over another card.

The two men groaned.

A third blond gentleman stood by the damask-draped window at the opposite end of the room, arms folded as he peered outside, frowning. The eldest brother, Charles presumed. He looked to be close to Charles's age, though not vastly dissimilar from the much older gentleman seated by the fire in company with a petite lady who could only be Kate's mother, Margaret Beresford, Countess of Allendale.

"Lieutenant Heywood and Miss Heywood," the butler announced.

The Beresfords all looked up in unison. One of the

spaniels uttered a low woof. The other spaniel stood, its tail wagging with interest.

Kate was out of her chair in an instant. She swiftly crossed the room to greet them, the skirts of her pale blue cashmere gown floating about her legs. "Lieutenant Heywood. Miss Heywood." She curtsied, smiling. "How pleased I am to see you! We all wondered when you would arrive. The roads are so uncertain this time of year."

Charles bowed to her. "Lady Katherine."

Hannah murmured a greeting of her own as she returned Kate's curtsy. Her cheeks were pink, her voice barely above a whisper. It was a sure sign she was succumbing to her shyness.

Kate seemed to recognize the symptoms. She took both Hannah's hands in hers. "How charmingly you look! I trust you had a pleasant journey?"

Hannah gave her a grateful smile. "Very pleasant. Thank you, my lady."

"Oh, do call me Kate. Everyone does."

The older lady and gentleman rose to join them.

"Mama? Papa?" Kate kept hold of one of Hannah's hands as she introduced them to her parents. "May I present Lieutenant Charles Heywood and his sister, Miss Hannah Heywood? Lieutenant Heywood, Miss Heywood, these are my parents, Lord and Lady Allendale."

"Lieutenant Heywood." Lord Allendale bowed. "Miss Heywood." He was a tall, lean gentleman with cool gray eyes and a lazy, leonine grace. The golden threads of his hair were finely wrought with silver. "You are very welcome."

"Indeed, you are," Lady Allendale said. Her mink-brown hair was as dark as her husband's was fair, her wide eyes the same shade of blue as her daughter's. "I'm sorry your parents couldn't join us. How fares your mother? I trust her health has improved?"

"Thank you, ma'am," Charles said. "She's all but recovered."

"My father insisted she remain at home," Hannah volunteered shyly. "He's very protective of her."

Lord Allendale exchanged a wry look with his wife. The glacial set of his countenance was briefly thawed by a flicker of tenderness. "I can understand the impulse."

Lady Allendale's mouth curved into a warm smile. "I shall have cook supply you with a restorative jelly to take back with you. She swears it's a cure for every ill."

"Restorative jelly." Jack Beresford pulled a face as he approached them. "Vile stuff, Miss Heywood. Don't let anyone tell you otherwise."

"You already know my brother, Jack, of course," Kate said. "And this is my second eldest brother, Ivo."

The bespectacled gentleman who had been standing behind Jack at cards acknowledged Charles and Hannah with a bow. "Lieutenant. Miss Heywood. Pleased to make your acquaintance."

"And that unsociable fellow by the window is my oldest brother, James, Viscount St. Clare." Dropping her voice, Kate whispered to Hannah, "You're not to take anything he says to heart during your stay. He lives to suppress all our fun."

Detaching himself from the window, St. Clare crossed the room to make his bow. He evinced no reaction to his sister's words. "Miss Heywood. Lieutenant. Welcome to Beasley Park."

Hannah stole a look at the viscount through her lashes. Her blush deepened.

Charles frowned. He supposed, to a young lady's eyes, St. Clare must be considered a dashing fellow. Fortunately, the viscount didn't appear to be the flirtatious type. Aside from a single impenetrable glance in Hannah's direction, he refrained from either staring or engaging with her.

The dogs milled around their legs, plumed tails wagging.

Charles reached to stroke their heads. Hannah joined him, her face brightening.

"This is Gem and that one's Jolly," Kate said, introducing them to each of the spaniels in turn. She cast a fond glance at her cats, still sleeping on the chair. "And there are Tabby and Major. Take no offense. They wouldn't rouse themselves to greet anyone, the selfish creatures."

"You'll be wanting to refresh yourselves after your journey," Lady Allendale said. "I'll summon Mrs. Kirby to show you to your rooms."

"I'll show them, Mama," Kate said. "Come, Miss Heywood." She tugged Hannah toward the door. "You've been given the room next to mine. It has the prettiest view."

Charles inclined his head to Lord and Lady Allendale and their sons before following after Kate and his sister.

Kate hadn't yet addressed him personally. Indeed, she'd scarcely looked at him. But all of that changed the instant she'd installed Hannah in her lavishly appointed bedchamber. No sooner had the door clicked shut than Kate turned on Charles with an air of breathless impatience.

"I wish to speak with you," she said.

He lifted his brows. They stood in the center of the hall. Maidservants and footmen bustled past, not so engaged in their duties that they couldn't spare a curious glance at their young mistress and her guest.

"Not here," Kate said. "In private." She led him

farther down the thickly carpeted hall. "Will you walk down to the stables with me?"

"When?" he asked.

"In ten minutes' time. Unless…" She gave him an uncertain glance as they approached the end of the corridor. "Do you need longer to refresh yourself?"

"Ten minutes will suffice."

"Excellent." She came to a halt in front of a wood-paneled door. "This is your room. I put you close to your sister."

And close to you, he nearly said.

To be sure, his bedchamber was located only a few doors from hers. It was a fact that would no doubt be plaguing him this evening as he attempted to find sleep in his bed.

"Will she be all right if we slip away awhile?" Kate asked.

"I'll speak with her," Charles replied.

"Very well," Kate said, satisfied. "I shall meet you in the downstairs hall in ten minutes." With that, she turned and strode away.

Charles stared after.

He hadn't seen her in a week. Not since the afternoon they'd parted in Gold Street. But he'd thought of her every day since.

And not only with irritation.

He'd imagined her face. Her voice. The lively intelligence in her eyes and the bold lilt in her smile. Those imaginings had been painfully vivid. And yet …

They paled in comparison to reality.

A troubled frown worked across his brow as he entered his room. He wondered, not for the first time, what the devil he was getting himself into.

Chapter Sixteen

Precisely seven minutes later, sturdy boots on her feet and a woolen mantle over her gown, Kate descended the stairs to the marble-tiled entry hall. But it wasn't the tall, dark, and serious ex-naval lieutenant who awaited her there. It was her equally sober-minded brother, James.

He stood at the door, clad in his black winter overcoat, his hat in hand. His face was set with grim resolve.

"You're not looking for me?" she asked as she stepped down into the hall.

"I'm not looking for anyone. I'm going out." He opened the front door. There were no servants about to open it for him. Not that James would have insisted upon it. For all his pompous respectability, he was no spoiled aristocrat.

The wind whistled into the house, bringing with it a flurry of snow.

"Now?" Kate asked in chagrin. "But our guests have just arrived!"

James cast a sardonic glance over her own heavy mantle. "Which is why you're going…where?"

"For a walk with Lieutenant Heywood."

James's gaze sharpened. "And his sister?"

"What about his sister?"

"Who will be entertaining her in your absence? Jack? Ivo?" James cocked a brow. "Myself?"

"Miss Heywood has no need for entertainment. She's refreshing herself in her room. When I return, I'll go and fetch her. You can see her again then."

He stilled. "What makes you imagine—"

"I saw the way you looked at her," Kate said. "The lieutenant and Miss Heywood mayn't have noticed, but I know you, James. She's the first young lady I've ever seen you offer a second glance."

Her brother was silent a moment. "Her eyes don't match."

"That shouldn't have been a surprise. I warned you they didn't."

"Yes, but…" He frowned. "You said nothing about all the rest of her. She's—"

"She's shy. Painfully so. You must endeavor to be sweet to her."

A glimmer of suspicion darkened his face. "Are you matchmaking, Kate?"

"Goodness no," she said. "I wouldn't dream of it. We all know you intend to go to London next season and find yourself a duke's daughter or a princess or some equally illustrious personage who will marry you and set herself up as the most admired hostess in the country."

"One of us must do our duty. Our family requires respectability. Something you'd do well to remember."

"When have I ever forgotten it?" Kate gave a sharp tug to her mantle, straightening the fabric over the skirts of her woolen gown. "You still haven't said where you're going in such a hurry."

"If you must know," James said tightly, "I'm going after Ivo."

"Ivo's left the house as well?" Kate expelled an exasperated breath. Were none of her brothers going to remain long enough to entertain their guests?

"He has," James said. "He made his escape not fifteen seconds after you departed the drawing room. I saw him from the window, walking toward Letchford Hall."

Kate recoiled. "Not Miss Burton-Smythe again?"

"I fear so. Now"—James settled his hat on his head—"if you would allow me go in peace, I may yet have time to catch him."

"By all means." She stepped back. "Do what you must."

Her brother slipped out the door.

Kate remained on the threshold, staring after him, the icy winter wind biting her face as he crossed the drive in the direction of the boundary Beasley Park shared with Letchford Hall.

Good Lord.

Did Ivo have no brains in his head? He couldn't seriously imagine that anyone would sanction a match between him and the daughter of Sir Frederick Burton-Smythe?

Papa certainly wouldn't.

He despised Sir Frederick with a passion. Indeed, Kate had once heard the servants whispering that, in her father's scandalous youth, he and Sir Frederick had engaged in fisticuffs on more than one occasion.

Kate well believed it.

Her father was an old dear, but when riled, he wasn't a man to be trifled with. Only a fool would get on the wrong side of him. Her oldest brother was much like their father in that regard. If anyone could resolve the problem with Ivo and Miss Burton-Smythe, it would be James.

A booted footstep sounded on the stair behind her.

"Leaving without me?" a deep voice inquired.

Kate turned from the open door. Her heart gave an excited leap as Charles Heywood approached. Like her brother, he was dressed for the out of doors in a heavy overcoat and gloves. Unlike James, however, Charles's dashing appearance provoked an unholy swarm of butterflies in her stomach.

Foolish.

He wasn't the first good-looking gentleman she'd ever seen.

No, she thought wryly. Only the *most* good-looking one.

At least, he seemed so to her.

It was a strange alchemy. Something about him that satisfied her sensibilities in every regard. No other gentleman had affected her thus. With most, she was bored to sobs in the first ten minutes.

"Not at all," she said, collecting herself. "I was only seeing my brother off. He's, er, gone to call on a neighbor."

It wasn't entirely a lie.

Charles caught hold of the door in one large black-gloved hand, relieving her of the weight of it. He held it open for her. "It's getting colder out."

"Yes. Isn't it lovely?" Exiting the house, she made her way down the snow-covered front steps. The frigid air numbed her cheeks, making it hurt to smile. She smiled nonetheless. "I adore this time of year almost as much as I enjoy the spring and summer."

"Despite the frost and the damp?"

"Despite everything." She thrust her hands into the

long sleeves of her mantle. "The stable is just around the corner. It will be warmer there."

Charles walked alongside her, his boots crunching on the gravel. "How is your horse?"

"Much improved. Jonas brought him home from Tiverton yesterday. Three nights confined to a loose box at the White Horse, coupled with thrice-daily hoof soakings, have all but cured him. He's to rest another week here at Beasley before I ride him again."

"A wise course."

"Indeed. I daren't risk laming him. One can't be too careful with a horse's hooves. It's like the proverb says: 'But for a hoof the kingdom was lost.' Or something like that."

A shadow of amusement edged Charles's mouth, but he didn't correct her, though she knew she'd misquoted.

Kate liked him all the better for it.

There was nothing so tedious as a gentleman who was always correcting a lady. Men who set themselves up as experts, offering unsolicited advice, opinions, and masculine guidance to women who never asked them for it in the first place.

She led him into the expansive stone stable block where her maternal grandfather, the late Squire Honeywell, had once housed his famous bloodstock. Straw was scattered about the floor, the air warm from the bodies of the lazily dozing horses in the long rows of loose boxes.

"Here," she said, taking him to Ember's box. "You can see for yourself."

The big bay gelding stuck his head out. His dark eyes glimmered with irrepressible curiosity.

Charles stroked Ember's neck. "He's a handsome fellow."

"Yes, he is." But Kate wasn't looking at Ember. She was looking at Charles—at the strong line of his profile and the sensitive glint in his somber gaze as he examined her horse.

She moistened her lips to speak. The words wouldn't come. Not the right ones, anyway. She was reduced to scratching Ember's velvety nose in uncharacteristic silence.

It wasn't like her to be reticent with a gentleman. But Charles Heywood wasn't just any man. He was the fellow she'd chosen all on her own. The one she'd pursued and was very near to catching.

Or so she hoped.

It wouldn't do to say the wrong thing. One ill-spoken phrase—one clumsy misstep—and she'd ruin everything. And then where would she be? Back on the marriage mart again, amid the same dreary crop of lords and sirs who had paid court to her during her debut.

A dispiriting prospect.

It emboldened her to find her voice.

Charles spoke before she could do so. "By the way," he said in an offhand manner, "my sister doesn't eat animal flesh."

Kate's brows lifted. It seemed an odd non sequitur. "Doesn't she?"

"I trust it won't be an issue with your cook. I wouldn't like Hannah to be embarrassed."

Kate's heart melted a little more. Just when she thought it wasn't possible to like him any better, she discovered he wasn't only heroic, noble, rich, and handsome, but he was a caring brother, too.

"Leave it with me," she said.

"Thank you. I will." He paused. "You had something you wished to say to me?"

She exhaled a breath. "Only that I've been beside myself with curiosity since we parted. You must tell me what's being done about Satterthwaite Court."

"I wrote to my family's solicitor on the matter inquiring about Mr. Catmull's claim on the property."

"And? How did he reply?"

"I haven't heard back from him yet. However, if all is as it should be, I've instructed him to make the man an offer."

"You'll buy the house, then?"

"If there's no underlying issue, yes."

"And that will be that?" Kate was incredulous. "What about the grievous wrong done to your mother?"

"What about it?"

"Aren't you the least bit interested in discovering what it was?"

Charles let his hand fall from Ember's neck. "I went to Tiverton, didn't I?"

"That was just the beginning, surely. You haven't yet found out who's behind the letter. And you've made no strides in uncovering the injustice it alluded to."

"I expect they were merely referencing the loss of my mother's childhood home. It was an injustice, by all accounts, though not of the legal variety."

"If that was the case, why mention a grievous wrong at all? Why talk of writing to you at risk to their own safety? No one has ever been in danger from uttering an acknowledged truth."

"It doesn't follow that there's a secret to uncover."

"You haven't tried very hard to discern one." Kate studied his face. "Or have you?" A fleeting glimmer of resolve in his eyes alerted her to his true intentions. She brightened with triumph. "I knew it! You *are* trying to uncover the secret, aren't you?"

"I'm making efforts," he admitted.

"What sort of efforts?"

"Discreet ones. My family's history with the family of the villain who inherited the house is complicated."

"Edgar Townsend."

Charles nodded. "He was a ruthless man who would have sold my mother to the highest bidder to further his own aims. When she married my father instead, Townsend's fortunes plummeted. I suspect that's why the entail was broken. He must have been in desperate need of money."

"So, he sold Satterthwaite Court," Kate mused. "Pity your parents didn't know of it at the time. They could have purchased it themselves." She chewed her lip. "Will you question Mr. Townsend?"

"Townsend is dead."

"Oh." That *was* inconvenient. "What about your mother and father? Surely they must know something—"

"I won't have my parents distressed by troublesome recollections from the past," he said firmly.

"Well then?" she prompted him. "What next?"

He hesitated a moment. And then: "Townsend's daughters, Elizabeth and Abigail, are still living. If there was any wrongdoing on their father's part in relation to Satterthwaite Court, there's a chance they'll know of it."

"You must question them, of course."

"I intend to," Charles said. "Starting with Abigail. She and her husband were on good terms with my parents for a time. I expect I'll have better luck where she's concerned."

"Do they live in the West Country?" Kate was already imagining herself accompanying Charles on his fact-finding mission.

"They're in London," he said. "I wrote to her there a few days ago."

Kate couldn't hide her disappointment. "You wrote to her," she repeated. "And that's all?"

Charles leaned his back against the side of the loose box. He folded his arms. "What else would you have me do, Kate?"

She warmed a little at his use of her name. It was a reminder that they were friends—or something very like it. "You must go to London yourself. You can interview Abigail and Mr. Catmull and—"

"I've no desire to return to London."

"Why not? I'll be there next month."

He gave her one of his unreadable looks. "At this time of year? Whatever for?"

"The Dowager Duchess of Chesham is having a ball. Her birthday falls on Valentine's Day. She always celebrates in lavish style. She's turning sixty this year, so the ball will be grander than ever. There have been whispers that the Queen and Prince Albert might come."

"And you've been invited?"

"Through the auspices of my parents' friends, Viscount and Lady Mattingly. It's an opportunity I won't be permitted to miss. Afterward…I'm to remain in London for a time."

"For the season," he said flatly.

"Yes."

"Because you must find a husband."

"Ostensibly, yes. But that's neither here nor there. The fact is, I'll be in London. If you were to come, we could investigate the mystery together."

"On no account," he said. "This isn't a game we're playing. And a visit to London is out of the question. I've only just returned to Somersetshire. I can't be leaving again on some fool's errand."

Her spirits flagged. She quickly rallied. "I'll be there, in any event. I could ask Mr. Catmull—"

"You'll do no such thing," he replied with sudden sharpness. "I mean it, Kate."

"You'd rather let the matter drop?"

"I haven't let it drop. I went to Tiverton. I've consulted with my solicitor. If all goes well, I shall soon possess the deed to Satterthwaite Court. The rest scarcely matters in comparison."

Kate couldn't conceal her frustration. "You would buy the estate and set up house, simply ignoring the fact that it all started with a sinister letter that made references to grievous wrongs and personal peril?"

"I'm hardly ignoring it. I've written to Abigail, haven't I?"

"You've *written* to her. It isn't the same as chasing down the mystery in person. Have you no sense of—" She broke off, an alarming thought occurring to her. "Just why *are* you buying the house? Is it purely out of sentiment?"

"Not purely, no," he said. "I'd intended to purchase a property of my own now I'm back in England. It may as well be this one."

A knot of inexpressible emotion twisted in her breast. Had she misread him? Misunderstood his meaning when he'd helped her into the coach in Tiverton?

She recalled the things he'd said. The way he'd taken her hand.

No, she couldn't have been wrong. She *couldn't* have.

"You've never mentioned settling down before," she said. It was practically an accusation.

His mouth quirked faintly. "When could I possibly have mentioned it? More to the point, why would I have?"

She glowered at him. "You might have indicated if you

had marriage plans in mind. If there's some young lady with whom you have an understanding—"

"There's no young lady."

The knot in her chest eased a little. "Oh. Well… that's…"

"Though how it's any of your business, I can't begin to imagine."

"Of course it's my business! We both know what this is. Do me the courtesy of—"

"What this is," he said gruffly, "is the height of absurdity. I've been a fool to indulge it this long."

Her face fell. "Is that what you've been doing? Indulging me?"

He raked a hand through his hair. "Lord knows what I've been doing. From the moment I set foot in Bond Street, my life has been in chaos. I wish to heaven I'd never encountered that wretched dog."

"Now who's being absurd." She advanced on him, only coming to a halt when the front of her full skirts bowed against his legs. "You rescued that poor dog for one reason only. If not for that—"

"I went after him because he was on the verge of harming himself, or someone else. He bit you to start. Five minutes longer and—"

"You rescued him because you're a hero. Not just the kind who fights in a war or who performs some grand act for public acclaim." She took hold of the lapels of his greatcoat, giving them a forceful tug. "You didn't care a whit what anyone thought. And you certainly made no effort to endear yourself to us. You acted purely for the good, regardless of the muck, and filth, and inconvenience of it. How could I not set my sights on you? I'd be a fool—"

He closed his hands over hers, silencing her. "You don't know me, Kate."

Her heart beat hard. She was almost afraid to say it. Almost afraid to ask. But, after all, faint heart never won fair gentleman.

"I'd like to know you," she said. "Don't you want to get to know me?"

He stared at her for a long moment. "Yes," he said finally. "God help me."

She brightened. "Then we're of the same mind."

Frowning, he let go of her hands. "I doubt that very much."

She released his lapels, briefly smoothing her hands over the wrinkles she'd made in his greatcoat before stepping away from him. "You know what I mean. We both of us wish to know each other better. And we've three days in which to do it."

Charles straightened from the wall of the loose box. "I have a suspicion that three days won't be near enough."

"Oh? How long do you suppose it will take?" she asked.

"Three years," he answered solemnly. "Perhaps three decades."

She laughed at his seriousness. "Nonsense. I'm not that complicated." She gave her skirts a shake. "Shall we return to the house? Doubtless your sister will be wondering where we are. I shouldn't like her to feel I've abandoned her."

He wordlessly offered her his arm.

Kate took it, still smiling, as they walked from the stables. He was grumpy, to be sure. Grumpy, gruff, and occasionally disobliging.

But he was going to be hers.

She was determined.

Chapter Seventeen

That evening, Kate sent her lady's maid, Yvette, to assist Hannah with readying for dinner. Kate followed a half hour later. She knocked softly on Hannah's bedroom door before entering.

"May I come in?"

"Please do." Hannah was seated in front of the dressing table mirror as Yvette put the finishing touches on her coiffure.

The lady's maid had arranged Hannah's auburn tresses in a heavy, interwoven roll at her nape, securing it with a single, artfully twisted plait. The elegant simplicity of it was a perfect complement to Hannah's understated gray silk dress.

"I brought this for you to wear this evening." Kate crossed the room to the gauze-draped dressing table, a silver filigree hair comb displayed in the palm of her hand.

She'd selected the ornament with care from the many bits and baubles in her collection. Unlike the expensive jewels she'd been given by her parents, the little silver comb was something Kate had bought with her own pin money. It was wrought in the delicate shape of a butterfly.

"It will glitter nicely in your hair," she said.

Hannah's face lit up. "Oh! It's lovely."

Kate glanced at Yvette. "If you've finished?"

"Oui mademoiselle," Yvette replied.

"Thank you, Yvette," Kate said. "You may go."

Yvette quietly withdrew, shutting the door behind her.

"It was kind of you to send her to me," Hannah said. "I didn't imagine I'd need a maid for so short a visit. I'm accustomed to looking after myself at home."

"As am I." Kate anchored the comb into Hannah's hair. "But one can still appreciate the little luxuries of life." She smiled. "There. What do you think?"

"It's beautiful. Thank you."

"Consider it my gift to you."

Hannah's eyes went wide. "You're too kind. But I couldn't—"

"Nonsense. Now I've seen how well it suits you, I'm persuaded it was destined to be yours." Kate stepped back to examine the full effect of Hannah's toilette. "How well you look with your hair in that style! Yvette has such a deft hand. When you go to London for the season, you must hire a French maid of your own to look after you. They're known to be the best."

Hannah's gaze slid away from Kate's in the mirror. "I'm not going to London." She stood from her chair. "I fear it must be Bath for me."

Kate gently touched Hannah's arm. "No! You can't mean it."

"I do."

"But why?" Kate led Hannah to the window seat. It was lined with oversized feather cushions. Kate sat, drawing Hannah down beside her. "It's not because of the expense?"

"No, not that."

"What, then?"

"I simply don't have the temperament for London." Hannah held up a hand, anticipating Kate's objections. "No, no. I know it to be true. Indeed, I would prefer Bath. It's still daunting, but I believe I can manage my shyness better there."

Kate was sensitive to Hannah's shyness, but she didn't entirely understand the cause of it. "What have you to be shy about? You're from an excellent family. You're kind and well-spoken. And you're lovely. To be sure, when you first arrived, my brothers couldn't stop staring at you."

Hannah blushed mightily. "Please don't say that."

"It's the truth," Kate said. "I share it in the hope that you might be tempted to reveal something of your own brother's feelings."

"Charles?" Hannah's mouth lifted in a bemused smile. "I'd have thought his feelings were evident. He's here, after all."

"Mere politeness," Kate said dismissively.

"Not Charles. He's civil, yes, but he's never before done something merely to be polite. Not so long as I've known him." Hannah paused. "Of course, he *has* been away a good many years. I suppose he may have changed."

"How many years has it been since last you saw him?"

"Four altogether. He stopped at Heywood House on leave for just a few weeks, then. He was but four and twenty and I only fifteen. I feared it would be a long while before we met again. And it has been."

"I can't imagine one of my own brothers disappearing for years on end," Kate said. "Though sometimes I *have* wished them to Hades."

"Charles wasn't meant to disappear. He was supposed to go to Cambridge."

"And instead, he joined the Navy. Yes, Mr. Trumble mentioned something to that effect."

"My parents weren't at all pleased," Hannah said.

"Surely they didn't expect him to remain close to home forever?"

"No, indeed. Charles didn't like the peacefulness of the countryside as well as we did. Not then."

"And now?"

"He speaks of purchasing an estate and settling down right here in Somersetshire," Hannah said doubtfully.

Kate came to attention. "You don't believe him?"

"I don't know. I hope he'll choose to settle here, but…"

"But?"

"In the past he was drawn away by his thirst for adventure."

Kate's brows notched. She recalled Charles mentioning his attraction to adventure on their return journey from Satterthwaite Court. He'd spoken of it as being part of his past. "Perhaps he's changed, as you said."

"Perhaps." Hannah plucked at the silk covering of one of the cushions. She was loyal to her brother, that was plain, and was clearly regretting having already revealed too much. "I expect only time will tell."

"As diplomatic an answer as any." Kate took Hannah's hand. "Be easy. I won't spend the whole of your visit interrogating you about your brother. However," she added with a cheeky grin, "if you want to know anything about one of mine, you need only ask."

CHARLES WAS RETURNING TO HIS ROOM TO CHANGE FOR dinner after a game of billiards with Ivo and Jack when he passed the Earl of Allendale on the stairs. Thus far, the two of them had only met in company. There had seemed no need to solicit a private interview with the man. At least, not this early in Charles and Kate's acquaintance.

But Lord Allendale, it seemed, had other plans. "Heywood," he said. "Well met. Join me in my study a moment, if you please."

Charles could hardly refuse. He followed the earl back down the hall. His study was a darkly masculine room furnished with leather, mahogany, and claret-and-gold-threaded Aubusson. A branch of candles flickered on the mantelshelf, illuminating another portrait of Lady Allendale.

It was a similar painting to the one Charles had observed in the drawing room, though this portrait was smaller and obviously of a more intimate nature. The countess's hair was loose over her shoulder and she was half turned, as though casting a private glance at the viewer.

That viewer being her husband.

Lord Allendale's desk was situated directly across the room from his wife's portrait, presumably so he might look at it while he worked. Another indication of the happy state of their marriage.

It put Charles in mind of his own parents. Arthur kept a portrait of Philly as well. Except the painting of Charles's mother had been done in miniature, making it easier for his father to carry it with him always.

Lord Allendale sat down behind his desk, motioning for Charles to take a seat. "You'll forgive a father's curiosity, but hearing of your association with my daughter, I took the liberty of writing to a friend of mine at the Admiralty."

Charles remained standing. "I see."

Lord Allendale extracted a letter from his desk. "I believe you know Admiral Dixon?"

Charles stiffened. "You must know that I do."

Lord Allendale glanced up at him. "Come. Sit down. I won't torture you any more than your own father would torture a gentleman who had become entangled with your sister."

Charles reluctantly took a seat in one of the chairs in front of the earl's desk. His mouth settled in a grim line. "That's not very reassuring."

Lord Allendale chuckled. "I know something of your father. His reputation with a pistol exceeds my own. He fought in the Peninsula, did he not? And was wounded there."

"That's right."

"Your family has a history of serving the crown. But not you. Not any longer. You were obliged to leave the Navy."

Charles glanced at the letter in Lord Allendale's hand. He could only imagine what Admiral Dixon had written to the earl. Something about Charles's lack of patriotism, no doubt. "I resigned my commission," he said. "Many officers, do."

"The way I understand it from Dixon, you were compelled to resign."

"It was suggested to me," Charles acknowledged. "But there was no compulsion in it. Had I felt it was right to remain, I'd have done so, regardless. I acted then—and have always acted—in accordance with my own conscience."

"Admiral Dixon mentioned that as well. Indeed, he

describes the strength of your character in rather eloquent terms." Lord Allendale held the letter up in the light from the candle on his desk so he could read it aloud. "'My unofficial opinion of Heywood is that he's an entirely noble, imminently heroic, and unquestionably unrelenting pain in the arse.'"

Charles suppressed a grimace. "Is that all?"

The earl lowered the letter. "He claims you suffer from an excess of compassion. A liability in battle, apparently. His criticisms are limited to your failure to follow orders."

"I suppose that's fair."

"A soldier must do what he's told."

"So everyone keeps reminding me."

"If you dispute the policy behind those orders, you're better served entering politics."

"I have no ambition in that regard," Charles said.

"Pity. The country could use men of conscience. Though noble sentiments mean little if one is unable to occasionally listen to those who know better."

Charles's jaw tightened. He wasn't vying for Kate's hand. He nevertheless felt the need to defend himself in the eyes of her father. "You're not to think I make a habit of defying my superiors in every respect. I had good reason for objecting to certain orders in the Navy."

"Yes. Dixon said. You disagree with the concept of Empire. You're not the only one." Lord Allendale studied Charles's face. Something he saw there appeared to satisfy him. "In any case, I never did care much for gentlemen who practiced blind obedience. A man must have a will and a mind of his own—especially if that man means to court my daughter."

Charles shook his head. "You've mistaken my reason for being here. It was my sister Lady Katherine invited, not me."

"No, I don't believe I have mistaken it. You see, I know my daughter." Lord Allendale returned Admiral Dixon's letter to his desk drawer. "Kate is formidable, like her mother. She's also very young. A twenty-year-old heiress is vulnerable to all manner of fortune hunters, rascals, and rogues. You don't appear one of them. Still, I must warn you that my daughter is not unprotected. If any man were to meddle with her, he'd have me to answer to. And once I was finished with him, her brothers would have their turn with whatever was left. You won't find the Beresford men a forgiving lot. We're not known for letting insults lie."

Charles's fingers flexed on the arm of his chair. He didn't relish the idea of having to fight Kate's father or her brothers on account of some imagined insult. Nor did he fancy informing Lord Allendale that, if there had been any impropriety thus far, Kate had been the one guilty of instigating it.

"I have no evil intentions toward your daughter," he said instead. "I have no intentions whatsoever. The moment I develop any, you may be certain I'll be calling on you."

Lord Allendale smiled slightly. "Be sure that you do."

Chapter Eighteen

A single night spent at Beasley Park was enough to confirm Charles's suspicions: the Beresfords were nothing like the Heywood family. The house's gilded ceilings and elegantly papered walls housed a peculiar brand of affectionate chaos, characterized by tart words, physical competition, and good-hearted bickering.

Not that affection was lacking in the Heywood family. Far from it. But where Charles's parents were quiet and thoughtful, addressing their children with tender gravity, Kate's were loud and boisterous, verbally jousting with each other as they dined, played cards, or engaged in rambunctious after-dinner games of charades.

They were no less fond of each other.

Lord and Lady Allendale held hands with the same frequency as Charles's parents. Indeed, much like Arthur and Philly, the earl and his countess seemed to have a way of communicating all their own—an entire language made up of private glances and lingering touches.

Theirs was a love match, it was clear. One where the fires of passion were still blazing brightly.

"They've known each other since they were children," Kate explained the next day as she and Charles set off on an early morning ride across the glistening, snow-covered grounds of the park.

Lord Allendale kept a fine stable. Charles was mounted on a gleaming, brawny chestnut warmblood, while Kate rode her mother's hunter—a majestic ebony mare with a wild light in her eye.

The two of them weren't alone. Hannah trotted ahead with Kate's brothers Ivo and Jack, both of whom were talking and laughing with her as though she were their newly adopted little sister.

Only Kate's brother James had refrained from joining them, choosing instead to ride out on his own into the village on some errand or other. He seemed a solitary sort of man, one with little patience for the high spirits of his siblings.

Charles wasn't sorry to be absent his company. The viscount's cool gaze had settled on Hannah once too often during dinner last night. Though he'd shown no marked preference for her, never talking to her or teasing her like his younger brothers, it was plain that she'd caught his attention. And it was equally plain that the viscount had made an impression on Hannah. Since their arrival, she hadn't once met the man's eyes, not that Charles had seen.

It wouldn't do.

When Hannah wed, it must be to someone as warm and compassionate as she was. A man who would nurture her gentle nature, not snuff it out with his coldness and distance.

"They grew up here together at Beasley," Kate said. "They were practically inseparable. It's why they prefer their own company to anyone else's."

"Not to yours and your brothers, surely," Charles said.

163

Kate smiled. "Oh yes, even to us. Mama and Papa would never admit to it, but it's true." She brought her mare alongside his gelding. "They'd have joined us on our ride, but they rarely leave their room before midmorning. Not if they can help it."

It was an indecorous admission. Charles wondered it didn't put Kate to the blush. But she seemed to have no compunction about referencing her parents' unfashionable affection for each other.

"They're soul mates," she said. "Destined to be together."

He looked across at her. "A romantic notion."

"It's the truth." Kate squinted against the glare on the snow. She hadn't worn her hat or her riding veil this morning. Without them, the sun shone over her face unfiltered. She appeared both very beautiful and very young. Far younger than her bold ways would attest. "Don't you believe in soul mates?"

"No," he said frankly.

"Not even a little?"

Charles didn't like to disabuse her of her fancies. But there was no point in pretending. "I believe that two people of a similar mind and temperament can be happy together if they're lucky. That's all."

"Similar temperament, bah," she scoffed. "Naturally a couple must be aligned on the fundamentals—just as we are—but—"

He couldn't contain a smile. "Are we, indeed?"

"It's obvious enough if you look at our characters objectively. We both prefer the country to town. We both love animals and the out of doors. And we neither of us are content to sit back when a situation calls for action."

"All of which you've deduced from our limited acquaintance."

"And from talking to your sister. Hannah tells me you're resolved to live a quiet life in the country, despite the fact that, in the past, you were always seduced by adventure."

Seduced.

It was as good a way of putting it as any. Even now, back in the familiar tranquility of the West Country, the thrill of discovering the origins of the mysterious letter beckoned.

As did Kate.

To be sure, Charles was as drawn to the adventure of her as he'd ever been to anything.

But it was a weak man who couldn't control his passions.

"I am," he said.

"As am I," she replied promptly.

His lips twitched. "I suspect our ideas of what constitutes a quiet life might differ in the extreme."

Kate dismissed his doubts with a wave of her gloved hand. Her mare pranced beneath her. "We needn't be identical in every regard. Imagine how dull that would be. Only look at my parents—or at your own. Are they so much the same?"

"They are actually," he said. "They began as friends. Marriage came later."

"And love?"

"That as well," he acknowledged.

A hill rose ahead of them, covered in a blanket of pristine white snow. Hannah, Jack, and Ivo broke into a canter on their ascent.

Kate held her mare back from joining them. "Do you want to know what I believe?"

"I suspect you're going to tell me."

"I believe in Plato's theory, that men and women were

originally one being. He writes about it in *The Symposium*. He says that, fearing their power, Zeus broke humans in two and scattered them about the earth. That's what a soul mate is—your missing half. Not the same as you, but the parts you're lacking. The pieces that make you whole."

Charles thought of the unnamable emptiness he'd felt since leaving home eight years ago. That odd sense of being lost and incomplete. He'd been searching for fulfillment ever since. Looking for a purpose—not a person.

The idea that any one individual could make another whole was romantic nonsense. It bordered on ludicrous. And yet…

What would his father be without his mother? Their relationship had begun as a friendship, it was true, but Arthur had been a broken man when he met Philly, too shattered from the war to find life very much worth living. If not for her, he'd have given up on it entirely.

Charles checked his horse. "You've read Plato's *Symposium*?"

"Of course," she said, as though it were the veriest commonplace. "I've studied every subject my brothers have. My parents believe in a broad education for ladies."

"You don't strike me as a bluestocking."

"I'm not. I simply enjoy pursuing my interests, wherever they take me."

He wondered if she included him in that category. He presumed so. "And mythology is one of your interests?"

"Don't change the subject." Wind whipped over the hill, causing her horse to start. Kate gave the mare's neck a reassuring stroke. "You must have observed that my parents aren't identical. My father runs cold and my mother burns hot. Yet they're deliriously happy together."

"Is that what you aspire to? Delirious happiness?"

Her eyes met his as they caught up with the others. "I'll settle for nothing less."

Charles supposed he was on his mettle.

Kate rode on over the rise along with Jack and Hannah. Charles didn't keep pace with them, choosing instead to fall back with Kate's brother Ivo.

Ivo wasn't as jolly as Jack, but he was less frosty than James. He'd been in Europe the past several years and had returned possessed of a multitude of progressive ideas for the future of British industry. He'd shared some of them with Charles over a glass of port last evening.

"If my sister suggests a race," he said, "I'd advise claiming indisposition."

Charles's mouth quirked in an amused smile. "Is she likely to suggest one?"

"If she doesn't, then Jack will. You can beat him. You're riding Fury. Jack's horse is no match for him. But Kate can beat anything, regardless of the horse she's riding."

"She's that good?"

"She's that strategic," Ivo said. "*And* she's determined. She's been winning wagers since she was in leading strings. There's no challenge too great that she won't pick up the gauntlet."

Charles's smile dimmed.

Is that what he was to her? A contest? A challenge?

He'd be a fool not to recognize it. Not to see that her pursuit was inspired as much by the thrill of it than by her genuine interest and attraction.

She was young—only twenty. And he was weary. He didn't need a young lady leading him a merry chase. When he married, he required someone steady and dependable. Someone who could hold the course. He'd had enough adventure for a lifetime.

"Some wagers are impossible to win," he said.

"Kate finds a way. She's the baby. She's accustomed to getting what she wants." Ivo gave him a sympathetic grimace "Whatever she has planned, you'd best be on your guard."

"I thought this was just a morning ride."

"It's never just a ride," Ivo replied feelingly.

They joined the others over the rise, trotting down a short path alongside a snow-flocked woodland. A small cottage was visible in the distance, surrounded by a broken stone wall. Kate and Jack led the way toward it.

Ivo grinned. "So that's what she has in mind. I might have guessed it."

Charles cast him a quizzical glance. "Are we paying a call on someone?"

"Not on a person," Ivo said. "That cottage is where the gamekeeper stores his guns."

<hr />

"WON'T THE GAMEKEEPER BE UPSET IF WE BORROW HIS rifles?" Hannah asked as she followed Kate into the icy interior of the stone cottage. It was neat and tidy, with a plain wood kitchen table, an old stuffed sofa and chairs, and several worn, rag-carpets covering the slatted floor.

Kate passed through to the gun cupboard, the skirts of her riding habit tossed over one arm. "They're not his. They belong to the estate. And Mr. Gridley doesn't mind our using them. It was he who gave me the keys to the cupboard."

"Will he be loading for us?"

"No indeed," Kate said. "He was asleep in the kitchens

when last I saw him. Which is precisely how I prefer him. We don't require his advice. We can load for ourselves."

She unlocked the cupboard, revealing the hodgepodge of weaponry inside. There were rifles and muskets and even an ancient horse pistol or two from her father's time.

Jack joined them inside after securing their horses. He selected an elegant polished rifle with a thirty-inch barrel from the cupboard. It was Kate's favorite. "Where shall we set the targets? On the wall?"

Kate plucked the rifle from Jack's fingers. She loaded it herself while he chose another. "Of course not. That would be no sport at all."

"Sport enough for some among us." Ivo entered the cottage with Charles. "Not everyone enjoys a shooting contest, Kate."

He gave her a significant look, silently reminding her of the trouble she'd got into during her ill-fated dawn shooting contest on the Heath in London. Aunt Jane had revealed every detail in her letter to Kate's mother, much to Kate's chagrin. On learning of it, the whole family had joined in criticizing Kate for exposing the Beresford name to censure.

She lifted her chin in defiance. "This isn't a contest. We won't be vying for stakes."

"Pity," Jack said. "I could use a few quid." He loaded his rifle. "Do you like shooting, Hannah?"

Hannah blushed. "I don't *dis*like it. Not so long as it's target shooting and not hunting."

Jack's hand stilled on the ramrod he was using to push the lead ball, powder, and cartridge paper into the muzzle of his rifle. "You object to hunting?"

"I object to any sport in which animals are harmed," Hannah replied.

"None will be harmed today," Kate said. "We can shoot at pine cones."

Charles chose an old rifle for himself from the cupboard. He tested the weight of it in his hand.

Kate met his eyes as he loaded it. "I trust you don't object to a little good-natured competition?"

His mouth hitched in a wry smile. "What makes you think I'm up to it?"

"Sailors can shoot, can't they?"

"Not all of them. And not all of them well."

Kate appreciated his modesty, but she saw no need for it. "Don't pretend you're among that class. Gilbert Trumble has already revealed all."

"Ah," Charles said. "Is that what's prompted this diversion?"

"You're a good shot, I take it," Ivo said in sudden understanding. "This begins to make sense."

Jack led the way out of the cottage, his rifle in hand. "I daresay Kate imagines she can best you. She's an excellent shot herself."

Charles arched his brow at her. "Is that a fact?"

"Don't look so surprised. Shooting has more to do with skill than physical force, as you must be well aware." Kate strode past him to join her brothers, with Hannah close behind.

Charles came after them. "Good vision helps."

Ivo squinted at the stone wall ahead. "Mine is abominable."

Jack laughed. "He *has* spectacles. He's just too vain to wear them outside of the house."

"It's not vanity," Ivo retorted. "I simply prefer the world to be out of focus. The streets are cleaner this way and the prettiness of the village girls is greatly improved."

Jack and Kate exchanged a look. She supposed Ivo

counted Meg Burton-Smythe among the pretty village girls of his acquaintance. Pity he hadn't been wearing his spectacles when he met her. He might have recognized that she was forbidden to him.

"Shall I collect pine cones for us?" Hannah asked.

"I'll help you," Kate said gamely.

It wasn't difficult to find them. Most of the trees had shed their pine cones weeks ago. Kate and Hannah collected enough to line up along the top of the wall. It was less than fifteen yards from the cottage. Scarcely any sport at all. But Kate wouldn't embarrass Hannah by insisting on setting their targets at a greater distance.

"Do you practice much?" Kate asked.

"Rarely," Hannah said. "But I do know how to hold a rifle and shoot it."

"Did your brother teach you?"

"My father."

"It was my mother who taught me." Raising her rifle, Kate pointed it at the farthermost pine cone and fired. There was an acrid cloud of smoke as the ball discharged. The pine cone shot off the wall with a satisfying crunch.

"Well done, Kate!" Ivo called out.

Jack applauded. "A direct hit."

Kate looked to Charles.

His eyes gleamed with appreciation. He inclined his head to her in acknowledgment of her skill.

Pride swelled within her. "It was nothing," she said, reloading her rifle. "A mere twelve yards at best."

"But such a small target!" Hannah said admiringly.

"You go next, Miss Heywood," Ivo said. "Ladies choice."

Hannah reluctantly accepted the rifle from Kate. "I can't strike one of them from this far."

"Move closer," Charles said, coming to stand behind his sister.

"Oh, but I couldn't," Hannah told him. "It wouldn't be fair to everyone else. If twelve paces is the minimum—"

"Nonsense." Kate urged Hannah forward. "We make our own rules."

Hannah haltingly closed the distance, stopping a scant two yards from the wall. She took her time sighting the pine cone before firing. The force of her shot sent her staggering back several steps. She might have fallen if her brother hadn't been there to brace her. But her aim held true. The ball struck the edge of the pine cone, sending it spinning.

The four of them cheered Hannah's effort with enthusiasm.

She lowered the rifle, handing it back to Kate with a bashful smile. "It shouldn't count for as much as a shot from farther away.

"I propose that Heywood make up the difference," Jack said. "He can consider it a handicap."

"Fair enough," Charles said.

Jack went next. Positioning himself at an angle, he aimed and fired down the length of the wall, striking three of the pine cones at once. "Ha ha!" he crowed. "Top that, Ivo!"

"You know I can't," Ivo said sourly.

"You can try." Jack reloaded his rifle and passed it to his brother.

Squinting at the nearest pine cone, Ivo pointed and squeezed the trigger. When the smoke cleared, his pine cone remained standing.

Jack burst out laughing.

Ivo scowled. "Had I known we'd be shooting today, I'd have brought my spectacles."

"The loser's lament," Jack said. "'If only I'd worn my specs, Jack wouldn't have won.'"

"Jack *hasn't* won," Ivo retorted. He looked to Charles. "I'm counting on you to humble him Heywood."

"Two and twenty yards," Jack reminded Charles. "That's Kate's twelve plus Miss Heywood's ten."

Charles glanced at the cottage, frowning.

Kate at once grasped his dilemma. "It's impossible from here," she said. "Unless you take your shot from inside the house."

"That won't be necessary." Charles turned back to the wall. He looked past it, focusing on the woods that loomed in the distance. "How far would you say that pine tree is?"

Kate came to stand beside him. She followed his gaze. "Good Lord! That's easily more than forty yards. Surely you're not proposing to hit it?"

"No," Charles raised his rifle. He pointed the muzzle toward the single remaining pine cone that was nestled, almost invisibly, in the tree's branches. "I'm proposing to hit *that*."

Her eyes widened as he took aim and fired. His shot struck the pine cone, sending it flying out of the branch.

Ivo, Jack, and Hannah converged upon Charles in an excited rush.

Kate stared up at him in wonder, all but forgetting her own sense of competition in the face of such extraordinary skill. "How—?"

"Practice," he said simply, lowering his weapon.

"Bollocks." Jack slapped Charles on the back. "That, my friend, is God-given talent."

"He can do it with both hands," Hannah informed them proudly. "Can't you, Charles?"

Charles gave Kate a lopsided smile. "Would you like to see it?"

Kate's heart raced. Competence was a powerful allurement. But this level of mastery quite took her breath away. "Oh yes. What shall you aim at next?"

"You choose," he said.

"What about that icicle?" It hung from the same tree on a branch high above the ground. "That's not too difficult, is it?"

In answer, Charles reloaded his rifle. Taking it in his opposite hand, he sighted the icicle and fired. The icicle shattered into the snow.

Kate clapped wildly as her brothers cheered, the smoke from the rifle billowing around them.

Charles set down his weapon. "With that, I respectfully withdraw from competition."

"As you should," Ivo said. "Leave the rest to us mortals."

Hannah collected another batch of pine cones and, with Ivo's help, assembled them on the wall while Jack busied himself reloading.

Kate remained with Charles, her blood still humming merrily.

His smile broadened. "I see I've impressed you."

She had the sense that he'd *wanted* to impress her. Indeed, unless she was mistaken, he'd been showing off a little. "You have," she said. "Are there no end to your talents?"

"That's the extent of them."

"Nonsense. You can shoot. You can ride. You're excellent with animals. And you're a marvelous brother, as well. It leaves me to wonder…"

"You were expecting something more?"

"Only one thing," she said. "I trust you can waltz?"

Chapter Nineteen

After dinner that evening, Kate had the drawing room cleared for dancing.

"I'd have rather we used the ballroom," she said, sinking down on the velvet-covered stool in front of the satinwood pianoforte. The voluminous flounced skirts of her white tarlatane muslin evening dress pooled around her slippered feet. "But it's shut up this time of year. We've had no balls or parties large enough to warrant opening it. Winters at Beasley are rather isolated."

Charles stood over her, poised to turn the pages of her music. "My sister and I passed a thriving village on our journey here. We saw several great houses, as well."

"Oh yes, there are a great many villagers and prosperous farmers hereabouts. We host a Harvest ball for them every autumn when we're in residence. As for the local gentry, the only family worth inviting to anything is that of our neighbor, Sir Frederick Burton-Smythe, and he and my parents don't get on."

It was a vast understatement, but Charles didn't need to hear the whole of it.

Kate wanted him to see only the best of her family during his visit.

She spread her fingers over the keys. If this were a larger gathering, there would be someone else volunteering to provide the music while she and the others danced. But there were only eight of them altogether—five gentleman and three ladies. It was a number that included her parents.

Kate wasn't the only one among them skilled at the pianoforte. However, the dancing had been her idea. She felt duty-bound to take the first turn at the instrument.

Outside, the snow swirled in lace-patterned flurries against the windows. A chill seeped through the glass, creeping into the edges of the room. Only the blazing fire in the cavernous marble hearth kept it at bay.

"Play it allegretto, Kate," Jack said. "It will warm us up." He stood in the center of the room across from Hannah Heywood.

James was beside him, lined up facing their mother.

Mama wore a blue moiré evening dress, embellished with a rich fall of lace at her bosom and sleeves. Papa stood by the hearth, regarding her with a smile, while Ivo wandered near the doors of the drawing room, too restless to sit still.

"You don't have to turn the pages," Kate said to Charles. "I know most of this one by heart."

"It's no trouble," he said.

Kate began to play a Scotch reel, performing the piece as her brother had bid her, fast and lively, at a pace commensurate with an energetic country-dance. It wasn't too difficult. She was a creditable hand at the piano and harp. What she lacked in skill, she made up for with energy and enthusiasm, lending a boisterous quality to the chords that harmonized with the laughter and stamping feet of the dancers.

James and Jack changed partners at intervals. Hannah's face flamed each time she took James's hands, and James's smile dimmed, his eyes becoming guarded, whenever he gazed down at her in turn.

Charles watched them, frowning.

"She's safe with my brother," Kate said. "He'd as soon blow his brains out than commit an impropriety."

Charles's brows lifted. "A vivid metaphor."

"An apt one. For all I know, he'll one day be prime minister. He's that straitlaced and decent. It's quite dull really."

"Decency is dull?" Charles inquired, turning the page of her music.

Kate fumbled a chord. She swiftly corrected herself. Over-corrected, in fact. She corrected her overcorrection just as gamely. "It can be."

"If that's the case," he said, "I'm amazed you can tolerate my company."

"Oh, you're not decent," she replied without thinking. "You're…"

Amusement flickered in his eyes. "What am I?"

She gave him a roguish smile. "That's what I'm attempting to discover."

He didn't reply, only looked at her, that same amused light softening his stern expression. At some point in the course of his visit, the frown he'd worn during their earlier encounters had begun to fade away, replaced with a look of something resembling affection. Indeed, since arriving at Beasley, Charles Heywood had smiled at her—and *with* her—with increasing frequency.

Perhaps he was beginning to see how well they suited

one another? Perhaps—just perhaps—he was beginning to like her?

Kate glowed with optimism.

When the song came to a close and the dancing ceased, her mother crossed the room to the pianoforte. She was flushed from exertion, her eyes sparkling like twin jewels. In her youth, Mama had suffered an illness to her lungs. She'd been all but an invalid. Even now, after all these years, she could still get breathless from exertion.

"Up you get," she said to Kate. "It's my turn to play."

Papa came to join her. "An excellent idea. Shall I fetch your music, love?"

"Would you, my dearest? I've a new waltz in the top drawer of the desk."

A waltz.

Kate stood from the pianoforte, her heart thumping hard.

Her mother was lending her support. She wouldn't have suggested a waltz otherwise. Not this early in the evening.

Kate impulsively kissed her cheek. "You're an angel, Mama."

Her mother gave her an absent pat before waving her away. "Don't hover, darling." She took Kate's place on the seat in front of the pianoforte. "I have this well in hand."

Kate met Charles's eyes. "Will you—" She immediately stopped herself. It was one thing to take the reins on every other occasion, but asking him to waltz was a bridge too far.

Charles appeared to comprehend her predicament. He offered her his hand with all solemnity. "Would you care to dance, my lady?"

Kate smiled broadly as she took it. "I thought you'd never ask."

She followed him out onto the makeshift dance floor, her pulse skipping with excitement.

Jack relinquished Charles's sister to James. A scorching blush swept up Hannah's bare throat and into her face as his arm circled her waist. The waltz was still a trifle scandalous. There was no other dance where two people were so close, moving together in a closed hold, all but embracing.

Kate feared she was blushing a little herself when Charles's arm closed around her. She set her hand on his shoulder. It was solid as stone beneath her fingertips. As solid as all the rest of him. His finely tailored evening clothes did nothing to disguise it. He was a sailor. A man of action. Of unwavering and determined strength.

"I'm out of practice," he admitted as he swept her into the first turn.

"I'm not," she said.

He stared down at her steadily. "Shall I let you lead?"

She bit back a laugh. As if he wasn't already! She may not be steering him in the dance, but it was she who was plotting the course of their journey in every other respect.

For the time being, Charles seemed disposed to let her.

Kate beamed up at him. It took a confident gentleman to allow a lady to helm the ship. Her father often permitted her mother to do so. But Kate had never yet met another gentleman willing to cede his power to a female. After her dismal season in London, she'd begun to doubt such a man existed.

"Not when dancing," she said. "I prefer not to think at all."

He guided her into another sweeping turn. "You must have waltzed a great deal during your season."

Her skirts swayed in a graceful arc. "I did. Including with your Mr. Catmull."

The amused glint in Charles's eyes dwindled. "Unhappy thought."

She would have liked to press him on the subject of Mr. Catmull. Or perhaps even tease him a little about the possibility of his being jealous. But they weren't in a London ballroom. They were in her parents' drawing room at Beasley Park, with her father and mother only yards away and her overbearing older brother even closer.

James held Hannah as formally as a dancing master. Indeed, Kate would wager that if she measured the distance between the two of them with a ruler, it would come out to the same prescribed number of inches her old instructor, Monsieur Laurent, had told her must be maintained in a closed hold. That didn't stop Hannah from blushing rosily as James led her into every turn, her mismatched eyes fixed at the approximate level of the top button of his waistcoat.

Kate's father turned the pages of her mother's music, ushering the chords of the waltz toward a swelling close.

"Did you have occasion to waltz much during your time in the Navy?" Kate asked Charles.

His mouth tipped at one corner in a smile so faint she might have missed it if she wasn't gazing up at him so intently. "My sister asked me just the same at Christmas."

"And your answer?"

"I was on a ship, Kate. Whom do you suppose I was waltzing with?"

"Did you never come off your ship onto dry land?"

"I did," he said grimly. "But not for dancing."

Kate searched his face. He was referencing fighting, presumably. She would have asked him about it, but the family's butler, Selby, chose that moment to make an appearance. She caught sight of him as Charles waltzed her past the entrance to the room.

Ivo was there as well, having spent the past two dances lingering conspicuously by the doors.

Selby's usually inexpressive face was pained. "Miss Burton-Smythe, sir," he said, as though reciting the line of a play he'd been forced to practice in advance.

Meg Burton-Smythe entered the room behind him. Her red hair was caught up in a thick coil of plaits, secured with a tortoiseshell comb that complemented the pale apricot of her simple silk dress. The candlelight danced over her profile, bringing light to the liberal sprinkling of cinnamon-colored freckles that dusted her face.

Kate stumbled at the sight of her, briefly losing track of her steps. Charles's arm tightened around her waist, instantly steadying her.

"Bloody hell," Jack muttered under his breath. "What the devil is Ivo playing at?"

Mama brought the waltz to an abrupt close. She rose from the pianoforte to stand alongside Papa. Despite Jack's indecorous outburst, their expressions were inscrutable.

Kate remained with Charles on the dance floor. James stood nearby alongside Hannah. His frame was taut with barely concealed anger.

Ivo approached his guest with a smile. "Mother, Father." Taking Miss Burton-Smythe's arm, he drew her into the room. "Seeing as how we were short of ladies for the dancing this evening, I took the liberty of inviting Miss Burton-Smythe to join us. Meg, you remember my parents, Lord and Lady Allendale? And doubtless you recall my sister, Kate, and my brothers Jack and James."

There was an awful silence. Kate's stomach tensed. She had the feeling they were all of them standing atop a tinderbox. One wrong word—one wrong move—and the entire situation would explode.

"Miss Burton-Smythe," Mama said at length. "This is indeed a surprise."

Miss Burton-Smythe curtsied prettily—and a bit bashfully. She gave every indication of being as embarrassed by Ivo's stunt as Ivo should rightfully have been himself. "M-my lord, m-my lady," she said in a voice nearly too soft to be heard. "I was honored t-to receive your invitation."

Kate had forgotten Meg's stutter. It was an endearing trait, really. One that softened Kate's heart toward the girl a fraction. It wasn't, after all, Meg's fault that Kate's brother was such an unremitting arse.

"Miss Burton-Smythe," Papa said, with a curt bow. "How fares your father?"

Kate inwardly winced. Leave it to Papa to cut straight to the heart of the matter.

"His gout is t-troubling him, m-my lord," Meg replied, her stutter worsening. "He's b-been abed all day."

And was still abed, Kate suspected, probably fast asleep, under the influence of laudanum or some such drug, blissfully unaware of his daughter's defection. It was likely the very circumstance that had allowed Miss Burton-Smythe to slip away for the evening unnoticed. Were he awake and coherent, Sir Frederick would never have permitted his daughter to set foot in Beasley Park. He despised Kate's father as much as Papa despised him.

Which was no fault of Miss Burton-Smythe's, really.

Dropping Charles's arm, Kate stepped forward to greet the girl. "Miss Burton-Smythe. It's been an age."

"Lady K-Katherine." Miss Burton-Smythe bent her head.

"Kate, please. And may I call you Meg? Miss Burton-Smythe is so dreadfully formal."

"Oh yes," Meg said. "If you p-please."

Ivo drew Meg closer. "Allow me to introduce Lieutenant Charles Heywood, grandson of the Earl of Gordon. And this is Lieutenant Heywood's sister, Miss Hannah Heywood. They're staying with us until tomorrow."

Charles and Hannah exchanged polite greetings with Meg.

Ivo stood by, exhibiting not an ounce of shame. "Now that our numbers have evened up," he said to Mama once the introductions were dispensed with, "James can take over your duties at the pianoforte while the rest of us dance. You won't mind, will you, James? We can't spare any of the ladies."

James plainly minded very much. To be sure, Kate's normally unflappable eldest brother looked as though he were a hair's breadth from throttling Ivo.

"An excellent idea," Kate's mother said. She took Papa's hand, her fingers threading through his. She gave his hand a meaningful squeeze. "Shall we, my love?"

Kate's father held Ivo's gaze for a long moment before allowing Mama to draw him away.

Ivo didn't flinch. "Play something jolly, won't you?" he said to James.

Kate held her breath. But James didn't rise to the bait, thank goodness.

He strode to the pianoforte and sat down. Unlike Kate and her mother, he didn't require someone to turn the pages of his music. He didn't require music at all. James had a prodigious memory and could play most pieces entirely by ear. He did so now, pounding out the opening chords of a march with bone-rattling strength.

Jack approached Hannah. "Would you do me the honor, Miss Heywood?"

"Yes, of course," she said.

Charles lined up across from Kate. He couldn't fail to

recognize the peculiar tension in the room, even if he didn't understand the source of it.

Kate resented the fact as much as she resented Ivo for inviting Meg.

The last thing she wanted to be doing during the Heywoods' brief visit was explain her family's scandalous history. She was trying to persuade Charles that she was a worthwhile partner, not the reverse.

Though whether Charles would even ask her about it was an open question. A gentleman who was serious about her would surely want to know. One who was genuinely contemplating an alliance. But...*was* he?

A frown tugged at her mouth as she crossed places with him in the dance. Herein lay the danger of being the pursuer instead of the pursued. One could never guess what the other person was thinking or feeling. For all she knew, Charles didn't care one way or the other about her family's history. About any of them.

About her.

The prospect sank her spirits far more than any ill-advised stunt pulled by her brother.

Kate wasn't the only one whose spirits were waning. As the eight of them joined and separated again in the pattern of the dance, she observed that Mama's smile was brittle and Meg's face was aflame. Even Hannah was looking out of sorts, her eyes perpetually flashing to her brother as if seeking reassurance.

Oh, but it was all a disaster!

When Kate linked hands with Ivo in turn, she scowled at him. "Are you satisfied?" she asked under her breath.

"Immensely," he replied. "I've often found that the best way of enacting change is to force it upon the resisting parties."

"You may have ruined my plans."

"Really? My own are going swimmingly," he said unre-morsefully as they parted again.

Meg Burton-Smythe remained for another two hours, dancing with each of Kate's brothers and even Kate's father. All was painfully polite and excruciatingly civil. But there were no more waltzes. No more flirtatious looks or easy conversation. The pall over the room never lifted, not even after Ivo departed to see his controversial guest safely home.

Kate feared that, when he returned, her brother would be in for the scolding of his life.

Chapter Twenty

L ater that night, Charles descended Beasley Park's
curving staircase. The distant light from the crystal
chandelier illuminated his steps in the darkness. It
was half past eleven. He'd retired only a short time ago,
bidding good night to Kate in the hall before withdrawing
to his room. Once inside, he'd got no further than
removing his coat and cravat before recollecting that he
needed something to read.

His first night at Beasley Park had been spent tossing
and turning, too preoccupied with thoughts of Kate and
the business with Satterthwaite Court to get more than a
few hours of sleep. Tonight, he didn't doubt that sleep
would prove equally elusive without a book to aid him. It
needn't be anything too riveting. Some dry text on agricul-
ture or philosophy would serve the purpose.

With that in mind, he made his way to the library.

The wall sconces were still lit along the corridor, flickering candle flames casting long shadows over the
carpeted floor. Charles had gone no more than a few steps
when the sound of raised voices—male voices—stopped

him where he stood. And not only that. There was a figure in the hall.

It was Kate.

She stood half-hidden in the shadows, leaning against the wall outside the library doors, listening as her father and brothers argued.

"I warned him to keep clear of her," James was saying. "I told him he was putting us all at risk. My reputation—"

"You're not my father," Ivo shot back. "For God's sake, you're only two years older than me!"

"Your brother was right to warn you off," Lord Allendale said in a voice that cut through the din. "To encourage a connection with that family is a great piece of folly."

"I'm not encouraging anything. I merely invited a neighbor for a bit of merriment on a cold winter's evening. We needed another lady for dancing and—"

"Whom do you think you're addressing, Ivo?" Lord Allendale asked in a tone of perilous calm. "Do you imagine I'm not up to every trick?"

Ivo fell silent.

"Your brothers and sister are of an age to marry," Lord Allendale said. "I'll not have the old gossip started up again."

"Meg doesn't care about any of that," Ivo replied. "She's never mentioned—"

"Miss Burton-Smythe's father won't show such forbearance," Lord Allendale said. "He has no love for the Beresfords."

"He cares for Mother," Ivo said sullenly. "He named Meg after her, didn't he? It follows that he must have some fondness for Mother's children."

"*My* children," Lord Allendale said. "Your mother's and *mine*. Fred hasn't changed so much in the intervening years that he'd refrain from destroying the lot of you. He wouldn't view it as hurting your mother. He'd view it as hurting *me*."

"If you won't think of me," James said, "think of Kate. She's barely out of her first season and still seeking a titled lord for a husband. She can't afford to have someone questioning her legitimacy."

"Kate's given up on a title," Ivo said. "She's interested in Heywood now."

"She's toying with Heywood," James said. "She'll soon grow tired of him. When she does, she won't thank you for tarnishing her good name. If you'd given a thought to her—"

Kate chose that moment to turn away from the door. The flames from the nearest wall sconce danced in her eyes, revealing the alarming glint of tears.

Charles's chest tightened.

His first instinct was to withdraw back into the darkness. He'd caught her in a rare moment of vulnerability and had no wish to cause her embarrassment.

But it was too late.

Before he could move—before he could breathe—Kate's glimmering eyes locked with his. Her face paled in the candlelight. Straightening from the wall, she came to meet him.

Despite the troubling words he'd overheard, Charles's first thought was only for her. His voice sank with concern. "Are you—?"

Kate motioned for him to be silent. Catching hold of his arm, she tugged him away from the library, pulling him into a small anteroom near the end of the hall.

The furnishings within were shrouded in darkness. Only the luminous shimmer of moonlight through the cracks in the heavy draperies allowed Charles to see Kate's uncharacteristically solemn face.

"How long were you listening?" she asked quietly.

"Not as long as you were," Charles replied, equally quiet. He had no desire to draw attention to their presence. To be found here, alone with Kate at this hour, would do neither of them any favors.

He stood by the cold hearth as she found a box of friction matches and moved to light a candle.

"How much did you overhear?" she asked.

"Enough," he said.

She set the candle on the mantelpiece. The flame flickered in the draft from the empty hearth. "Enough to believe I'm illegitimate?"

Charles was silent. He'd been too long from England to be aware of the latest society gossip. If there was some scandal associated with Kate's birth, he hadn't yet heard of it. Until he did, he saw no point in jumping to conclusions.

"It isn't true," she said before he could answer. "I'm perfectly legitimate. My brother James was referencing a different kind of illegitimacy." She exhaled an unsteady breath. "If you must know, he was talking about the title."

His gaze sharpened. "Your father's title?"

She paced to the center of the anteroom, her figure all but disappearing in the darkness. Only the rustle of her skirts betrayed her continued agitation. "There have long been rumors that my father was born on the wrong side of the blanket. They're perpetuated by another claimant to the title—a very distant cousin of his. It's largely sour grapes, but...the truth is...the rumors aren't wholly unfounded."

"I see."

"You can't possibly." She continued pacing. "My great-grandfather had a reputation as an adventurer. And his son, my grandfather, was a known rogue who even turned highwayman for a time. It was quite the scandal, made worse by my own father having spent most of his life abroad. When Papa finally returned to England, he was a man grown. Many people claimed he was an imposter. Never mind that he looked exactly like his father and his grandfather before him."

Charles remained by the fireplace, unmoving. "Malicious gossip, then."

"That's all it is." Kate returned to him, coming to a halt in the small halo of candlelight. Her arms were folded at her waist. "It's still enough to cast a shadow over my father's claim. That and the fact that his mother was of low birth. She was a maidservant, if you must know."

"Ah." It was, objectively, a shocking detail. One that might understandably be a source of personal mortification. To Charles, however, it was nothing very horrifying.

He'd been raised to give more weight to a person's character than to their pedigree. It was a precept instilled in him by his parents. One that had only been strengthened in adulthood. Some of the best men he'd known in Her Majesty's Navy had been of dubious birth.

He contemplated a suitably reassuring reply.

Kate didn't seem to require one. "You can't imagine what it's like," she went on in the same agitated tone. "If any of us ever set a foot out of line, that's what it's blamed on. On the fact that my grandmother was no better than she ought to be. It should be ancient history, but no one has forgotten. It's why my brothers must marry well. It's why *I* must marry well."

"To a gentleman with a title." That small detail hadn't escaped him.

She didn't deny it. "Ideally. As far as my family's concerned, that's always been the goal."

Charles had already discerned as much from what her father and brothers had said. He didn't require it to be made any plainer. Kate required a titled husband. Anyone else was merely a momentary diversion—someone with whom to while away the winter while she was consigned to the country.

He'd long suspected this was a game to her, and here at last was proof of it. Her own brother had confirmed it. Kate had been amusing herself with Charles. Indulging in a flirtation as surely as she might indulge in a game of whist or a wager at the races.

A strange stillness settled into Charles's veins. Having his suspicions confirmed shouldn't be surprising. It shouldn't *hurt*.

But it did.

"A titled husband is indeed a worthy goal," he said at last. "I wish you luck in your pursuit of him."

<hr />

KATE WASN'T SO VAIN AS TO IMAGINE THAT CHARLES would be devastated to hear of her family's aspirations for her. His lack of reaction to the news was no less vexing. "Is that all you have to say?" she asked.

He stood by the fireplace, gazing down at her with the same impenetrable frown he'd often worn before coming to stay at Beasley Park.

But no.

She realized suddenly that it wasn't the same at all.

There was a strange air of vulnerability about him tonight. Something in the way his raven hair was rumpled. In the way his jaw was shadowed with evening stubble and his clothes were—

Goodness.

He was in his shirtsleeves!

Kate hadn't noticed it before. But she noticed it now. It was impossible *not* to notice. She'd never seen him absent the armor of his dignified black coat and cravat. He looked younger. Handsomer.

"You were anticipating something else?" he asked.

"Well…yes," she admitted. "What about us?"

"Us," he repeated flatly.

She stifled a huff of impatience. He was being purposefully difficult. One would think she'd offended him somehow. "We spoke of it only yesterday," she reminded him. "In the stables, if you recall. You said—"

"I *know* what I said." A rare spark of heat infiltrated his voice.

The knot in Kate's stomach eased a little. Indifference might rout her, but anger she could handle. She knew how to fight. "Then why—"

"That was before I was made aware of your ambitions," he said.

Ah. So that was it.

She might have known such mercenary desires would put his back up. He was too noble to comprehend the baser side of courtship.

"Not my ambitions," she said. "My family's."

"I see."

"You don't, clearly." She moved closer to him. "The rumors about my father's title may well follow his descendants into future generations. It's up to my brothers and me to stop that from happening. Alliances with powerful families will help strengthen our own. That's why I'm supposed to marry well—to wed someone titled and wealthy who can help lend legitimacy to the family name."

His brows lowered. "Because your parents insist

upon it?"

"No. Which only makes it worse. They'd sacrifice everything for my happiness if it came to it. I should do no less for them. Indeed, I fully intended to. Until…"

"Until what?"

A rueful smile curved her lips. "Until I met you."

There was an endless pause. Kate's emotions teetered on the precipice of it. And then—

"It needn't be mutually exclusive," he said. "Your happiness and marriage to some rich, titled lord."

Her smile froze. "I beg your pardon?"

"There must be dozens of eligible viscounts, earls, and marquesses about. Perhaps even a duke or two. You have every chance of making an enviable match."

She drew back from him, stunned. Had he really just said that? Had he really just encouraged her to meet and marry someone else?

Hurt constricted her throat.

It was too much. She'd all but declared herself to him and here he was, offering sensible, brotherly advice, completely unmoved at the prospect of her slipping from his grasp forever.

"Don't you even *care* that I might marry someone else?" she asked.

He looked down at her steadily, a brooding look in his eyes.

"I suppose you're indifferent," she said. "It was *I* who chose *you*, after all, not the other way round." She turned to walk away. "My mother warned me. You're only here to oblige your sister, not because—"

He caught her by the arm before she could take another step. His fingers curved around her, pressing gently—achingly gently—into her bare flesh. "Wait."

Her breath stopped. So did her heart for an instant.

She marshaled her senses. "You needn't humor me, sir."

"When have I ever done so?"

"You might have been doing it all along. Being gentlemanly and polite—"

"Hardly." His hand remained around her upper arm, holding her fast, holding her close. He moved the pad of his thumb over her bare skin in a slow caress.

Butterflies swarmed in her stomach.

Drat him!

She might have known how tender he would be from the way he'd settled Ember in Tiverton or how he'd calmed that crazed little dog in Bond Street.

But Kate was no flighty horse or feral dog to be pacified thus.

"It's probably the only reason you're here now," she said petulantly. "Out of politeness."

Reluctant humor glinted briefly in his eyes. "Now you're just being contrary."

"I'm not. I'm being logical. It stands to reason—"

"Kate." His voice deepened with gruff sincerity. "I've never in my life been anywhere I don't wish to be."

She gave him a doubtful look. "Even here at Beasley Park?"

"Even here in this room."

She stilled. It was the closest he'd ever come to admitting his feelings for her. "Then why do you…" Her voice trailed off as he lifted his hand from her arm to cradle her cheek.

A breath trembled out of her.

Oh, heavens.

It took an effort to keep her countenance. To refrain from blushing or swooning or pressing her face into the warm curve of his palm.

"Why do I what?" he prompted.

She swallowed hard. "Why do you always appear indifferent to me?"

His mouth hitched in a faint, apologetic smile. "An excess of caution, I suppose."

"Because you're afraid I'll trap you into marriage?"

"It's you who'd be trapped." He stroked her cheek. "You're young, Kate, and you're rather magnificent. You deserve a future as bright and exciting as you are. Not a dull, dreary life in the country with me."

"Who says life with you would be dull and dreary?"

"I do. My adventures are over, sweetheart. I'm ready to retire into a quiet, comfortable obscurity. But your life is just beginning."

Sweetheart.

Kate's pulse leaped. She was so thrilled by the endearment that she little heard the rest of it. "You're not *that* much older than me. You're only eight and twenty."

"I'll be nine and twenty soon."

"And I'll be one and twenty. That's how time works, always moving forward. Fascinating, isn't it? Before either of us know it, you'll be fifty and I'll be two and forty. A negligible difference at that age, you must agree." She brought her hands to his chest. "And you're wrong to assume I want excitement. I've told you before, I prefer the peace and quiet of the countryside just like you do."

"Yes, I'm sure you do," he said wryly.

"Charles—"

He shook his head. "Don't tempt me, Kate. I can't keep resisting you forever."

"I wish you wouldn't resist me at all," she said. And clenching her fingers in the fabric of his waistcoat, she pulled him down to her and brazenly pressed her lips to his.

Chapter Twenty-One

K ate hadn't planned to kiss him. She rarely planned anything, truth be told. It was often better, she'd found, to throw herself fearlessly into the fray and contemplate the consequences of her actions in the aftermath. It was an instinctive strategy. One that generally worked for her. She was at her best in the midst of the maelstrom.

But she hadn't reckoned for what happened next.

Charles received her chaste peck on the lips with gentlemanly forbearance, only the rigidness in his frame betraying his surprise. But when Kate moved to draw away from him, satisfied with her virginal bit of boldness, he didn't let her go. Instead, his arms came around her in a crushing embrace and, bending his head to hers, he kissed her back.

"*Oh.*" Kate exhaled a trembling breath. The sound was part pleasure and part surprise.

She'd imagined this moment. How it would feel. How *she* would feel when it happened. But nothing had prepared her for the overwhelming intimacy of it.

He was so close—his body warm as a furnace in the icy anteroom. His lips were warm, too. Firm, warm, and utterly perfect. They shaped to hers with passionate certainty, as though he'd kissed her dozens of times before. As though he knew just what to do to make her melt into his arms.

Her hand drifted up to his shoulder, fingers curving around the strong column of his neck. His *bare* neck. It was hot beneath her fingertips.

"Oh, Charles," she sighed.

Heaven knew what else she said. His name again? Murmured words of praise? Of affection? Kate hadn't the slightest notion. Kissing him was that glorious. That wonderfully sweet. She could have kept at it forever.

But, alas, it wasn't to be.

All too soon, Charles returned to his senses.

He broke their kiss, his breath coming hard. "There, you see." He rested his forehead gently against hers. A huff of laughter rumbled in his breast. "That's the undignified truth of it."

She threaded her fingers in the thick hair at his nape. "What's the undignified truth of it?"

"That I'm not indifferent to you," he said. "I doubt any man could be."

She refrained from telling him that he was wrong. Plenty of gentlemen were indifferent to her. Not to her fortune, perhaps, but definitely to her character. Though indifferent might be the wrong word. Disapproving would be better.

Or possibly appalled.

"Are you saying," she inquired, "that I have cause to hope?"

"I don't want to encourage you," he said.

"It's a bit late for that, sir. After a kiss like that—"

The sound of footsteps in the hall arrested Kate's speech.

She stiffened in Charles's arms.

Good Lord. It was her father! Or worse yet, James. Either would be a disaster. And not because she feared being caught in a compromising position but because her father and brother would undoubtedly ruin things. She wanted to treasure this moment, not spend the rest of her life looking back on it with mortification.

She stared up at Charles in frozen, wide-eyed silence until the footsteps faded, disappearing into the distance.

A breath of relief shuddered out of her.

"Goodness," she said shakily. "I thought they'd come in here."

Charles frowned. "They might easily have done so."

"Yes, but they didn't."

He slowly released her from his arms. "I won't compromise you, Kate."

Kate reluctantly slid her hand from his neck as he backed away from her. She felt the loss of his warmth as keenly as if she'd been removed from a cozy place in front of the fire and thrust out of doors, straight into the snow.

"You haven't compromised me," she said.

Though, admittedly, it had been a very near thing.

Charles put a respectable distance between them. "From now on, our friendship—or whatever it is—must be conducted with absolute decorum."

She smoothed her rumpled gown. "How dreary that sounds."

"I mean it," he said.

It was her turn to frown. "Yes, I can see that you do."

"It's not my habit to…to…"

"To passionately kiss young ladies?" she volunteered helpfully.

"No," he said, scowling. "Not the ones I'm serious about. I respect you too much to—"

"I'd rather you respected me a little less."

"Kate—"

"But if you insist on conducting our friendship—or whatever it is—with absolute decorum, then...I suppose you'll have to court me properly."

Charles lapsed into silence.

Kate refused to be discouraged by it. "You'll have to come to town next month and call on me in Duke Street. But only if you're serious about me. Only if that kiss was something more to you than a careless liberty taken in the moment—"

"You know it wasn't," he said fiercely.

"Then come to London. Pursue me there, as I've pursued you."

He looked at her intently. An expression of resolve gradually settled over him. "If I pursued you, then I'd have you. There would be no turning back."

Her heartbeat quickened. It was practically a threat.

A *romantic* threat.

"I'm all anticipation," she said.

"This is no jest, Kate." He tilted her chin up with his fingers, forcing her to meet his eyes. His gray gaze was as solemn as a vow. "I don't take on a challenge idly. When I set my mind to something, I see it through to the end."

"So do I." A smile tipped her mouth. "And here you thought we had nothing in common."

Chapter Twenty-Two

Charles and Hannah left Beasley Park the next day. The Beresfords all assembled on the snow-covered front steps to bid them farewell, wishing them a safe journey and inviting them to return with their parents as soon as they were able.

Kate embraced Hannah like a sister. "You must come again when I return from London. We had so little time together this visit to discuss your come-out." She kissed Hannah's cheek. "Promise me you won't depart for Bath without talking to me first."

"I promise," Hannah said. "And don't forget—" She whispered something in Kate's ear.

Kate laughed and whispered something back. Whatever it was brought a swift smile to Hannah's lips.

"I promise," Hannah said. "Goodbye until then." She waved to the rest of the Beresfords. "Goodbye!"

James, Viscount St. Clare, stood at the top of the steps, apart from his brothers and sister. He inclined his head to Hannah.

Hannah managed a shy smile in return before climbing into the waiting carriage.

Kate extended her hand to Charles. "You'll think about what I said?"

Charles took it. It was such a small, delicate little hand. One might easily imagine that its owner was small and delicate as well.

But people underestimated Lady Katherine Beresford at their peril.

She was no fragile flower. She was, as he'd told her in the moments before kissing her, rather magnificent.

"I will," he said.

Indeed, he already had. He'd spent most of last night lying awake thinking about following her to London. That is, in the few moments he wasn't dwelling on the blood-simmering details of that unexpected, and surprisingly scorching, kiss.

But he'd made Kate no promises then. And he made her no promises now.

He'd believed himself to have come home a changed man, no longer susceptible to the siren song of adventure. He realized as he climbed into the carriage with his sister, that that wasn't the case at all. Romantic adventure still had the power to lure him. Only this time, it wasn't in the guise of a dangerous voyage or a noble fight on some distant shore. It was in the form of a woman.

Lady Katherine Beresford wasn't the quiet, demure, biddable young lady he'd envisioned for himself during his last year at sea. She wasn't what he was supposed to want. But, by God, he wanted her all the same. The mere thought of her returning to the marriage mart—dancing with someone else—*kissing* someone else—made Charles want to put his fist through a wall.

She was made to be his.

Once he'd accepted that fact, the decision to chase after her came easily enough.

It was a decision that was solidified later that afternoon when he and his sister arrived back at Heywood House. There, he was met by a letter from Mr. Inch in Taunton. Charles waited until he was alone in his room to open it.

Dear Lieutenant Heywood,

Per your instructions, I investigated the legality of Mr. Elias Catmull's ownership of Satterthwaite Court in Devonshire and have determined that his title is in good order. Having done so, I tendered your offer on the property to Mr. Catmull through his attorney, Mr. Arbogast in Tiverton without delay. I regret to inform you that your offer has been summarily rejected. I took the liberty of inquiring as to whether Mr. Catmull might be amenable to a larger sum and was told, in no uncertain terms, that Mr. Catmull has no desire to sell the property to you.

If you wish to discuss the matter further, you will find me at my office through the first of February, after which I will be leaving for my annual holiday in Scotland. Until such time, I am at your disposal.

Yours, etc.,

Jeremiah Inch, solicitor

Charles lowered the letter, utterly perplexed. Catmull had rejected his offer? And he was refusing to consider a larger offer? It made no sense.

Were it any other property, Charles might have been willing to let the matter go. But this was Satterthwaite Court. If it was for sale, he was determined to have it. No mysterious, capricious owner was going to dissuade him. Certainly not a man who had spent the last year relentlessly chasing after Kate.

A snake, she'd called him.

Charles would rather anything than be bested by the man.

The next morning, he saddled a horse and rode into Taunton. Mr. Inch's office was in the high street. A relatively young solicitor, he'd got his start in London as a clerk to Mr. Ombersley, the aged solicitor employed by Charles's grandfather, the Earl of Gordon. When Inch had set up his office in Taunton over a decade ago, it had been only natural for the Heywoods to employ him.

He was a good attorney, as far as Charles was aware. Not as savvy, perhaps, as Ombersley, but sufficient enough for estate matters and minor contract disputes.

"Lieutenant Heywood," he said, welcoming Charles into the warmth of his small office. "I might have known you wouldn't let the grass grow under your boots."

He was a hearty man, with thick muttonchop whiskers and a pronounced double chin.

"Inch." Charles inclined his head to the solicitor before taking a seat. "This business with Satterthwaite Court—"

"Yes, yes. Excessively vexing." Inch sat down. "Your offer was more than generous for an estate of that size. As I said to the man Catmull has representing him in Devonshire, this Mr...."

"Arbogast."

"Mr. Arbogast, yes. A decent chap. I told him you'd be willing to go higher if Catmull insisted upon it. But Arbogast informed me—rather extraordinarily—that it wasn't the sum his client objected to, but to you personally."

Charles stilled. "To *me?*"

"That's the rub of it."

"I've never met the man."

"No?" Mr. Inch's mouth flattened. "That *is* peculiar."

"It's irrational," Charles said.

Inch scratched his side-whiskers. "You haven't any idea why the man has taken against you?"

"He has no good reason to have done so," Charles said. "Perhaps I should speak to Arbogast again?"

"It sounds to me as though the matter is out of his hands. If Catmull is refusing to do business with you, that's an end to it." Inch cleared his throat. "And there's a second issue to contend with."

Charles's eyes narrowed. "What issue?"

"Arbogast confided that Catmull is in receipt of another offer. It falls short of your offer by seven hundred pounds, but given Catmull's unpredictable nature, he may well accept it regardless."

Charles muttered an oath.

"It is unfortunate, to be sure," Inch said. "I regret there's nothing else to be done."

"Oh, but there is." Charles stood. "I'll speak with Catmull myself."

Inch's face shone with approval. "An excellent idea. I might have suggested it myself, given time to consider the matter."

Charles wondered. When it came down to it, Inch was no Ombersley. The latter could have devised a solution to the thorniest problem. Whereas Inch seemed disposed to accept every defeat without a struggle.

"I can furnish you with his address in Russell Square." Inch dipped his quill pen into the inkpot on his desk and dashed off a note. He handed it to Charles. "Though it may prove a wasted journey."

Pocketing Catmull's address, Charles bid the solicitor good day.

This wasn't over. Not by a long chalk.

When Charles arrived in London, he'd confront the matter of Satterthwaite Court in person. He would question Abigail. He'd even interrogate Elizabeth, if he could discover her whereabouts. But first, he'd deal with Elias Catmull.

Had Charles met the man somewhere before?

Charles thought not. Nevertheless…

He supposed it was possible there was some tenuous connection between the pair of them. Catmull might well be a relation of one of the sailors Charles had had cause to discipline in the Navy. Or possibly an uncle or a cousin of some lad Charles had unwittingly snubbed at Eton or the Royal Naval College.

Either might be cause for Catmull to have taken a dislike to Charles without having met him. But neither reason was sufficient to refuse Charles's offer on the estate.

His very generous offer.

By God, he'd been willing to pay the entire asking price! It was fifteen thousand pounds altogether. Surely no man would forego such a sum over a trifling quarrel.

Not a man in his right mind.

Chapter Twenty-Three

London, England
February 1844

K ate stood at the raindrop-streaked window of the confectioner's shop, a velvet embossed mantle cloak over her shoulders and a velvet muff dangling from one hand. She gazed out at the flooded street. "Rain, rain, go away," she murmured. "Don't come again until Lady Day."

Christine set a hand at Kate's waist, ushering her to a table in the corner. "It always rains in London in February. One of the hazards of returning to town before the spring." She glanced back at her lady's maid. "Plum? Go to the livery stable and tell Driscoll to bring the carriage round. He may collect us in half an hour."

"Yes, Miss Mattingly." Plum bobbed a curtsy before hurrying out into the storm, armed with a sturdy black umbrella.

The sky had been clear enough when Kate and Christine had left the Mattinglys' townhouse this morning for a final fitting on their ball gowns, but the moment they'd emerged from the modiste's shop in Bruton Street, the heavens had opened up. Ducking into the confectioner's for a hot cup of tea and a warm bun while they awaited the carriage had been Christine's idea.

"It always rains in London full stop." Kate sat down at the table. "At least in the country, one can be out of doors in the mud and muck. Here, we're obliged to remain inside, perfectly tidy at all times."

Christine joined her. "I thought you enjoyed the elegance of town life."

"I do," Kate said. "But things were just starting to get interesting in the country."

Christine's lips thinned. "With Lieutenant Heywood, I presume."

Kate remained silent while the shop's proprietor served them a pot of tea and a plate of currant buns. On returning to London, she'd confided in Christine about her various encounters with Charles in Somersetshire, sharing all the details of what proved to be the beginning of Kate's first serious romance.

Well…perhaps not *all* the details.

Kate had left out the bit about her pretending to be Charles's wife in Devonshire. And she'd refrained from sharing anything to do with the kiss she and Charles had shared at Beasley Park. Some things were too private to share, even with one's dearest friends.

"Why must you sound so disapproving whenever you mention him?" Kate asked when she and Christine were alone again.

"How can I sound otherwise?" Christine poured out

their tea. "He made a less than favorable impression on our first meeting."

"That's long past."

"It was less than two months ago."

"Yes, quite so. An absolute age." Kate took a bite of her currant bun. "He improves greatly on acquaintance. You'll see for yourself when he arrives."

Christine refrained from replying as she sipped her tea. Her silence spoke volumes.

"He *is* coming," Kate said.

Christine lowered her teacup. "Did he say he would?"

"No. Not in so many words. But—"

"Then you can't know."

"I know," Kate said firmly.

She *hoped*, anyway.

What was the point of it otherwise? Of attending Lady Chesham's ball on Wednesday? Of wearing her spectacular new silver-blue silk gauze ball gown? Kate was no longer looking for a suitable gentleman to wed. She'd already found one. No other man could compare.

She prayed she hadn't put Charles off by issuing what was, undeniably, an ultimatum. Goodness, she'd told him it was *his* turn to pursue *her*! It had seemed a good idea at the time. But now…

Here she was in London, waiting on him to act instead of acting herself. An uneasy state of affairs. She wasn't accustomed to doing nothing.

"Even if he does come," Christine said, "it doesn't follow that he'll attend the ball. Invitations were sent weeks ago and Lady Chesham wasn't inclined to hand them out to just anybody."

"Lieutenant Heywood isn't just anyone," Kate said. "He's the grandson of the Earl of Gordon. *And* he's a famous naval officer. He earned a fortune in prize money during his time at sea. A man lacking in courage could never have done so. If he wants to see me, he'll find a way to be there."

She spoke confidently enough, but as Kate drank her tea, niggling doubts began to eat away at her peace of mind.

Christine's expression softened. "Upon my word, Kate. If I didn't know you better, I'd suspect you of pining. You really do like him, don't you?"

"Is that so hard to believe?" Kate asked.

"I confess, I had my doubts in the beginning. But if you're sure of him—"

"I am."

Reaching across the table, Christine clasped Kate's hand. "Then I shall support the match with my whole heart."

Kate pressed her friend's fingers in gratitude. "You're a darling."

Christine squeezed her hand in return before releasing it. "I'm practical. I realize that once you've set your heart on something, you won't rest until you have it. I'd be foolish to stand in your way."

"If only my feelings were the sole concern. It's his that are at issue. He may not like me as well as I like him. Not well enough to exert himself."

"I don't believe it."

Kate scarcely did herself. She feared she'd lost control of the situation—and of her emotions. It had made her strangely vulnerable. "I only wish he was here now. I've been in a town nearly a week already and he's yet to show his face."

"What you need is diversion," Christine said. "Sir Lawrence has promised to take us to the theater tomorrow night. There's a dramatization of Mr. Dickens's *A Christmas Carol* that is sure to be delightful."

Kate mustered a show of enthusiasm. She refused to let her anxious mood diminish her friend's enjoyment. "I look forward to it," she said.

As she and Christine finished their tea, the door of the confectioner's shop opened. A thin, angular-faced gentleman stepped in from the rain, removing his curly-brimmed hat and shaking out his silk umbrella. His close-set eyes found Kate immediately.

She inwardly groaned. It was Mr. Catmull.

He wasted no time in approaching their table. "Lady Katherine. Miss Mattingly. What a happy accident it is to encounter you here."

Kate joined Christine in greeting the odious man, wondering all the while if his appearance truly *was* an accident. Had he been watching her since her arrival in town? Marking her movements along the strands of his web like a spider stalking a fly?

"A storm is brewing," he said. "I see you're without your maid or footman."

"My maid has gone to fetch the carriage," Christine replied. "She'll be back directly."

He pulled out a chair. "Allow me to offer my protection while you await her return."

Kate stiffened. As if they required his chaperonage!

But Christine was in no position to rebuff a gentleman who was in business with her betrothed. She offered Mr. Catmull a gracious smile. "An excellent idea, sir."

"I consider it my duty." Mr. Catmull sat down beside Kate. His leg brushed the swell of her skirts beneath the table. "Were it up to me, no young lady would set foot out of doors unescorted."

"Then we should be grateful it isn't," Kate said. "This

isn't the dark ages, sir. We ladies are accustomed to exercising a degree of independence."

"You may rightly accuse me of being old fashioned, my lady," he replied. "I hold to the belief that females are the weaker sex. It needn't be viewed as a failure on your part. It's simply how you were fashioned. Your bodies and brains aren't equipped to handle the rigors of life without a man's guidance and protection. It is our moral duty to look after you."

Kate exchanged an affronted glance with Christine.

"A laudable sentiment," Christine murmured politely.

"That's one word for it," Kate said.

Christine shot her a warning look. She liked Mr. Catmull no better than Kate did, but it wouldn't do to insult the man. Not so long as Sir Lawrence and Mr. Catmull were on terms of cordiality.

Kate raised her teacup to her lips, her fingers clenching tight on the handle. She wasn't interested in Mr. Catmull's strictures about a man's dominion over women, the swine. But there was *something* about him that interested her.

An idea struck her all at once.

"Mr. Catmull," she began. "It's recently come to my attention that you—"

"You there!" Mr. Catmull snapped his fingers at the shop's proprietor. "Another pot of tea, and be quick about it!"

The proprietor hastened to oblige him. "Apologies, milord." He brought them a fresh pot, steam swirling from its spout. "Is there anything else—"

"That's all." Mr. Catmull waved the man off with a flick of his hand.

Kate lowered her teacup very precisely back to the table. It took all her strength not to remark on Mr.

Catmull's behavior. She abhorred rudeness to servants and shopkeepers.

Her parents had always said that one could tell a lot about a person by how they treated those they perceived to be beneath them. Papa knew this firsthand, having begun his life in a less than elevated position.

Did Mr. Catmull not realize Kate's own paternal grandmother had been—at best—a scullery maid?

He waited while Christine dutifully poured out his tea. "That will do," he said to her before she'd finished.

"Kate?" Christine held up the pot.

"Yes, please." Kate permitted Christine to freshen her half-empty cup.

Mr. Catmull's gaze returned to Kate's face. "You arrived back in town on Tuesday last?"

Kate bristled. Naturally he knew the day. She wouldn't be at all amazed if he knew the precise time of her arrival as well. "I did."

"I trust your visit to Somersetshire was of a pleasant variety."

Kate added milk and sugar to her steaming cup, stirring it slowly. She'd meant to question him outright, but perhaps a roundabout method was better? She had little choice when he wouldn't let her get a word in edgewise.

"It was, thank you." She brought her cup to her lips. "And you, sir? How did you spend your Christmas?"

"I remained in town for the holiday. Sir Lawrence and I had business to attend to. However, in January, personal inclination briefly took me to the West Country."

Her brows lifted. "Oh?"

"I have a property in Devonshire that's being readied for sale," he said. "Satterthwaite Court it's called. Perhaps you've heard of it?"

Kate nearly choked on her tea. Mr. Catmull had visited

Satterthwaite Court last month? *Good Lord.* It was a minor miracle he hadn't happened upon her wandering about the grounds, masquerading as Mrs. Heywood!

"Satterthwaite Court," Christine repeated thoughtfully. "Do you know the place, Kate?"

"The name *is* familiar," Kate acknowledged. "My parents' estate isn't too far away, I believe."

"Rather close by, in fact," Mr. Catmull said. "I contemplated calling on you there, but as I haven't yet been formally introduced to your parents, I thought it best to refrain." He paused, adding, "For the time being."

Kate suppressed a shudder at the thought of Mr. Catmull venturing anywhere near Beasley Park or her parents. "A pity you didn't. Though I daresay it was for the best. I was much engaged during my visit home."

"There will be other opportunities for us to meet," he said. "One of them in the not-too-distant future."

"The Chesham's ball. Of course." Kate had forgotten he would be attending.

"I regret we can no longer expect an appearance by Her Majesty," he said. "She'll undoubtedly be too grieved to make merry after the Duke of Coburg's death."

"Yes, so I've heard," Kate murmured.

Ernest I, Duke of Saxe-Coburg and Gotha, had been both Prince Albert's father and Queen Victoria's uncle. His death a fortnight ago had sent the royal household into mourning, all but assuring that neither the Queen nor any in her retinue would be attending Lady Chesham's ball.

"The ball still promises to be a momentous affair," Mr. Catmull continued, "despite Her Majesty's absence."

"I didn't know you were acquainted with Lady Chesham," Christine remarked.

"It's my mother who boasts the connection," Mr. Catmull said. "I'll be accompanying her to the ball."

Kate hadn't been aware Mr. Catmull had any near relations to speak of. None, that is, excepting his much-boasted-of uncle the viscount.

Christine seemed to read her mind. "I don't recall meeting your mother during the season."

"You wouldn't have," he said.

"Does she never come to town?" Christine asked.

"Mother doesn't move in society any longer," Mr. Catmull said. "She's been an invalid these many years, content to keep to her rooms. But I've persuaded her to bestir herself on this occasion."

Kate's felt a glimmer of apprehension. "I can't think why."

Mr. Catmull's mouth curled in a calculating smile. "Can you not my lady?"

"Good gracious, what next?" Kate stripped off her gloves and removed her bonnet. "Before we know it, Mr. Catmull will be calling the banns."

Christine divested herself of her own wet things, handing them off to the footman who had opened the front door of the Mattinglys' townhouse for them. "You mustn't make sport of it. He's clearly on the brink of making you an offer."

Kate preceded her friend up the stairs to the drawing room. "That's no concern of mine."

Christine flashed her a stern look. "It will be if he proposes. You must discourage him, Kate. Truly."

"I thought I had," Kate said.

It was after three o'clock. The Mattinglys' drawing room was newly empty, a dwindling fire crackling in the hearth and the lingering aroma of expensive perfume the only evidence of the guests who had gathered there an hour before. Aunt Jane hosted an informal salon every Thursday, where well-to-do society matrons discussed art and music. Kate and Christine must have narrowly missed their departure.

Sinking down on the drawing room sofa, Kate flopped back against the plump cushions with a sigh.

Christine joined her there. "You shall simply have to be firmer. Either that or unwittingly end up married to the wretched man, cursed to live out your days under the watchful eye of his mysterious invalid mother."

"His mother is indeed mysterious—as is that country house of his." Kate dropped her head onto Christine's shoulder. "I'm quite curious about it actually."

Outside the sky had darkened with storm clouds. A roll of distant thunder shook the windowpanes, announcing another surge of rain.

Christine rested her cheek against Kate's head. "The odd things that interest you, my dear. I shall never understand the whole of them."

"My interests aren't that diverse. In some respects, they've remained remarkably unchanged over the years."

"Oh yes. Horses, dogs, cats—"

"Beautiful gowns," Kate added.

"Reckless wagers," Christine countered. "Even more reckless adventures."

"I follow my star," Kate said. "It hasn't steered me wrong yet."

A few moments later, as she and Christine lazed amid the sofa cushions, talking together, the Mattinglys' butler, Pruitt, appeared at the door of the drawing room.

"There's a gentleman downstairs, Miss Mattingly," he said. "A Lieutenant Heywood, inquiring after Lady Katherine. Are you at home to him?"

Kate jolted up straight in her seat. Her heart leapt with elation—and no little relief.

Charles was here!

She'd told herself he would come, that he'd pursue her as she'd been pursuing him, but she hadn't entirely believed it until this moment.

Christine adjusted herself on the sofa, far more composed than Kate was herself. "Thank you, Pruitt. Please show Lieutenant Heywood in."

Chapter Twenty-Four

C harles stood at the door of the drawing room. He was windswept and damp from the storm. Not at his best, admittedly, though he'd been in perfectly good order when he'd departed from Grillon's an hour ago.

The chocolates were to blame.

They'd been a ridiculous, romantic afterthought. Had he not had the idea of stopping off at the sweet shop on the way to Duke Street, he'd never have been splashed by that passing four-wheeler or jostled in the cab of that blasted omnibus. There'd been no time to return to his hotel. He'd been that impatient.

He hadn't seen Kate in nearly a fortnight.

She stood alongside her tall friend in front of the over-stuffed drawing room sofa, a faint tremble on her lips, and her blue eyes very wide as the butler announced him.

Charles's chest tightened in an unexpected rush of emotion.

She'd been uncertain of him. He realized it now with a savage sense of irony. It was he who had been uncertain of her, all these days past, alone in the wilds of Somersetshire as he'd planned his trip to London. He'd been half convinced that, when he finally arrived, he'd find she'd forgotten him. That her impulsive nature would have led her to fix her interests on some other fellow who may have caught her fancy.

But no.

Kate may be spirited and impulsive, but she wasn't inconstant. Not if the way she was looking at him was to judge.

"Lady Katherine." He bowed.

"Lieutenant Heywood." She dropped into a perfunctory curtsy. She wore a dusky blue silk dress with a darker blue silk ribbon belt at her waist, not too dissimilar from the dress she'd been wearing the first time they'd met. "May I present my dear friend, Miss Mattingly?"

Charles crossed the room to make his bow to the tall young lady. "Miss Mattingly and I have met before, I believe."

Miss Mattingly smiled. "We have, sir. I'm resolved to forget that unfortunate encounter so we might start anew."

"I'm obliged to you."

"Please sit down." Miss Mattingly relinquished her place beside Kate. "I must step away a moment to speak to Pruitt. If you'll excuse me?"

"By all means," Kate said. "Take as long as you require."

Charles waited until Miss Mattingly had gone and he and Kate were alone to withdraw the crushed box of candy from the inner pocket of his coat. "I brought you something," he said, offering it to her. "My apologies. It's a bit worse for wear."

Kate took the dented box with a bemused smile. "Sweets?"

"Chocolates."

She opened the violet-ribbon-trimmed lid. The dainty chocolates inside were ornamented with even daintier pieces of candied ginger. "Ginger creams!" she exclaimed in genuine delight. "My absolute favorite." Her smile turned quizzical. "How did you know?"

"I didn't," he said. "I guessed."

Among a shop filled with cloying sweetness, the ginger creams had seemed an appropriate selection. Like Kate, they contained a dash of fire.

She popped one into her mouth, eyes closing briefly with the pleasure of it. "Oomph. How divine."

Charles suppressed a grin. "I'm pleased you like them."

"I beg your pardon. Would you like one?"

"Thank you, no."

She flashed him an apologetic look, partially covering her mouth with her hand as she finished chewing. "I suppose I should have waited to eat them until I was alone."

"You needn't suspend your pleasure on my account."

She took a seat, setting the box aside. "I shall restrain myself. It's you who commands my attention, not your gift, much as I adore it." Brushing the chocolate dust from her fingers, she extended a hand to him. "When did you arrive?"

"This morning." He took her hand in his, holding it gently as he sank down beside her. "I've taken rooms at Grillon's."

"Will you be staying long? Or—" She broke off. "Don't answer that. I don't want to think of your leaving yet. It's only that, this whole last week, I waited and—"

"I couldn't leave Somersetshire immediately. I was detained for a few days on business too important to delay."

"What business? Was it about the estate or—" Again she stopped. "It doesn't matter." Her eyes shimmered with unexpressed emotion. "I'm just so dreadfully glad you've come."

His thumb moved over the curve of her knuckles. "Did you doubt me?"

"Well…I confess I did. But not because of you. It was because of me. I shouldn't have given you an ultimatum."

"I wasn't aware you had."

"But I did. When I told you that you must pursue me to London."

"Ah."

"No doubt you felt duty bound to come here. After what happened that night at Beasley Park…"

Her words trailed off as he drew her hand to his lips and pressed a kiss to it. "I *am* dutiful."

Her breath caught. "Charles—"

"I told you what would happen if I pursued you."

"I remember."

He lowered her hand from his lips. "I also told you I wouldn't compromise you." A frown worked its way across his brow. "The truth is…I've already done so nearly half a dozen times."

She blinked in surprise. "You haven't!"

"I have," he assured her. "In Tiverton. At Satterthwaite Court. And again, that night at Beasley Park."

"Oh, those don't count. No one observed them."

He arched a brow. "Arbogast is nobody? His coachman is nobody?"

She made a dismissive sound. "They didn't know who I was. And as long as no one knows it was me in that carriage or under that oak tree or—"

"In that anteroom?"

Color suffused her cheeks. "Yes, exactly. To compromise someone, the misdeed must take place in front of witnesses. Otherwise, there's no one to force a gentleman to do the right thing."

"Excepting himself," Charles said gravely.

It didn't matter that no one had observed them. Had he been behaving as a gentleman, he'd have traveled to Beasley Park immediately after parting ways with Kate in Tiverton. He'd have gone straight to Lord Allendale and asked for his daughter's hand. If not then, then certainly after Charles had kissed Kate in the anteroom.

Redeeming her honor, some would call it.

That Charles had lost his heart to Kate shouldn't even come into it.

But it did.

It had.

He'd been delayed in coming to her for precisely that reason.

Though now was plainly *not* the right time to enlighten her.

She slipped her hand from his, her expression growing wary. "I trust you're not getting any foolish ideas."

"A great many, in fact," he told her.

Her eyes narrowed. "None to do with honor and self-sacrifice, I hope."

"You may believe that self-sacrifice doesn't come into it."

"I'm serious, Charles. If you've come to pursue me, I won't have it be because you feel some tedious obligation."

"Obligation is the last thing I'm feeling at the moment. Bewilderment, more like it. How is it that we're quarreling about this?"

Outside the storm worsened. Rain beat against the windows, streaming down the glass in zigzagging rivulets.

"Because," Kate said determinedly, "it's important to

me that I'm wanted for myself. Not for my fortune, or my family name, or even for the way I look. And certainly not because a man feels himself duty bound by some antiquated notion of masculine honor."

"I see." Charles thought he did. "It's a good thing, then, that I want you for none of those reasons."

Suspicion darkened her brow. "Don't you?"

"No. It was your spirit that first attracted my interest."

"My spirit," she repeated doubtfully.

"You are beautiful, Kate. You're also valiant, warm-hearted, and maddeningly unpredictable. A delicate confection, with a bite to it. Rather like those chocolates I gave you."

A reluctant smile edged her mouth. "Or like your dog."

He smiled in return, relieved he'd managed to leaven the moment. "My sister's dog now. I hesitate to call him delicate."

"How is Hannah?"

"Very well. She sends her regards, as do my parents."

"They know you came to see me?"

"We didn't discuss it, but I suspect so. I told them I had business in town. It's not entirely untrue." Charles explained, "Mr. Catmull refused my offer on Satterthwaite Court."

"Oh no!" she said. "But why?"

"Because he's taken a personal dislike to me, apparently." Charles gave her an abridged version of his conversation with Mr. Inch in Taunton.

Kate shook her head, unable to make sense of it. "I don't understand. Are you quite certain you've never met Mr. Catmull before?"

"Not that I'm aware," Charles said.

"You'd recall if you had. His appearance isn't of the variety a person easily forgets. The way he looks at one!"

She gave an eloquent shudder. "Miss Mattingly and I had the misfortune to cross paths with him at the confectioner's shop today and you'll never guess. He was at Satterthwaite Court when we visited it in January."

"*What?*"

"Yes, I was rather taken aback myself."

Charles recalled the rifle shot that had hit the tree branch above them. He understood, all at once, why he'd experienced the same heightened sense of awareness he'd felt in battle. That odd prickle at the back of his neck that told him he was in an enemy's sights. It hadn't been the shot itself that had caused it, it had been the intention he'd sensed behind it.

If Catmull had been in residence at the time...

"You don't suppose he saw us?" Kate asked.

Charles had no intention of alarming her with his suspicions. "I don't expect so," he said. "But I daresay anything's possible."

"When I think of what might have happened if he'd encountered us under the oak tree—"

"Did he give you the impression he had?"

"Not outright, no. Though I did discern a certain calculation in his manner. Then again, he always seems calculating. Especially now I know there's a mystery afoot." Kate gave Charles an expectant look. "Have you heard back from Mr. Townsend's daughter, Abigail?"

He shook his head. "Not yet. I wrote her again before leaving Somersetshire, informing her I'd be in town. I'll call on her while I'm here. As for Catmull—"

"He's brought his invalid mother to town with him to attend Lady Chesham's ball," Kate said abruptly. "He's threatened to introduce me to her."

"Has he." Charles frowned. Introducing a young lady to one's mother wasn't an action most gentlemen would take lightly. He certainly hadn't. "Are you at all interested in meeting her?"

"I have no interest in anything related to Mr. Catmull," Kate said. "Exactly the opposite. I can't stomach the man." She retrieved her box of chocolate from the seat cushion beside her, carefully re-affixing the beribboned lid. "When will you call on him?"

"In the morning," Charles said. "With luck, I'll be able to persuade him to sell the estate to me."

"And if you're successful? What then?" She asked the question with seeming unconcern. "Will you remain in London?"

Charles felt a surge of tenderness for her. "You needn't doubt me, Kate."

She exhaled a soft breath. "I don't. It's just that—"

"It's I who should be unsure of you, not the other way round."

Her gaze flashed to his, vaguely disgruntled. "I don't know why. You could have anyone."

Charles looked steadily back at her. A smile hitched his mouth. "That's the trouble, sweetheart. I don't want just anyone. I want you. Why else do you suppose I'm here?"

Chapter Twenty-Five

Elias Catmull resided in a nondescript townhouse on the southern side of Russell Square, amid the well-to-do lawyers and merchants who populated the neighborhood. Rain flashed over the brick façade, flowing in a continuous river toward the pavement.

Charles was left standing on the topmost step, only his greatcoat and hat to protect him from the elements while a footman conveyed his card to Mr. Catmull.

He wasn't kept waiting overlong.

The footman returned momentarily. His face was void of expression. "Mr. Catmull is not at home, sir."

"When might I expect him in?" Charles asked.

He was met with unambiguous silence.

"I see," Charles said. "Very well." He didn't argue with the man. There was little point in doing so. Leaving his card, he exited the house and made his way back out to the street.

So, this was how it was going to be.

Not only was Catmull rejecting Charles's offer on

Satterthwaite Court, he was now refusing to grant Charles an interview.

What in blazes was going on?

Charles was resolved to find out.

Despite the foul weather, the street approaching the British Museum was thick with passing carriages, carts, and wagons. The minute Charles spotted a hackney, he flagged it down.

The cab slowed to a halt in front of him. An elegant carriage behind it, sporting a gilded crest on the door, was briefly obliged to slow as well. Its velvet window curtain twitched and an older lady peeped out. At the sight of Charles, her mouth opened on a gasp. The curtain promptly closed again.

Charles inwardly grimaced He supposed he did look rather like a half-drowned bilge rat. Damn Catmull for leaving him languishing on the front step in the middle of a storm!

"Grillon's Hotel," he said to the jarvey before climbing into the cab.

"Righto, sir." The jarvey clucked his horse into action.

Back at Grillon's, Charles washed and changed. Then, he dashed off a note to Gilbert Trumble.

Kate had referred to Gilbert as Charles's old school friend. It had been stretching the truth to the point of hilarity. But Charles and Gilbert *were* acquainted. They'd crossed paths occasionally at Eton. Back then, Gilbert had been part of a fashionable sporting crowd. The sort of young man who knew everything about everyone. And with Charles's uncle and grandfather currently in the country, Charles needed a good source of information.

As luck would have it, Gilbert was sufficiently at his leisure—and sufficiently curious about Charles's motives—

to join Charles for drinks at his club in St. James's Street later that afternoon.

The club was unusually full when Charles arrived, rain having driven most gentlemen indoors to nurse their cigars and brandy. Smoke filled the main clubroom, billowing over red leather chairs grouped around crackling fires or tucked away in private corners, shielded by potted palms and pillars displaying bronze busts of storied club members of old.

Gilbert Trumble was seated in an alcove, not far from a grizzled elderly gentleman dozing by the fire and a heavy-set fellow who had retreated behind a copy of the *Times*. He looked much as Charles remembered him from school—pale, fair, and entirely uncomplicated.

"Oh, Catmull's not a member here," he said after he and Charles had ordered drinks and dispensed with the necessary reminiscences about their days at school. "Not sufficiently high in the instep. He belongs to the Venturists'."

Charles had never heard of the place. "It must be a new club."

"It was formed a few years ago by a group of fellows keen on finance. That's what they do over there, as far as I can tell, talk about financial matters and investing in the newest schemes. It's all excessively commercial. Not for our sort, though there are a few men of breeding among the members. Sir Lawrence Glade is one of them. That's him over there behind the newspaper." Gilbert nodded in the direction of the portly gentleman reading the *Times*. "He's recently betrothed to my cousin."

"Perhaps he might be willing to provide me with an introduction to Mr. Catmull?"

"Don't see why not." Gilbert raised his voice. "Glade!"

Sir Lawrence lowered his paper. "What's that, Trumble?"

"Come and have a drink with us."

Sir Lawrence folded his paper and rose to join them.

"I say, Heywood," Gilbert remarked as they awaited him. "You're awfully keen to meet Catmull."

"Is that so unusual?" Charles asked.

"It is rather," Gilbert replied. "He's the sort of chap most people avoid."

"He has something I want," Charles said.

Gilbert squinted. "Lady Katherine, you mean?"

Charles gave him an alert look.

"She mentioned you before Christmas," Gilbert explained. "Something about a dog in Bond Street. I told her I'd known you at Eton."

"What has that to do with Catmull?"

"Only that some fellows say he'll catch her one of these days," Gilbert said. "Stupid, if you ask me. Kate's not the sort to be caught."

Charles's temper kindled at the thought of anyone being so disrespectful as to bandy Kate's name about—and in connection with Catmull of all men.

"Better she should end up with Fenwick or the Duke of Whitney's heir," Gilbert went on, oblivious to Charles's darkening mood. "They'd have her for her beauty. But Catmull's different. I reckon he wants to put her in her place. Show her he's lord of the manor or whatnot. He's got a chip on his shoulder the size of Gibraltar, that one."

Sir Lawrence approached them. "Trumble."

"Glade," Gilbert answered. "This is Lieutenant Heywood. I was at Eton with him. Heywood, Sir Lawrence Glade."

Sir Lawrence shook Charles's hand. "I'm acquainted

with your uncle, Lord Carlisle. He's spoken of you often, with a good deal of pride."

"My uncle is generous with his praise," Charles said.

"Heywood is looking for an introduction to Elias Catmull," Gilbert told Sir Lawrence. "He's had the devil of a time pinning the fellow down."

Sir Lawrence sat down in a vacant leather chair next to him. "That's Catmull to a T. Slippery as an eel when he wants to be. Is it the canal scheme you're interested in?"

"Are you seeking new investors?" Charles asked.

"Can't have too many," Sir Lawrence said. "It's a long-term investment. We've seen no earnings as yet, but those of us who have the fortitude to persevere will reap the benefits in the decade to come. Success is all but guaranteed. Catmull assures me of it."

Charles wondered. "Have you known him long?"

"A year or two," Sir Lawrence said. "He was abroad before then."

"In the Navy?" Charles asked, still trying to place the man.

Gilbert choked on a laugh.

Sir Lawrence chuckled along with him. "Catmull?" He scoffed. "Not him, sir. Catmull isn't a fellow who can stomach the front lines. Prefers to work behind the scenes. That's where his strength lies."

"Does it indeed," Charles murmured.

"He's a dab hand at finance," Sir Lawrence said. "Not entirely out of the top drawer, but worth keeping in one's pocket. Be happy to introduce you tomorrow evening at the Chesham's ball. You *will* be in attendance?"

"I'm planning on it," Charles said. "Though it's late in the day to expect an invitation."

"Nonsense," Sir Lawrence replied. "If her ladyship

won't oblige you, then his lordship will. Chesham!" he called to the small gray-haired gentleman dozing beneath a nearby potted palm. "The Earl of Gordon's grandson is in town. You must see he's invited to the ball."

The little gray-haired gentleman snuffled awake. "Excellent notion," he said. "Capital, capital."

"Deaf as a post," Gilbert confided in a low voice. "But I'll see his secretary gets your particulars. Can't have you missing the ball."

Charles had no intention of doing so. "Incidentally," he said, before either gentleman could depart. "I understand Catmull claims a viscount for an uncle."

Gilbert laughed. "He mentions it enough!"

"Is he anyone of note?"

"Viscount Darly," Sir Lawrence said. "An amiable chap. He's married to Catmull's aunt."

"*Viscount Darly?*" The intelligence hit Charles like a thunderbolt. "Are you telling me that Catmull's mother is Elizabeth Townsend?"

"Don't know his mother," Gilbert said. "She doesn't come up to London."

"She's here now," Sir Lawrence informed them. "He's brought her to town for the ball. I reckon he means to introduce her to Lady Katherine."

Charles stood. He scarcely knew what he said in taking his leave. The next moment, he was back on the street.

The pieces began to fall into place. Not the note—that much was still a mystery. And not the breaking of the entail. But all the rest of it.

Charles now understood why his offer on Satterthwaite Court had been denied. Why Catmull had refused to receive him here in London. Charles even knew why someone might have stooped to take a shot at him beneath that oak tree in Devonshire.

His father had said gossip lived forever. So did grudges, apparently.

Elias Catmull was Edgar Townsend's grandson.

Chapter Twenty-Six

Later that evening, Charles dressed for the theatre. Kate had mentioned that Sir Lawrence was escorting her and Miss Mattingly to the Adelphi. Charles hadn't been formally invited to join their party, but he was determined to be in attendance. At the very least, he could pay his respects to Kate. It was past time he made a public show of his interest in her.

He would address Catmull, Catmull's mother, and Lady Darly in the morning. Charles was certain that between the three of them lay the answer to this mystery.

He'd just finished tying his neckcloth when a knock sounded at the door of his hotel room. He opened it, still in his shirtsleeves.

A hotel footman stood on the threshold. "A message for you, Lieutenant Heywood. It was just delivered to the front desk." He extended a cream laid envelope.

Charles took it, turning it over in his hand. The envelope was sealed with red wax, imprinted with a strangely familiar family crest. The handwriting was familiar too. It spelled out Charles's name on the back in a spidery script.

"By whom?" he asked.

"A man from Viscount Darly's residence, sir. Shall I await your reply?"

"That won't be necessary." Charles thanked the footman and, tipping him a few coins for his trouble, closed the door. He tore open the envelope.

My dear Charles,

I comprehend you are at last come to London. It is a good thing, for I have long been meaning to speak with you on a matter that has troubled me greatly. Do me the courtesy of joining me for dinner this evening in Eaton Place. My husband and children are away and I am quite on my own. I shall expect you at half eight.

Fondly,

Abigail, Lady Darly

Charles lowered the letter. He realized two things simultaneously: why he'd recognized that crest and where he'd seen that handwriting.

A surge of quiet fury went through him.

The theatre would have to wait.

"HE'S NOT HERE," KATE MURMURED IN DISAPPOINTMENT as she gazed out over the railing of the box Sir Lawrence had engaged for them.

Christine sat next to her in a plush high-backed chair, wafting her pink feather fan. It was a chill night out of doors, but inside, the gaslight and the crowds had conspired to make the air exceedingly warm. "Surely you can't tell. It's such a crush this evening."

The Adelphi was a popular theatre, known primarily

for the burlettas, ballets, and pantomimes it produced during the winter and spring season. Lords, ladies, and the gentry were often in attendance, along with a wide swath of less elevated society. The pit and gallery seats below were jam-packed this evening, everyone having turned out for the dramatization of Mr. Dickens's *A Christmas Carol*.

Sir Lawrence had gone to fetch them a glass of lemonade at the interval, leaving Kate and Christine briefly on their own. They'd both dispensed with their lacy wraps, revealing the low necklines of their fashionable bronze silk and rose-pink satin evening gowns.

"Of course I can tell," Kate said, still peering over the rail. "Were he here, he'd be sitting in the Earl of Gordon's box."

It was a box that was presently empty.

"Not necessarily," Christine said. "Lieutenant Heywood seems an unpretentious sort. Perhaps he's taken a seat below?"

Kate doubted it. Charles may be unpretentious, but he wasn't an idiot. The people in the pit and gallery were packed together like tinned sardines. Surely no one would subject themselves to the crush if they had a more comfortable alternative.

"What's this about Heywood?" Sir Lawrence reentered the box, carrying their beverages in his hands. He was garbed in black and white evening dress, his graying hair arranged with a liberal application of pomade. Lemonade sloshed over the rim of the glass he offered to Christine.

Christine took it, delicately wiping the rim with her handkerchief. "Lady Katherine and I hoped we might see Lieutenant Heywood here this evening. He's recently arrived in London."

Sir Lawrence handed Kate her glass. "Quite so. Saw him this afternoon at my club. A serious fellow, and not in town for long." He resumed his seat next to Christine. "I daresay he's got better things to do this evening than attend the theater."

Kate stiffened. "Does he."

"And there's naught to bring him here, is there?" Sir Lawrence continued. "Nothing save a capital ghost story."

Christine gave Kate a bracing look. "Well, he doesn't know what he's missing, does he? I declare, this is the best dramatization I've ever seen. The ghosts are extraordinarily lifelike. And what a jolly scene it was at Mr. Fezziwig's warehouse."

Kate sat back in her chair, her lemonade held, untasted, in her silk-gloved hand. Who could think of the pleasure of Mr. Dickens's tale at a time like this?

Yesterday Charles had told her that he'd traveled to London specifically for her, but it seemed, when it came to the point, he hadn't time for her at all.

She wasn't worthwhile. She wasn't interesting enough or engaging enough. If she were, he'd be here now. Never mind that he hated polite society. That he'd never wanted to come to town in the first place. Kate's attendance should be sufficient to command his presence.

But it wasn't, apparently.

Her mother's warning during their ride together at Beasley echoed in Kate's mind. *A gentleman who cares, who's truly worth your effort, will make an effort of his own. He'll seek you out. He'll endeavor to win you.*

Quiet settled over the theatre once again as the gaslight dimmed and the stage curtain rose. The play resumed, depicting more ghosts, more gaiety, and even the sumptuous Christmas dinner of Bob Cratchit, complete with roast goose, smoking potatoes, and a plum pudding. But Kate was no longer distracted by it. She was too vexed.

No, not vexed.

She was hurt.

Chapter Twenty-Seven

"My sister Elizabeth tells me we should despise the French," Lady Darly said, "but Anton came so highly recommended. He makes the most decadent soufflés, you must agree."

Charles lowered his fork to his plate. He regarded the viscountess from across the heavy mahogany dining table. The candles had burned low during their meal—an hour-long parade of rich courses cooked to perfection by the Darlys' new French chef.

Lady Darly had chattered through the whole of it.

"Dinner was excellent, ma'am," he said.

Her ladyship gave him an anxious smile. She was a small, brown-haired woman, rapidly approaching fifty. A lady who compensated for the drabness of her narrow features by adorning herself in the richest silks, the largest jewels, and the most elaborately plaited coiffure Charles had seen in a decade.

They were alone in the crimson and gold dining room in Eaton Place. Lady Darly had dismissed the two liveried footmen after they'd served the final course. She'd been nervy ever since, fidgeting with her tableware, toying with her food, and fairly jumping out of her skin at the slightest sound.

"I'm pleased you enjoyed it," she said. "Would that my husband could have joined us. Alas, Darly and the children won't return from the country until next week. I shall have to tell him how greatly you take after your father. He won't credit it. The resemblance is uncanny."

She wasn't the first to comment on it. Charles had spent the whole of his life being compared to his father, just as Hannah had often been favorably compared to their mother.

"Indeed," she added with a tittering laugh, "when I saw you from my carriage window this morning on the way to the British Museum, I thought you *were* your father. What a shock it was!"

"As you've said." Charles folded his napkin to lay beside his plate. He'd hoped she'd broach the subject of her anonymous letter herself and that he'd be spared the necessity of confronting her. But so far, Lady Darly had been either unable or unwilling to come to the point. His patience was waning. "Your note mentioned that something's been troubling you?"

"Oh. That." Her smile vanished. "Yes. It has, rather." She fingered the stem of her wineglass. "It's been bothering me since the autumn. I knew I must write to you, for I wouldn't dream of approaching your mother or father on the subject. After all these years, such news would scarcely be welcome. Not from me of all people. What they might think! But I can't hold my tongue any longer."

Charles waited in silence.

Lady Darly inhaled a steadying breath. The dwindling candlelight flickered across her face, twinkling in the diamonds that circled her neck and the ruby-encrusted brooch that adorned her upswept hair. "It's about that estate of your mother's. The one in Devonshire."

"Satterthwaite Court," Charles said. He'd gathered as much.

"It was entailed on my father, Edgar Townsend." A shadow passed over Lady Darly's brow as if the recollection was an unpleasant one. "Perhaps you've heard of him? Or perhaps not. Your parents mightn't have mentioned his name. They weren't terribly fond of him."

"I understand they had reason."

"Undeniably. He used your mother very ill. It was her own good fortune she eloped with your father. Regrettably, my own father's fortunes were destroyed as a result. The Duke of Moreland saw to that. He blamed my father for the humiliation he'd suffered at your mother's hands. Within a year, Moreland had crushed all of father's business ventures. No one dared risk investing with him anymore. They stopped coming to the house for his advice. In time, we lost the house altogether. Elizabeth was obliged to marry a wealthy businessman to save us from ruin."

"Mr. Catmull, presumably."

Lady Darly nodded bleakly. "A boorish fellow. He was aged and not much to her taste. I wed Lord Darly but a year later—a happier union. Had we married earlier, I could have saved my sister from sacrificing herself. Elizabeth has never forgiven me." She raised her glass to her lips, finishing the remainder of her wine. "But that's all in the past. It's the house that concerns me now."

Charles studied her face. "Is that why you sent that letter to me in Somersetshire?"

Her countenance paled. She returned her empty wineglass to the table. "You knew it was me?"

"I recognized your handwriting on the note you sent to

Grillon's. What I don't understand is what you meant, or why you felt it necessary to conceal your identity."

"I had to. It was the only way to do right by you and to keep my name out of it. My loyalties are such that were I to come forward—" She stopped herself. "But all I've done is confuse the matter, haven't I?"

Abruptly, she rose from her chair.

Charles moved to stand.

She waved him back to his seat with a diamond-encrusted hand. "It's delicate," she said as she came around the table. "They're my family and I do care for them. But one can't remain silent. The injustice is simply too great."

Pulling out a carved mahogany chair, she sank down beside him.

"At the end of my father's life, he had little left of value except for Satterthwaite Court. He was determined that, on his death, the estate would come to Elizabeth's son, Elias. Father spent much time with Elias when he was a boy, instructing him in all he knew of the financial world and, I fear, instilling him with a hearty sense of grievance over the events that had transpired with your mother."

"In other words," Charles said, "Catmull has been raised to despise the Heywood family."

"To resent you, certainly. My father made Elias his heir. I held my tongue at the time. So long as the estate remained in the family, I could live with what my father had done. But now…Elias must raise money for his canal project. I entreated Darly to give him a loan, but my husband refuses to bestow any more money on Elizabeth or her son. Elias has been obliged to resort to other methods to raise the necessary funds."

"And this is what's prompted him to sell Satterthwaite Court?"

"Nothing but desperation could have compelled him to do so."

So much for Sir Lawrence's insistence that Catmull's scheme was guaranteed to make a fortune. It began to sound like the venture was riskier than the investors realized.

Abigail leaned forward in her chair. "I thought, if you could purchase the estate for yourself, all could be made right without creating a scandal. It's why I sent you to Mr. Arbogast. I knew Elias would be announcing the sale and I wanted you to be the first to know of it." She smiled hopefully. "I expect you've accumulated your own fortune during your time at sea. Sailors often come back to England rich as Croesus. And if you were to buy Satterthwaite Court—"

"Your nephew refuses to sell it to me," Charles said.

Her face fell. "You've made him an offer?"

"A generous one. Catmull rejected it out of hand." Given that Charles's last name was Heywood, he was beginning to comprehend why.

"But he *can't* refuse you," Lady Darly said. "The estate should be yours. Indeed, had things gone differently, it *would* be yours."

Charles stilled. "What is it you're implying?"

She bit her lip. "I can't. I've already said too much."

"You've said nothing at all."

Her shoulders slumped. "There's no point in it. If Elias won't sell you the estate, there's nothing that can be done." She moved to rise.

Charles caught hold of her hand, gently restraining her. "My lady, if you're in possession of information about a wrong done to my mother, I beg you would tell me the truth of it."

The anguish of indecision was evident in Lady Darly's

eyes. "I *can't* tell you. It would bring disgrace on my family."

"Was my mother not your family, too?"

Her ladyship's mouth wobbled. "You will blame me for having kept the secret. I shouldn't have done. I know that now. But I was never able to stand up to my sister."

It had been Elizabeth, then. She was the one responsible for the injustice alluded to in Abigail's anonymous letter.

"Has she threatened you?" he asked. "Or is it her son whom you fear?"

In her letter, Abigail had claimed she wrote at risk to her own safety. Charles could believe it. Unless he was mistaken, Catmull had gone so far as to take a shot at him. A cowardly maneuver. But then, in Charles experience, a coward was often the most dangerous breed of villain.

"Elias would be furious to know I'd revealed our family's secrets," she said. "He can be spiteful. Cruel. I despair of him finding out."

"Surely your husband—"

"Yes, Darly would protect me. He'd also demand to know the why of it." Her eyes pooled with sudden tears. "When I think of the disappointment he'll feel when he learns the truth of my weak character… It doesn't seem right to cause him such pain. And what difference can it make now? If Elias won't sell you the house—"

"Honor and integrity always make a difference," Charles said. He'd discovered that for himself. It's what had drawn him to the Navy—*and* what had compelled him to resign from it. "It's never too late to do the right thing, my lady. But you already know that. Your conscience commands it. It's why you wrote me that letter."

Lady Darly hung her head. "Yes," she acknowledged quietly. "Yes. You're right. I can't keep the secret any longer." Sliding her hand from his, she inhaled a steadying breath. "I found the papers when I was clearing out my father's safe after he died. *Legal* papers. I read what I could of them in the moments before the documents were taken from me. They showed that it wasn't my father who broke the entail. It was Sir Charles."

Charles stared at her. Whatever he'd been expecting, it hadn't been *that*. "That's impossible. Your father was the heir. He would have had to agree to it." Arbogast had explained as much when Charles met with him in Tiverton.

"I expect he did agree—for a sum. At the time, he would have valued ready money far more than he'd have valued the future promise of property. For all Father knew, Sir Charles might have lived another dozen years."

"If what you're saying is true," Charles said, "the estate should have gone to my mother."

"No. Not according to Sir Charles's original will. My father was named in it as the heir to Satterthwaite Court. A necessity, I suppose, since the property had been entailed upon him for eons. But when my father died, I saw another will among the documents in his safe. It had Sir Charles's name on it quite clearly."

"There was a second will?" Charles was stunned. "I don't believe it."

Lady Darly poured herself another glass of wine from the decanter on the table. Her hand was trembling. "I know what I saw. It was there along with the papers about the entail. Father must have come into possession of them before the contents of both could be made public. Without those documents, the estate and most of Sir Charles's fortune came to him, leaving your mother all but destitute."

Charles shook his head. "It's impossible," he said again.

"There would have been a solicitor involved. Witnesses to the will. Someone would have spoken up if Townsend had attempted anything illegal."

Lady Darly's mouth quivered into a sad smile. "You didn't know my father. He had tremendous power once. He could have made any man bend to his wishes, from the lowliest copy clerk to a duke of the realm. A country solicitor and a handful of unschooled witnesses would have been as nothing to him."

"Does Catmull know about this?" Charles asked.

"I should think so," she said. "It was he and his mother who spirited the documents away after I found them."

Chapter Twenty-Eight

K ate linked her arm tighter in Christine's as the two of them navigated their way through the crush. Lady Chesham's ballroom was packed full to bursting. Everywhere they turned, they bumped up against the full skirts of some lady's sumptuous ball gown or the pointy elbow of some elegantly clad gentleman.

Aunt Jane glanced back at them. She was tall and lithe, like her daughter, with a plain face made beautiful when lit with the animation of her splendid character. "Mind your dresses, girls."

Kate caught up her ribbon-bow-festooned silver-blue silk gauze skirts in one hand as she and Christine soldiered on. A lively galop had just ended, and couples were departing the floor before the next dance began. Kate's dance card hung at her wrist. It contained more blank spaces than it did names. She'd been reserving as many dances as she could for Charles, though the infuriating man had yet to show his face this evening.

"Here," Aunt Jane said, guiding them to a trio of upholstered chairs at the edge of the ballroom. "These will do nicely." She sat down, flicking open her painted fan. "Just a brief respite to catch our breath."

Kate and Christine took the vacant chairs on the left of her.

"Perhaps he couldn't manage an invitation?" Christine said quietly. "It *was* all very last minute."

"I refuse to believe that anything is beyond him," Kate stubbornly whispered back, "least of all something so trifling as an invitation to a ball."

"Not so trifling. It's important to you, isn't it?" Christine gave her a sympathetic smile. "You mustn't despair. He may yet show his face. The most tonnish gentlemen often come late. It's why I don't expect Sir Lawrence to arrive until after eleven."

Kate refrained from pointing out that Sir Lawrence hardly qualified as a Bond Street Beau. If her friend was happy, Kate must be happy for her, too. In any case, Christine was right. The ball had only begun at ten and wouldn't end until the wee hours of the morning. So long as Charles appeared before the one o'clock supper, Kate would be satisfied.

She would have to be.

Never mind that he hadn't called on her since Monday. Or that he hadn't sent her a Valentine's Card. Even Sir Lawrence had had the good sense to perform that small loverlike task. Christine's Valentine had arrived with today's post—a lacy, heart-shaped confection, which proclaimed:

The day when first I saw thee, love,
The hour when first we met;
I never did forget my love,
I never shall forget.

It was all so much treacle. A pit had nevertheless formed in Kate's stomach as she'd read it. Would it have been so difficult for Charles to have bought a similar Valentine for her? Such cards were displayed in the windows of every periodical shop in London at present.

"I'm engaged with Lord Barrow for the next dance," Aunt Jane said. "Who do you have down, my dear?"

Christine consulted her card. "Mr. Whitely."

"And you, Kate?" Aunt Jane asked.

Kate didn't need to consult her dance card. "My next dance is free."

"If that is so," Mr. Catmull said, emerging from the milling crowd, "I shall count myself the most fortunate of men."

Kate's stomach sank.

"Lady Mattingly." Mr. Catmull bowed to Aunt Jane. "With your permission?"

"If Lady Katherine doesn't object," Aunt Jane said.

Kate had no way of doing so. The rules of ballroom etiquette didn't allow for refusing a gentleman's invitation. Not if a lady was at liberty. "Very well." She dutifully marked his name down on her dance card.

"And the waltz," he added silkily. "If I may be so bold."

Kate snapped her card shut. "My waltz is spoken for, sir."

"There are two this evening, my lady," he said.

"Both reserved," she replied.

His eyes glittered in a rare display of irritation. It wasn't like him to respond to Kate's rebuffs. He usually met them with a deaf ear and a benign expression.

But not this evening.

Along with his thinning hair and the shadows cast by the opulently gilded chandelier overhead, the odd glint of anger in his eyes gave his cadaverous face the impression of a death's head.

"Pity. We shall have to make up for it." He extended his hand to her. "If you will?"

The orchestra struck up a spirited melody, well-suited for a livelier quadrille.

Kate set her hand in Mr. Catmull's, allowing him to lead her out onto the floor. They joined with three other couples, making the necessary formation for the dance.

Mr. Catmull fixed her with an unnerving stare as he led her into the first turn.

Kate wasn't troubled by it. Despite his sinister manner, he posed no danger to her, so long as they were in a public place. She danced with him just as she'd dance with any other London acquaintance, an inscrutable smile on her face that bespoke neither friendliness nor outright dislike.

"Valentine's Day is an auspicious day," he said when they came together once again after separating.

"Is it?" she asked politely.

"A day for lovers," he said.

Kate suppressed a snort of contempt. She wouldn't give Mr. Catmull the satisfaction of inspiring any particular emotion. "A day for shopkeepers," she said. "And for pranksters. There were more vinegar valentines sent today, I'd wager, than ones professing noble sentiments."

"And yet," he said, "many impetuous acts performed today will be attributed to cupid's dart."

Kate was glad when they separated again. Christine had warned her about Mr. Catmull contemplating a proposal. Kate was beginning to think her friend had been right. Why else would a gentleman speak of such things to a lady?

But when Mr. Catmull reunited with her, taking her hands for the final turn, his attention was no longer focused entirely on Kate. He was looking toward the doors of the ballroom, a gleam in his eye.

Kate followed his gaze. A slim older lady stood at the entrance. She wore an exquisitely cut amethyst satin gown, the effect of which was somewhat spoiled by the dated silk matron's cap on her head and the slight hunch in her spine. She had the same wispy hair and close-set eyes of Mr. Catmull—eyes that immediately found Kate from across the room.

Mrs. Catmull, undoubtedly. It could be no other.

The instant the music came to a close, Mr. Catmull's gloved hand curved around Kate's bare upper arm with inexorable force.

"My mother is anxious to meet you," he said, steering her toward the doors. "If you would do me the honor."

"I would be pleased to," Kate replied, "if you would but loosen your grasp."

Mr. Catmull's fingers eased, but he didn't relinquish his grip. "I won't risk you slipping away. A lady could easily become lost in such a crush."

Kate wished it were so. She'd have rather disappeared in the crowd than suffer the indignity of being introduced to Mr. Catmull's mother. From the looks of the woman, she was as adder-like as her son.

"Elias," she said as he approached. "And none too soon." She locked eyes with Kate. "Can this be the mysterious Lady Katherine I've been hearing so much about?"

"It is, Mother, at long last. May I present Lady Katherine Beresford, daughter of the Earl of Allendale. Lady Katherine, my mother, Mrs. Catmull."

Mrs. Catmull bowed. "My son has done you a disservice."

"Ma'am?" Kate inquired after returning the brief salute.

"He described you as a diamond of the first water, but I see you're something more than that. In my day we would have called you an original."

"I shall take that as a compliment," Kate said. "Now, if you'll excuse me. My chaperone will be wondering where I am." She moved to take her leave, but Mr. Catmull maintained his hold on her. There was no way to free herself without creating a scene.

A flutter of fear caught in Kate's chest.

It wasn't fear of him or of his equally encroaching mother. It was fear of causing a scandal. Which she most certainly *would* do if she stamped on his foot or delivered a hard knee to his nether regions (a trick her brother Jack had told her would reduce any impertinent fellow to a whimpering heap on the floor).

She cast about for Christine or Aunt Jane or anyone, really, who might come to her aid and extricate her from her predicament. But the ballroom was altogether too chaotic to find anyone easily. There were raised voices and laughter, instruments twanging, and people pressing past in preparation for the next dance. Kate wished she were taller so she might see over the crowd.

"Nonsense," Mrs. Catmull said. "Lady Mattingly and her daughter are engaged for the polka. I see them by the terrace doors with their partners. They'll not notice your absence." She addressed her son. "The air isn't fit to breathe in here, Elias. I find myself becoming quite ill."

Mr. Catmull's fingers tightened on Kate's arm. "Do you indeed, Mother. Shall we step into the conservatory?"

"An excellent idea. Come, my dear." Mrs. Catmull slid her bony hand through Kate's opposite arm. She was quite strong for a reputed invalid. "You and I are due to become better acquainted."

Kate made one last discreet attempt to drag her heels.

But in the end, there was nothing to be done but to accompany the pair of them.

Kate bided her time, privately seething. It was one of the many things she despised about fashionable society—the inability for a lady to exercise basic self-preservation. If a female screamed or made a fuss, it was she who was blamed for the outrage, just as much as she was blamed if she went along willingly to her own ruination.

There were no good choices. Not publicly anyway.

But woe betide Mr. Catmull when Kate got him alone.

Chapter Twenty-Nine

The Cheshams' conservatory lay at the back of the house, down the hall from the ballroom and past the closed doors to the library. It had been adorned with decorative Chinese lanterns for the occasion, their dim light illuminating the simple collection of plants within the conservatory's three walls of paned glass.

"I must protest again, ma'am," Kate said as the three of them entered. "Lady Mattingly would never forgive me if I didn't inform her of my whereabouts."

"You're among friends," Mrs. Catmull said. "And dare I suggest, soon to be more than friends? I comprehend that you and my son have a private understanding."

Kate was at last successful in shrugging free of Mr. Catmull's grasp. "We have no such thing. Whoever told you so—"

"I told her so," Mr. Catmull said. His face was unrepentant. "It's common knowledge amongst the fashionable set."

Kate glared at him. "Is it, by God?"

Mrs. Catmull's mouth pursed in disapproval. Now the

three of them were alone, her façade of civility was rapidly slipping. So, too, was any pretense of illness. Rather than take advantage of one of the conservatory's chairs, she remained by the doors as though blocking the exit.

"They've all noticed us together," Mr. Catmull said. "At every event you've attended, I've been there, too. They've seen us dancing. They've observed us conversing in the park, at the shops, in the tearoom. Why else has my mother exerted herself to come to London after so many years retirement in Bath?"

Mrs. Catmull's disapproving moue curled into something resembling a sneer. "The groundwork has been laid all around your feet, girl, and you didn't have the wit to see it."

"Oh, I've seen it," Kate said. "I've marked every effort of your son's from the beginning. But what that signifies now——"

"He's caught you, madam," Mrs. Catmull replied. "It has all led up to this moment. Elias? I leave you to it. I shall return presently with the others." Sweeping up her skirts, she exited the room, with a spryer step than when she'd entered it.

Kate turned on Mr. Catmull. "Others? What others?"

"Witnesses," he said. "Once you're discovered alone here with me——"

Kate moved to stride away in the middle of his speech, but Mr. Catmull caught her arm, bringing her to a stumbling halt. She twisted in his grasp. "Let go of me, you ridiculous man!"

"You needn't make such a show of refusing me." His fingers dug into her flesh. "I know of your family's history. Your mother's wildness. Your father's secret shame. Is it any wonder no other gentleman has made you an offer? But I have no such scruples, my lady."

"For once you speak the plain truth, sir," she said. "You have no scruples at all."

"What choice will you have after tonight is over but to wed me within the month?"

"You're threatening to ruin me? Is that it?" Kate mustered a scornful laugh. "I beg you would try, sir, and see what happens."

"Oh, I don't propose to ruin you in fact. Only in the court of public opinion. When my mother returns and her band of society biddies find us here alone, your good name won't be worth a ha'penny. But all will be forgiven when we announce our engagement, which we'll do tonight, with Lady Mattingly's blessing."

"You're mad," Kate said. "And anyway," she added, provoked into falsehood, "you're too late to effect your plan, for I'm already engaged."

Mr. Catmull's face betrayed a flash of surprise.

Ha! Kate thought. That was something he hadn't reckoned for.

But as fast as the shock appeared in his eyes, it was gone, replaced by a veil of contempt. "A worthy effort, my lady, but I know better than that. You're entirely free to accept my proposals. And you will accept them." He hauled her closer. "Or else," he continued relentlessly, "by this time tomorrow, the whole of London will know I've had you."

"By this time tomorrow," Kate said, raising her knee as her brother had taught her, "you'll be in Westminster Infirmary, regretting you were ever born."

A gentleman cleared his throat.

Mr. Catmull's head jerked to the door of the conservatory.

Kate followed his gaze. Her heart performed a disconcerting somersault.

Charles Heywood leaned against the doorframe, his tall, commanding figure half shadowed in the waning moonlight. "You were about to propose to my betrothed, I believe," he said to Mr. Catmull. "Pray don't let me stop you."

<hr />

CHARLES HAD ARRIVED AT THE BALL NOT FIVE MINUTES earlier in company with Sir Lawrence and Gilbert Trumble. It hadn't taken him long to ascertain Kate's whereabouts.

It had taken him even less time to grasp Catmull's plan.

Finding him alone with Kate in the conservatory, holding her arm in a ruthless grip as he threatened to ruin her, made Charles's blood run cold with fury.

His first instinct was to do as he always did—to plunge straight into the fray. He wanted to haul the man up by his neckcloth and pummel him within an inch of his life. It scarcely mattered that they were at a ball, or that there was a lady present, or that the beating would likely do more to bring Kate's name into infamy than the mere fact of her being alone with Catmull in the first place.

But no.

Kate hadn't needed a man's help. That much was evident in the instant before Charles launched into action. Indeed, unless he was mistaken, she was a hair's breadth away from delivering a punishing knee to the man's groin.

He thought at once of her rambunctious family. Of her three older brothers—especially the youngest of them, with his rough spirit of play and questionable sense of decorum.

The next time he saw Jack Beresford, Charles resolved to buy the man a drink.

"Heywood," Catmull said. "We meet at last."

He was a smaller man than Charles had envisioned. One of the slight, wiry sorts who often proved the most dangerous to those they viewed as being less powerful—women in particular.

"Catmull," Charles said. "While I don't object to your proposal in theory, I must insist you release my fiancée's arm."

Catmull gave a derisive snort. "Your fiancée? Don't make me laugh. I know full well that you're already married."

Charles looked at Catmull intently. "So, you did see me at Satterthwaite Court. I suppose that was your gig outside Peartree's lodge? And your rifle shot that missed?"

Kate's eyes widened. She stared at Catmull in equal parts astonishment and disgust. "You shot at him?"

Catmull grudgingly released Kate. "A warning shot. If I'd wanted to kill you, Heywood, you wouldn't be standing here now."

"That good at pistols, are you? I'm pleased to hear it." Charles cast a hard glance at the red imprints of Catmull's fingers on Kate's arm. "I needn't feel guilty about meeting you at dawn."

Kate immediately moved between them. "There's no need for that," she said hastily.

"Accept a challenge from a Heywood? You must think me stupid. It's brains I have, not brawn. It's how I've won this. The house. The girl. Everything. And what are you left with? No family estate. No beautiful heiress. Only a bit of Navy prize money and a dowdy wife, more suited to the muck than a London drawing room."

Kate stiffened. "Not *that* dowdy," she said in rising

indignation. "I'll have you know the riding habit I wore that day was made new last season, *and* by one of the best tailors in London."

Catmull gaped. "That was you?"

"And I *am* more at home in the muck of the countryside, thank you," she continued hotly. "Something you'd have already realized if you'd taken the trouble to know me at all."

"The two of you..." Catmull looked between them. "When? How?"

"We've had a secret engagement of longstanding." Kate flashed a meaningful look at Charles. "Isn't that so?"

Charles's mouth quirked. "Quite right. A deeply secret engagement."

"If it is indeed a secret," Catmull said, "then it's not too late for a change of plans."

"Why on earth would I contemplate changing my mind?" Kate asked, affronted.

"Not you," Catmull answered. "Him." He faced Charles, a calculating gleam returning to his eyes. "You still want the house, don't you?"

Charles's attention sharpened to a knife's edge. "You would sell me Satterthwaite Court?"

"Only if you walk away," Catmull said. "Go now, forget whatever promises you've made her, and it's yours."

"You must imagine I hold my promises very cheaply."

"I know what I would do," Catmull said. "I would think of my mother. You must think of yours. Consider what it would mean to her to have her family home back in her possession."

Anger coiled in Charles's belly. A sense of injustice so great he could have easily forgotten his self-restraint and given Catmull the beating he so richly deserved. "It should have already been in her possession. It was her grandfather who broke the entail, with your grandfather's agreement."

Catmull froze. "Who told you that?"

"His grandfather?" Kate queried. "Who—"

"Edgar Townsend," Charles said.

Kate gasped. "No!"

Charles held Catmull's gaze. "It's the truth, isn't it? And a matter of judicial record, if one knows to look for it."

"What of it?" Catmull said. "Whoever broke the entail, it changes nothing."

"No," Charles admitted. "It wouldn't. Not unless Sir Charles had left a second will."

Catmull's mouth twitched in a smug smile. "Yes, but there is no second will."

Not anymore, he might have said.

Charles supposed he'd burned it. Either he or his mother.

Whoever had disposed of it, it hardly mattered now. There was nothing left but the word of Lady Darly, and despite her pangs of conscience, she would never muster the necessary courage to come out publicly against her family. Even if she did, and even if —after nearly thirty years—Charles could manage to track down the solicitor who had drafted the second will and the villagers who had witnessed it, the only recourse against Catmull would be in the Chancery Courts.

It was no recourse at all.

Cases regarding disputed wills were known to drag on for decades in Chancery, often beggaring the parties in the process.

"No," Charles said. "Pity. If there had been, Satterthwaite Court would have been my mother's."

"It can be hers again," Catmull said. "If you leave here."

Kate's gaze fixed on Charles in breathless anticipation. Her body was tense as a tuning fork.

Did she really think an estate—*any* estate—could compete with what he felt for her?

Charles would have to disabuse her of that notion at the first opportunity. "Tempting," he said to Catmull. "But no. If it comes to the house or the lady, I believe I must choose the lady. We are, after all, soon to be married."

Kate's shoulders visibly relaxed.

He held out his hand to her.

She came to him in a flurry of ribbon-festooned skirts, allowing him to draw her close, into the shelter of his arm.

"You're a fool, Heywood," Catmull said.

"And you're in need of an heiress," Charles replied. "It's why you're selling your assets. You're gambling everything you have on this canal scheme, very probably throwing good money after bad. It's made you careless."

"And stupid," Kate added feelingly. "Of all the heiresses you might try to trap, why in heaven would you ever believe you could trap me?"

"Oh, he is enamored of you, sweetheart, on that I have no doubt," Charles said. "He may be a snake, but he isn't a blind one."

A commotion sounded at the doorway.

"I've found them!" a lady cried, as though speaking for an audience. "My son and Lady Katherine are here in the conservatory!" She entered triumphantly—a thin woman in a purple gown with the same hollow features and calculating eyes as Elias Catmull.

It was Edgar Townsend's eldest daughter, Elizabeth. A lady who was now the widowed Mrs. Catmull.

The sight of Charles stopped her in her tracks. Recognition flashed over her. She plainly knew the look of him. It was the look of Captain Arthur Heywood, the very man who, along with Phyllida Satterthwaite, she considered to be the author of all her misfortunes.

"*You*," she said, making the single word an accusation. "You're their son."

"I have that honor," Charles said gravely.

"What's the meaning of this? The two of you together…" Mrs. Catmull pivoted from Charles and Kate to her son. "Elias?"

"Lady Katherine is engaged to Lieutenant Heywood, Mother," Catmull said.

"No!" Mrs. Catmull turned the shade of a bleached corpse. "I won't believe it. To have our fortunes ruined by another Heywood—"

"Scarcely ruined, madam," Kate said. "My money was never yours to begin with."

"And now it's his." Catmull gave a humorless laugh. "The irony."

Three other ladies appeared close behind Mrs. Catmull. It was Lady Chesham, Lady Mattingly, and Lady Mattingly's daughter, Christine. They entered the room, each of them quickly taking in the scene and drawing their own conclusions from it.

"Lieutenant Heywood," Lady Mattingly said. "How delightful to find you here. Mrs. Catmull would have had us believe Lady Katherine was alone with her son."

"Not for a moment," Charles said. "My betrothed has been well looked after."

"Excellent," Lady Mattingly said without so much as a flinch of surprise.

Christine's eyes goggled. "Your betrothed! But Kate—"

"I'll explain later," Kate said quietly.

"What's this I hear about a betrothal?" Lady Chesham

swept toward them, the diaphanous folds of her crepe gown brushing over the floor of the conservatory. Her manner was as commanding as an admiral assuming charge of a rogue crew. "A Valentine's Day match between the children of two great families? We must announce it at my party, of course. It promises to be the talk of the season."

"My dear lady," Lady Mattingly said. "We none of us would dream of eclipsing your glory on your birthday. Let us leave it to the Earl of Gordon and the Earl of Allendale to arrange the announcement of the engagement. The rest of us would do better to return to the ballroom before we draw undue attention to Lady Katherine's absence."

"A wise idea," Lady Chesham said. "One can't be too careful with one's reputation these days. We must all work to minimize any hint of scandal. Mrs. Catmull? If you will join us?"

Mrs. Catmull glowered. "It seems I was in error," she said stiffly, moving to follow them from the room. "Apologies, my lady."

Lady Chesham waved the apology away. "No harm done, my dear."

Christine took Mr. Catmull's arm. "I'm anxious to better my acquaintance with your mother, sir. Shall we join her?"

Mr. Catmull's face tightened. "We may as well. There's nothing for us here."

Lady Mattingly smiled back at Charles before exiting the conservatory. "Lieutenant Heywood, I shall allow you five minutes alone with Lady Katherine. After that, I trust you to return her to me."

Kate's face betrayed a glimmer of surprise. "I'm amazed she didn't drag me off straightaway," she said when everyone else had gone and she and Charles were alone.

The light from a waning moon shimmered through the glass walls of the conservatory, casting a luminous glow over Kate's face. She had a garland of flowers in her dark hair. White roses and deep blue forget-me-nots twined together to complement the silvery-blue of her frothy ball gown. She looked rather like something out of a fairy tale.

Charles's voice went gruff. "She wouldn't have done," he said, "considering we're engaged to be married."

She gave an eloquent grimace. "I don't know what possessed me to suggest such a thing. I daresay it was only to see the look of shock on Mr. Catmull's face. The swine. It was good of you to play along."

"I wasn't playing."

Her brows notched. "I don't understand."

"You asked me on Monday why I was late in coming to town. It was because I stopped off somewhere first."

"Where?"

"At Beasley Park," he said. "To speak with your father."

Her lips trembled.

"This afternoon, I was delayed from calling on you for a similar purpose." Charles reached into the interior pocket of his evening jacket, withdrawing the small velvet box he'd purchased earlier that day at a jeweler's shop in Bond Street. He pressed the box into her hand.

Kate opened it, revealing the sparkling ten-carat oval sapphire ring within. Surrounded by an equal weight of small diamonds, it had taken a substantial portion of Charles's prize money. Money he'd gladly spend again to see such a look on her face.

She caught her breath. "*Oh.*"

He smiled. "You're beginning to understand, I take it."

"Yes, but…" Her eyes met his. There was a peculiar

sheen in them. "You shouldn't have…," she stammered. "You needn't have… And to call on my father?" She made a choked sound, part laugh, part sob. "Oh, what is this?"

"It's whatever you want it to be," he said. "A proposal. A valentine. Both."

"Both," she answered.

He slipped the ring onto her finger. The diamonds sparkled and flashed. "At heart, it's a symbol of what I've come to feel for you since the day we met. Respect. Admiration. Friendship." He brought her hand to his lips. "Love."

"*Do* you love me?"

"Love you? I want to marry you, Kate. To settle down on a great rambling farm somewhere in Somersetshire with you and our horses, our dogs, and even—Lord save me—your cats. I dearly hope you want that too. That you want *me*."

"I do," she said, a little wistfully. "Oh, but I do!"

Charles moved closer.

She set a hand on his chest, stopping him before he could take her in his arms. "But is that really what you desire? The mud and the muck? The dull life of a country squire? One day you might wake up and realize you've made a mistake. That you're still the same man who left Somersetshire all those years ago in search of adventure."

"You're the adventure," he said gruffly. And then he kissed her.

Epilogue

harles and Kate's betrothal was celebrated in grand style a month later at Heywood House. His grandfather and Mrs. Ogilvy were in attendance, along with Uncle George, Aunt Prudence, and their two strapping sons, Walter and Daniel.

Kate and her parents came to stay the week. Jack Beresford accompanied them, riding alongside the stately Allendale carriage on his newly acquired roan hunter. James was to arrive the following morning, on the heels of a previous engagement in London. As for Ivo, he'd absented himself altogether, for reasons known only to Kate's family.

Charles suspected it had something to do with the titian-haired Miss Burton-Smythe. He said as much to Kate on the day of her arrival. After dinner that evening, the two of them slipped into the drawing room ahead of the others. It was their first real moment alone since parting in London.

They stood by the window, holding hands as they faced each other in the flickering light of a branch of beeswax candles. Flurry, Twig, and Odysseus wandered past, staking out their places on the hearthrug, a tufted ottoman, and a warm patch of carpet beneath an inlaid table.

"Ivo said he had an appointment in Bath," Kate confided. "But he took none of his horses and he left his valet behind. We found out three days ago that Miss Burton-Smythe had gone as well. We don't know where and we daren't ask her father."

"A proper mystery," Charles said, teasing her.

She leaned into him, their fingers intertwined. Her skirts bowed against his legs. "I'll leave the solving of it to my parents. I'm done with mysteries."

He pressed a kiss to her temple. "I thought you enjoyed solving ours."

"Did we solve it?" Kate wondered. "We know who wrote the letter and why. And we know what the injustice was. But we had no success in righting it."

"No," Charles acknowledged. "We didn't."

The last he'd heard, Catmull had sold Satterthwaite Court to the other interested party. It was out of Charles's hands now. Out of all of their hands.

"Still…" She returned the warm clasp of her fingers. "I don't count our collaboration a complete failure."

He bent his head to hers. "Rather the opposite."

She stretched up to meet his lips, returning his kiss.

"Must you be so indiscreet?" Jack asked, entering the room with Hannah. "There are children present."

"I'm not a child," Hannah said. Evangeline and Tippo were close at her heels. "And I think it's romantic."

"That's one word for it," Jack replied.

Charles and Kate broke apart, still smiling at each other.

The click of a cane announced the arrival of Charles's father. He entered the drawing room with Lady Allendale on his arm. Lord Allendale followed, escorting Charles's mother. The two sets of parents couldn't be more different, but they had so far got along famously, making every effort to support their children's match.

Charles's grandfather and Mrs. Ogilvy came in next, along with Uncle George, Aunt Prudence, and their sons. They all sat down on the chairs and sofas around the fire, the older family members still conversing on the same topic they'd been discussing at dinner. Something to do with the perpetual drainage issues on Uncle George's Northumberland estate.

Grandfather's rheumy eyes kept falling shut as he listened. In his middle eighties now, he was overtired from his journey, and would be requiring his bed soon.

"Your mother and I have a gift for you," Arthur said to Charles. "A wedding present of sorts."

Philly sat down on the sofa beside Lady Allendale. Her face was aglow. "It's your father's doing. I can claim no credit."

"Nonsense," Arthur said. "Your mother may not have known of the endeavor, but she was, as ever, my guiding light." He withdrew a document from his evening jacket. It was folded in thirds and secured with a rather formal-looking ribbon. He handed it to Charles. "For you and Kate, with our blessing."

"What's that?" Grandfather snuffled awake. "A wedding gift for Charles?"

Mrs. Ogilvy leaned in to whisper to him. Her once lush mane of brown hair was solidly gray now, but her eyes no less merry as she fussed over her longtime companion. "It's from Arthur and Phyllida, my darling. A document of some sort."

Charles and Kate exchanged a look as Charles untied the ribbon that bound the papers.

It was a deed.

Good Lord.

It was the deed to Satterthwaite Court!

Charles's shocked gaze lifted to his father's face. "It was you," he said in sudden understanding. "You were the other buyer."

Arthur raised his brows. "Was there another?"

Charles hadn't yet told him about his own failed attempt to buy the house, or about what he'd learned during his dinner with Lady Darly. He'd intended to, but the moment had never seemed right to impart such bleak news. Not when everyone was so happy about his engagement. "How did you manage it?" he asked.

"The entail had been broken," Arthur said. "The seller was a distant connection of ours—no one of consequence. Still, I thought it best to have Ombersley purchase the property in my stead. I saw no need to rake up the past."

"No, indeed," Charles murmured.

"Ombersley's an excellent fellow," Grandfather said. "Wouldn't employ another solicitor on any account. Not for the important matters."

"Quite right," Arthur agreed.

Ombersley was indeed an excellent solicitor. No doubt he'd ferreted out that it was Sir Charles who had broken the entail. Sir Charles's intention to leave his granddaughter his estate could easily be deduced from that fact. As for the existence of a second will…

Charles wondered how much his father knew, and how much he only suspected.

He looked from his father to his mother. Her eyes were glistening with tears of joy. "Your childhood home," he said. "Father returned it to you, of course."

"And now it's yours, my love," Philly said. "But only if you and Kate wish to live there."

"Oh yes," Kate said. "It's perfect." She hugged Charles's father and mother in turn. "And it's so close to Beasley Park!"

"For which her mother and I heartily thank you," Lord Allendale said. "We wouldn't find it easy to be too far from our girl."

Lady Allendale embraced her daughter. "Would that your brothers could be as happily settled."

"Give me time, mother," Jack said. "I've barely started looking yet."

"No," Lady Allendale said, "James must be next, for he's the oldest."

Charles and Kate exchanged another glance, both of them certain that it would be Ivo, not James, who next met his match.

Later, when grandfather and Mrs. Ogilvy had gone to bed, and the remainder of the company had settled into games of cards and music on the pianoforte, Charles and Kate sat down together in the relative privacy of the window embrasure, holding hands while Odysseus snored loudly at their feet.

"Are you happy?" Charles asked her.

Kate rested her head on his shoulder. "Deliriously happy."

Charles gazed down at her face in the candlelight. This vexing, magnificent, wholly beautiful person who was soon to be his wife. "So am I, Kate," he said.

And he meant it.

Author's Note

When Charles Heywood tells the meddlesome woman in Bond Street that the chase-mad stray puppy is a rare breed of dog that has recently arrived from Spain, it's a nod to one of my favorite scenes in Georgette Heyer's novel *Frederica*. In *Frederica*, the heroine's mongrel dog, Lufra, stampedes a herd of cows in a London Street. When the bystanders call for Lufra to be destroyed, Frederica defends him, claiming he's a valuable "pure-bred Barcelona collie" that has been delivered to England "at enormous expense." This becomes a running joke throughout the story, with Lufra first being identified as a Barcelona collie and then, ultimately, a Baluchistan hound.

The dog muzzle Lady Kate crochets as a cheeky gift for Charles was inspired by a pattern for a crocheted dog muzzle in an 1868 edition of *Godey's Lady's Book*. Made of wool, it was recommended for a lady's pet dog as an alternative to a harsher muzzle made of wire. I first discovered this pattern many years ago and, ever since, have been eager to use it in one of my stories.

Mr. Catmull's dubious canal investment scheme is a

nod to my novel *A Convenient Fiction*. In that story, set in 1860, the heroine's unscrupulous attorney loses most of her family's money investing in a similar undertaking. I envision that Mr. Catmull (by then substantially older) is the unnamed force behind that failed venture as well. Since, in *A Convenient Fiction*, the fraudulent nature of the scheme is uncovered by solicitor Tom Finchley, it's he who will be responsible for Catmull's eventual downfall.

Charles Heywood's experiences as a naval lieutenant during the Second Egyptian-Ottoman War were inspired by a real-life naval action led by Admiral Sir Charles Napier. Charles's description of events in Chapter Four is almost identical to what happened when Admiral (then Captain) Napier was patrolling the Lebanese Coast in 1840, defending British interests against the occupying Egyptian forces.

When the commander of the army became ill, Napier was tasked with leading the land force. It was during this time that Napier's superior, Admiral Stoppard, claimed his flag of truce had been fired upon. In response, he bombarded Beirut, killing many civilians in the process.

I don't go into great detail about all of this in the story. I didn't feel it was necessary in order to convey Charles Heywood's resulting disillusionment. At the time, Britain was expanding its empire. Coupled with the events of 1840, I felt that a man like Charles—a gentleman of conscience who was, at heart, a defender and a rescuer—would begin to question the purpose of his presence overseas.

This is why, at the start of the story, Charles has vowed to give up adventure. He doesn't like where it's led him in the past. However, his desire for adventure hasn't been entirely extinguished, as evidenced by his fascination with

Lady Kate—and by his determination to solve the mystery of the anonymous letter.

Finally, just to note, the names of Charles's ships are fictionalized, as is the name of the lady's magazine where Kate finds the crochet pattern.

An Excerpt from Appointment in Bath

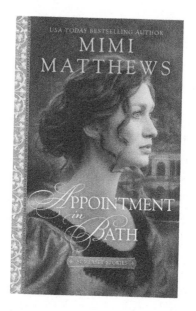

Turn the Page for a Sneak Peek of the next book in Mimi Matthews' Somerset Stories series, featuring Lord and Lady Allendale's forward-thinking son, Ivo Beresford, and Meg Burton-Smythe, the daughter of their longstanding rival.

Coming June 2023 and now available for pre-order.

CHAPTER ONE

Somersetshire, England
November 1843

"Are you hurt?"

Meg Burton-Smythe heard the question long before she spied the gentleman who asked it. She was half-sitting in the mud on the banks of the river by Sefton Bridge, the skirts of her sensible black wool riding habit hoisted above her knees as she examined her injured right ankle. At the sound of the stranger's deep voice, she hastily tugged her skirts back down over her half boots in a fruitless attempt at modesty.

It was too late. The gentleman had already seen her.

He rode up on an enormous white stallion, the late autumn sun at his back, its glimmering rays catching in the threads of his thick golden hair. He was a tall, athletic figure of a gentleman, with a devastatingly handsome face characterized by a strong chiseled jaw, lean cheeks, and firmly molded lips.

A knot formed in Meg's stomach. She was reminded of the fairytales she'd enjoyed as a child. Stories she still read occasionally, about dashing princes on their white chargers, riding to the rescue of damsels in distress.

Unhappy thought.

Given her present predicament, she'd have preferred to be rescued by one of the local farmers. Plain, ordinary, grandfatherly men who wouldn't care how she looked or what an idiot she'd made of herself.

"I've fallen from m-my horse," she said, rather unnecessarily.

Her stammer emerged just as it always did when she was anxious. She suppressed a grimace at the sound of it.

What she would have given to sound calm and collected in this moment!

"I can see that." The gentleman leapt from his own mount in one fluid motion. His finely made leather top boots squelched in the mud as he strode, sure-footedly, down the bank.

He was clad in tan Bedford cord breeches that hugged his long legs and a blue, broadcloth riding coat that accentuated the staggering breadth of his shoulders. When coupled with his honey-blond hair and beautifully sculpted features, he didn't just look like Prince Charming, he could have *been* Prince Charming.

Meg's mouth went dry. There was only one family in the county that boasted such golden splendor.

He must be a Beresford.

John Beresford, Earl of Allendale, and his wife, Margaret, owned Beasley Park, the estate that bordered Letchford Hall. Their eldest son, James, Viscount St. Clare was a cold, superior sort of gentleman with ice in his veins and their youngest son, Jack, was an unrepentant rogue with a devilish twinkle in his eyes. Meg knew them both by sight.

But Lord and Lady Allendale had another son. A middle son, Ivo Beresford, who had spent the last several years away from home, first at university and then abroad, enjoying a lengthy grand tour.

This was surely him, newly returned home to Somersetshire.

Meg privately cursed her terrible luck. It was bad enough that the gentleman coming to her aid should be gorgeous beyond imagination, but that he should be a member of a family as abhorrent to her own family as the Montagues ever were to the Capulets!

"What's her name?" He squinted as he approached

Meg's mare. In his boyhood, Ivo Beresford had worn spectacles. He wasn't wearing them now, but judging by the slightly unfocused look in his cool gray eyes, he still required them.

"Rowena," she said.

"Easy, Rowena," he murmured. "I'll not hurt you."

Rowena peered at him through her tangled forelock, glittering malice in her big brown eyes.

"She b-bites," Meg warned.

Mr. Beresford caught Rowena's reins. "She won't bite me." He held the mare's bridle tight as he gave her a pat on the neck. "Will you, old girl?"

Rowena's muzzle twitched. She plainly would have loved to sink her teeth into him.

It was Meg's own fault. She'd handfed Rowena too much when she was a filly. Meg had hoped to form a bond with her—to make her a friend, a partner. Instead, all she'd done was encourage Rowena to nip people's fingers.

Mr. Beresford lashed the mare's reins to a nearby tree before coming to Meg's aid. "Is it your ankle?"

Meg's cheeks warmed, knowing that he'd seen her with her skirts raised. "M-my right one," she said. "I c-can't put any weight on it."

He crouched down beside her on the bank, heedless of the mud. His hand touched the lacing of her brown leather riding boot. "May I?"

No longer warm, Meg's cheeks were positively scalding. "If you m-must."

He deftly unlaced her boot and slipped it from her foot. His strong fingers moved gently over her stocking-clad ankle and the curve of her instep.

She sucked in a sharp breath.

"Does that hurt?" he asked.

A pained breath trembled out of her as he manipulated her foot. "Yes."

"It's not broken," he said. "Only sprained, I'd guess."

"How c-can you t-tell?"

"If it was broken, you'd be screaming right now. But you're not." He smiled at her, revealing a glimpse of strong, white teeth. "You're only blushing."

Meg could have happily melted into the mud. She knew what she looked like when she blushed. Her entire face and throat turned scarlet. When coupled with her red hair and freckles, it gave her the appearance of a ripe tomato.

"I've n-never fallen from a horse before," she said. "That's why—"

"I don't judge." He slid her boot back on her foot, retying the laces in a loosened bow to better accommodate her injury. "I've been where you are countless times."

She gave him an uncertain look.

"In the mud," he explained. "On my backside." He stood and offered her his hand. "There's no indignity in it. So long as you get back up again."

Meg hesitated for an instant before slipping her gloved hand into his and permitting him to help her to her feet. "*Oh!*" A jolt of pain shot through her ankle the moment she put her weight on her right foot.

"Here. Let me." He slid his hand around her waist. His arm was as strong as a band of iron.

Meg flushed even hotter. At eighteen years of age, she'd only recently left the schoolroom. She wasn't formally out yet. She'd never danced with a gentleman or felt his arm at her waist.

Her heart raced and her tongue tangled over itself. She didn't know what to say, let alone where to look.

How disappointed Miss Adams would be in her! Meg's

beloved former governess had taught Meg all she knew of how to conduct herself in company. Meg was meant to be elegant, graceful, and articulate. The very opposite, in short, of how she appeared now.

Miss Adams had departed Letchford Hall in the spring. She was soon to be married in Bath. Meg was happy for her, though not so much for herself. In Miss Adams's absence, Meg had no companion at the Hall to keep her company. No one to leaven the dull days as one drifted inexorably into the other.

The only bright spot had been her solitary rides on Rowena. Unburdened by her governess's insistence that she have a groom accompanying her, Meg had traversed the countryside, galloping over the moors, jumping pasture gates, and exploring the hidden trails that wove along the river. Her daily outings were her sole taste of freedom. A seemingly harmless indulgence, which had now brought her to this.

"It will be less painful once you're in the saddle," Mr. Beresford said, bearing her weight.

Meg doubted it. She nevertheless allowed him to assist her back to her mare. Once there, he grasped her waist in his hands and effortlessly lifted her up into her sidesaddle. It happened so quickly, she had no opportunity to object to the familiarity. Not that she would have done. She'd never have been capable of mounting Rowena without his assistance.

She clumsily hooked her knee over the pommel. "Th-thank you," she stuttered. "Mr.—"

"Ivo Beresford," he said. "And I know who you are. You're Miss Burton-Smythe." He placed her left foot into her stirrup for her. "I'd recognize that red hair and those freckles anywhere."

Meg's already dwindling confidence withered still further.

So much for hoping she'd changed. That the intervening years had turned her from an awkward ugly duckling into a beautiful swan.

"You remember me," she said flatly.

"Of course, I do." Catching hold of his stallion, he vaulted easily back up into his saddle. "You and I are meant to be enemies."

Meg ducked her head, avoiding his gaze as she slowly gathered her reins. She was uncertain how to respond.

He rode up alongside her. "How's your ankle now?"

"Tolerably well."

"Can you manage the ride home?"

"I believe so, thank you."

Mr. Beresford didn't appear convinced. "I'll accompany you back just to be certain."

Her eyes flew back to his. "Oh no, you m-mustn't!" she cried before she could stop herself.

His brows lifted in amused surprise. "Mustn't I?"

Embarrassed, Meg once again bent her head. "I mean… I c-can manage. You needn't t-trouble yourself on m-my account."

There was a long and rather agonizing moment of silence.

"It's no trouble to me," Mr. Beresford said at length. "But I see it would be to you." He circled around her on his stallion, prompting Rowena to flatten her ears. "Very well, we shall part here."

Relief coursed through Meg. She couldn't imagine what her father would do if he spied her returning to Letchford Hall in company with a Beresford. The very thought of his reaction was too terrifying to contemplate.

"Shall I go first?" Mr. Beresford inquired. "I can gallop away in a trice, if you wish it."

She chanced another look at him through her lashes. "Yes, please. That is…if you would, sir."

Catching her shy glance, the same irrepressible smile pulled at his mouth. "Do you know what I think, Miss Burton-Smythe? I think we should be friends, you and I."

She stared at him, rendered speechless by the scandalous suggestion.

His grin broadened. "Consider it," he said. And then, kicking his stallion into motion, he cantered off over the rise.

Meg was left gaping after him, stunned.

Friends? How could a Burton-Smythe ever be friends with a Beresford? It was impossible. Unheard of. The two families hated each other and had done so since well before she was born.

But Mr. Beresford had been kind to her. More than kind. He'd been downright friendly.

And Meg was in desperate need of a friend.

Pre-order or Add this title on Goodreads

Acknowledgments

Writing a sequel to two of my most popular novels was a distinct challenge. When I ended *The Work of Art* and *Gentleman Jim*, I never intended to revisit those characters. Not because I didn't have more stories to tell in those worlds, but because I felt both narratives had wrapped up so perfectly. Then, sometime in early 2022, it occurred to me that both books were set in the same decade. They also both took place in Somerset. What if—just what if—the children of Maggie and St. Clare and Philly and Arthur were to meet and fall in love?

That was all it took for my imagination to take flight.

Many thanks to Deb Nemeth for editing; to James Egan for cover design; to Anne Victory and Crystalle for proofreading; to my gracious beta readers Flora, Sandy, Dima, Courtney, Dana, and Renee; and to my brilliant agent Kevan Lyon for all she does to get my books out into the world and into the hands of readers. I'm also so grateful to author Sarah Waldock for assisting me with research; and to my wonderful assistant Rel Mollet whose friendship, support, and encouragement were vital to me finishing this story.

Last but not least, extra special thanks to my beautiful mom—first-line beta reader, critique partner, and sounding board for all my insecurities (writing related and other-wise). And to my animal support group: Stella, Jet, Tavi, Bijou, and Asteria. This was a dog-filled story and my dogs (and all the rest of my menagerie) were present for every word of it. I couldn't do any of this without them.

About the Author

USA Today bestselling author Mimi Matthews writes both historical nonfiction and award-winning proper Victorian romances. Her novels have received starred reviews in *Publishers Weekly*, *Library Journal*, *Booklist*, *Kirkus*, and *Shelf Awareness*, and her articles have been featured on the *Victorian Web*, *the Journal of Victorian Culture*, and in syndication at *BUST Magazine*. In her other life, Mimi is an attorney. She resides in California with her family, which includes a retired Andalusian dressage horse, a Sheltie, and two Siamese cats.

Connect Online
MimiMatthews.com
Facebook: @MimiMatthewsAuthor
Instagram: @MimiMatthewsEsq
Twitter: @MimiMatthewsEsq

Want more?

Would you like to know when Mimi's next book is available?
Sign up for her newsletter (https://www.mimimatthews.com/
newsletter/) to keep up to date.

Join Mimi's exclusive Facebook group, Mimi Matthews'
Victorian Reading Room (https://www.facebook.com/groups/
mimimatthewsvictorianreadingroom), for exclusive access to
Mimi as she shares her love of writing, historical romance,
Victorian fashion, brooding heroes, independent heroines, and
of course, her beloved pets! Speaking of pets, Ignatius, the
Heywood's ancient mastiff in *Return to Satterthwaite Court* was
named by VRR member, Susan Snodgrass, following an
exclusive naming contest in Mimi's Victorian Reading Room.
Thank you, Susan!

Finally, the more reviews a book has, the more other readers will
discover it. Every review helps, so if you have a moment to post
your thoughts about this story, Mimi will be ever grateful.

Made in the USA
Monee, IL
15 May 2023

33736887R00173